THE VISITATION

SUE REIDY

SCRIBNER PAPERBACK FICTION
PUBLISHED BY SIMON & SCHUSTER

SCRIBNER PAPERBACK FICTION
Simon & Schuster Inc.
Rockefeller Center
1230 Avenue of the Americas
New York, NY 10020

This book is a work of fiction. Names, characters, places,
and incidents either are products of the author's imagination or are used
fictitiously. Any resemblance to actual events or locales or persons, living
or dead, is entirely coincidental.

First Scribner Paperback Fiction edition 1997
Originally published in Great Britain
Published by arrangement with Transworld Publishers Limited

SCRIBNER PAPERBACK FICTION and design are trademarks
of Simon & Schuster Inc.

Manufactured in the United States of America

1   3   5   7   9   10   8   6   4   2

Library of Congress Cataloging-in-Publication Data
Reidy, Sue.
The visitation / Sue Reidy. —1st Scribner Paperback Fiction ed.
p.   cm.
I. Title.
PR9639.3.R43V57   1997
823—dc21   97-16819
CIP

ISBN 0-684-83954-7

For Jenny, in loving memory

Acknowledgements

This novel grew out of my short story of the same name published by New Women's Press, Auckland 1989, in *New Women's Fiction 3*, edited by Mary Paul and Marion Rae.

I have not attempted to document literally the lives of saints and have deviated from and embellished upon my original sources.

The following books have been important in my research:

My source for the story of Marina de Jesus Paredes y Flores used in Chapter 1 was: *Saints: Their Cults and Origins*, Caroline Williams. Bergstrom & Boyle Books, London, 1980.

My source for the story of Blessed Clare of the Cross used in Chapter 10 was drawn from: *Powers of Darkness, Powers of Light: Travels in Search of the Miraculous and the Demonic*, John Cornwell. Viking, London, 1991.

My source for the story of St Maria Maddalena de' Pazzi used in Chapter 8 was drawn from: *The Bleeding Mind: An Investigation into the Mysterious Phenomenon of Stigmata*, Ian Wilson. George Weidenfeld & Nicolson, London, 1988.

The quotes from St Teresa of Avila and from Hildegard of Bingen used in Chapter 4 were quoted in *An Illustrated Encyclopaedia of Mysticism and the Mystery Religions*, John Ferguson. Thames and Hudson, London, 1976.

The quotation from St Teresa of Avila used in Chapter 23 is from St Teresa of Avila, *Life* 1565, tr. J. M. Cohen. Penguin Classics, 1957, quoted in *Catholics and Sex*, Kate Saunders and Peter Stanford. Mandarin, London, 1992.

The portrait of St Teresa of Avila by Juan de la Miseria described in Chapter 23 I have only ever seen used as a frontispiece in *Teresa of Avila*, Shirley Du Boulay. Hodder & Stoughton, London, 1991.

The extracts in Chapter 15 are from *On the Regulation*

of Birth, by Paul VI, third edition, from *Humanae Vitae*, St Paul's Publications, Sydney, 1981.

Keepers of the Keys. The Three Popes, John XXIII, Paul VI, John Paul II: Three Who Changed the Church, Wilton Wynn. Random House, New York, 1988.

El Corazón Sangrante. The Bleeding Heart. The University of Washington Press, Washington, 1991.

I would like to thank Fay Weldon and Jane Parkin who read the manuscript and gave invaluable advice and criticism. I have also appreciated the astute professionalism of my London editor, Averil Ashfield.

Particular thanks also to my partner Geoff Walker, who provided enormous encouragement and support, while still being totally mystified by anything to do with the BVM; to my agent Glenys Bean, who has been through thick and thin with me and stuck by me; to Paul Heywood, who provided encouragement at the beginning of the process, saying I would only get one chance at this story; to my sister Chris, who balanced me during the lows; to my parents, for whom my writing is 'not their cup of tea' (especially the 'sex bits') but who have been encouraging and have defended my right to be true to myself; to the women who have shared stories of growing up Catholic. And last, but not least, to my friend and fellow writer Lisa Greenwood, who always believed in me while agreeing that writing a book must surely be the most masochistic activity a person can ever indulge in, and why do we do it?

Because there's no choice in the matter.

I gratefully acknowledge the assistance of the QEII Arts Council of New Zealand, who awarded me two Literature Programme grants to complete this work.

'The words I speak come from no human mouth;
I saw and heard
them in visions sent to me.'

Hildegard von Bingen

'Sometimes I say to Him with my whole will: "Death or
suffering, Lord, that is all I ask of You for myself." It
comforts me to hear the clock strike, for then another hour
of my life has passed away, and I seem to be a little
nearer to seeing God.'

The Life of St Teresa of Avila by Herself

'Religious suffering is at the same time an expression of
real suffering and a protest against real suffering. Religion
is the sigh of the oppressed creature, the sentiment of a
heartless world, the soul of soulless conditions.'

Karl Marx, *Introduction to the Critique of
Hegel's Philosophy of Right*

Chapter One

THE VIRGIN MARTYRS

Lucy's eyes were stolen.
Joan was burned alive.
Agatha lost her breasts.
Barbara's father chopped her head off.
Agnes had her throat cut.

CHATTERTON 1966

Other children played 'Mothers and Fathers', 'Cowboys and Indians', or 'Cops and Robbers'. Catherine and Theresa Flynn played 'Martyrs and Suffering Virgins'. After school they changed out of their black serge gym frocks and slipped into their saintly roles as Maria, Rose, Anastasia, Agatha, Agnes, Joan, Lucy or Barbara.

All their heroes were women and most of them had died horribly – their deaths caused, naturally, by men.

'So what's new?' Smoking Nana shrugged her shoulders. Grace Malone was a barrel-shaped woman in her mid-fifties. Her faded green cotton gingham shift strained at her midriff and creased into sausages of fat when she sat. Over the dress she wore a rust-coloured home-knitted cardigan, the buttons of which were made from deer antler. Her hair was a bird's nest of spidery tufts gathered into an untidy bun at the nape of her neck.

Her son-in-law Terrence observed her sourly from the opposite end of the green Formica table. Grace held court while his children hung onto her every word as if it were manna from heaven. He might as well have been invisible for all the attention they paid him when she visited. She was enough to put anyone sensitive off their food.

'Men can't control themselves,' Smoking Nana told her granddaughters and she spread her buttocks out more comfortably on the vinyl chair.

They nodded in response, their eyes big with admiration and curiosity.

Terrence Flynn bit his tongue. He gave a little yelp of pain, but no-one heard him.

'They've just got to prove to everyone that *they're* in charge.'

'Am I bleeding?' Mr Flynn asked his wife.

'Even if they have to kill women to make the point.'

'I can't see anything.' Mrs Flynn squinted as she peered in. There were three teeth missing on both sides of his lower jaw. It was not a pretty sight.

'Don't get married, girls.'

'There's no blood? I don't believe it.'

'None, I'm afraid.'

'You'll only regret it if you marry. Go out and become brain surgeons or explorers instead.'

There was glory in dying the noble death of a martyr. It was a Test of Faith, the nuns said.

'The martyrs were Saved,' said Sister Mary Cecilia. 'They live now with God in heaven like one big happy family. *Your heavenly family*, who watch over you.'

'I don't want anyone watching over me, I want to be private and think my own thoughts,' argued Theresa. She wanted to be like Smoking Nana.

'Not a sparrow falls, but . . . ' replied her teacher.

St Agnes refused to worship at the altar of Minerva. She was punished by having her clothes removed in front of a crowd of spectators. She covered up her nakedness by letting down her long hair. Later she was stabbed in the throat. She was twelve years old.

Agnes was their favourite. In their Heroines of God book, dog-eared and worn from constant rereadings, St Agnes was depicted wearing a long ochre-coloured robe and carrying a sacrificial lamb in her arms. Her eyes were raised towards heaven. Her long wavy hair was haloed by soft yellow light. The wound on her white throat was clearly visible.

She was more beautiful than any fairytale princess and braver than Red Riding Hood, Sleeping Beauty, Cinderella or Snow White, all of whom had waited for someone to save them. Agnes saved herself by choosing to be a martyr. She suffered excruciating pain.

Suffering counted. It guaranteed immediate entry to heaven without first having to endure the flames of Purgatory.

What would it be like to die for someone you couldn't see? The drama and tragedy of the martyred girls fuelled their fantasies. Theresa and Catherine always argued over who was to play the part of the beautiful doomed Agnes and who was to be the cruel Roman soldier. The one who was relegated to being the soldier had to whip Agnes and drag her around the back yard where she was scorned and jeered at by the crowd consisting of Francie, Andrew, Tim and John. Toots lay in his pram snuffling and gurgling while they shrieked around him. Sometimes he projectile-vomited, and this always added an element of unpredictability to the proceedings.

They used cochineal for blood. The old sheets that they used for robes were already splattered with dark mulberry-coloured stains from previous games.

They entered easily into the spirit of it. The back yard disappeared and was replaced by dirt streets full of carts and beggars. Bloodthirsty soldiers strode about shouting and brandishing swords. The Flynn children used sharpened tomato stakes until Mrs Flynn noticed and confiscated them.

'You'd better give up Jesus, or else,' hissed Theresa the Roman soldier.

'You can't make me,' Catherine replied, clutching at the teddy bear that played the role of Sacrificial Lamb.

'Oh can't I just?' Theresa gave a tug on the rope that was tied around Catherine's foot. She changed voices when she swapped roles, becoming the young man who had fallen in love with Agnes. 'Marry me,' she pleaded. 'I'll save you if you do.'

'Never!' cried Catherine, beating her breast. Saints always beat their breasts. It added to the suffering. 'I belong to my Saviour alone,' she said. She eyed Theresa uneasily. Her sister often forgot it was only a game.

'Don't say I didn't warn you,' threatened Theresa.

'I'm just an ordinary girl,' moaned Catherine. 'Have mercy on me.'

'Never!' Theresa brandished a broom handle perilously close to Catherine's neck.

Francie ran to save Agnes. She never tired of playing 'martas', but often she forgot the plot.

Theresa experimentally poked Catherine in the neck with the broom. Francie attempted to wrestle it from her.

'Francie, stop it will you, Agnes is *supposed* to die.' Theresa dragged the broom away from her little sister.

'Let's see if your God will save you now, Agnes,' shouted Theresa.

'I want a different ending,' begged Francie.

'You're not allowed.'

Francie lurched forward and bit Theresa's hand.

Theresa was indignant. 'What did you do that for?'

'I got carried away,' said Francie.

14

                              *   *   *

When they had exhausted the possibilities of Agnes
they discovered St Rose of Lima. Rose wore a hair shirt
and she loved to whip herself. She whipped until she
bled.

Whip, whip, went Theresa with a branch against
her blouse. She saw blood splatter everywhere, as
it had with Rose of Lima. On the fence. Over the
cinerarias, their mother's washing.

'I want to play too,' said Catherine, determined not
to be left out. It was always Theresa who thought up
the most interesting games.

Dead women began to crowd the garden.

The back yard was awash with blood. It became
a struggle to reach the house. The younger children
swam out to join Theresa and Catherine. They watched
their father arrive home from work, climb out of the
car and wade through a red soup up to his ankles
until he reached the back door.

His black suit was iridescent red.

Catherine was repelled by the gruesome stories of
the young virgin martyrs, whereas Theresa relished the
descriptions of torment and suffering.

The martyrs had preferred death to relinquishing
their virginity. If an unmarried girl lost her virginity,
she became a 'fallen woman' – a woman who had
tumbled from grace. She had dropped out of God's
sight and into the devil's lap like a ripe plum.

'How does a girl lose her virginity?' asked Theresa.

'You're too young to know. When you're big girls
we'll tell you everything. But not now. Later,' promised
their mother.

'Later, always later. We want to know now. We *need*
to know now.'

'What's a Fallen Woman?' they asked Smoking Nana.
She was the only person in their lives who could be
relied upon always to tell the truth. Already they

understood there was Catholic Truth and Non-Catholic Truth and an abyss between them. Their grandmother was a non-Catholic and an atheist.

A disappointed woman, said their mother.

Godless, their father said.

Their family, they were told, was *God-fearing*. Their parents would have had a *Mixed Marriage* if their mother hadn't become a *Convert* immediately before marrying their father.

Did that mean that once their mother had been Godless, they asked. Or worse, a pagan?

'Certainly not,' snapped their father. Their mother had been of a *Different Faith* – Presbyterian – but fortunately for all of them, she had changed her mind and seen the *Light* and been given the Gift of Faith.

Which light? Electric light? Gaslight?

'The light of the One True Faith, of course.'

'A fallen woman,' said Smoking Nana, 'is a Loose Woman. A Fast Woman. A Woman of Easy Virtue. A Woman of Doubtful Reputation. A Scarlet Woman. A Painted Woman. One who is no better than she should be.'

'Yes, *yes*,' breathed Theresa. Why shouldn't they too become fast, loose, painted and scarlet? But there was more they could be.

Their grandmother pulled out a thick book containing thousands of tiny words and flipped the pages avidly. She called it a thesaurus. A labyrinth of words they might lose themselves in. So many choices, she told them, it made you dizzy. So many subtly different points of view to take into account.

'Wench,' she read out. 'Trollop, trull, tart, harlot, whore, strumpet, hooker, scrubber, cocotte, floozy, doxy, moll, temptress, vamp, Jezebel, Delilah. A Bit of Fluff. An odalisque.'

Odalisque?

'Female slave,' she said, adjusting her glasses and

16

frowning at the page. 'Oh dear, in my enthusiasm I seem to have strayed over into kept women and prostitutes. Forget about odalisques, will you, darlings.'

'I want to change the world,' wished Theresa.

'I want to be someone else,' decided Catherine.

'Who?' Theresa idly picked a scab on her knee.

'A nun.'

'Don't be stupid.'

'A martyr, then. I'll die young and everyone will weep buckets of tears. "Such a waste," they'll say.'

'It's worth becoming a martyr to be famous. But you can't be one,' said Theresa, 'because I've already decided that *I'm* going to be the martyr in the family. But you can be the nun if you like.'

'What's the point of being famous if you're dead?' retorted Catherine.

Mrs Flynn covered her ears. 'Spare me,' she groaned, 'this endless drivel. Why can't you go off and become something normal, like nurses, for instance? You can't possibly become martyrs. Don't be so silly,' she said, looking up from a crinkled pile of sliced silver beet. 'This is New Zealand, not Italy. That sort of thing doesn't go on here.'

'Why not?' persisted Theresa.

'Because I said so, that's why.'

'You always say that.'

'Do I?' Her mother's voice was vague, her attention already elsewhere. She scooped up a curl of fat from the enamel basin beside the stove, melted it in the large aluminium pan and added nine meagre mutton chops. She turned down the heat when they began to spit. Next she picked the eyes from seventeen peeled potatoes with a blunt knife, dropped them into an aluminium pot, covered them with cold water and a teaspoon of salt, put a lid on and set them to boil. Then she picked up a handful of the silver beet.

'If I can't become a martyr, I'll become a film star instead,' said Theresa.

Her mother sighed. 'Be what you like,' she said wearily. 'Just so long as you're happy and don't get into any trouble.'

The beautiful Marina de Jesus Paredes y Flores often yearned for death as she lay cocooned in her coffin of self-inflicted pain. Her life was devoted to sacrifice and denial. She stifled her emotions, never smiled or danced and lived like a nun, cloistering herself like a bat in a dark, lonely cell.

Every Friday she prepared for her weekly penance. She put on a clean black dress, an ugly sack-like garment she wore to disguise her slender figure. She polished the little gold cross which she wore on a chain around her neck and brushed her waist-length dark hair until it shone. She loved to feel the weight of her hair swinging against her straight back. It was her one concession to vanity.

After she had dressed she removed the dummy of a corpse from where it resided inside a coffin in her bedroom. She kept it there to remind herself of her own death.

She climbed into the coffin.

It was her custom to spend Friday nights lying enclosed in the coffin, her arms and legs bound with heavy chains. A metal belt encircled her waist. On her head she wore a crown of thorns made of iron spikes. The metal pinched her flesh in a cold embrace all night long but she endured it willingly, offering up her discomfort for the love and glory of her Saviour.

She ate only twice a day, once in the morning and again in the evening. Her first meal consisted of dry crusts of bread which she chewed slowly with her eyes shut, savouring every mouthful. Afterwards she drank two cups of water. The second meal consisted of a bowl of thin vegetable broth. During the afternoons she tried to ignore the rumbling gurgles of protest from her stomach.

Marina de Jesus's senses were finely tuned. She was able to hear the mice and insects mating. She heard rats gnash their teeth in the darkness.

Her eyes became like magnifying glasses. She saw spiders weaving lace curtains for the walls, flower petals open, bulbs shoot, mould spore and grow. She saw and heard all manner of sights and events she would have preferred to remain in ignorance of, yet was unable to prevent herself from knowing. She heard voices clamouring inside her head, warning her. She saw apparitions – demons, angry vengeful angels. Organisms grew and changed in front of her eyes. Fragments of others' thoughts drifted over from the neighbouring houses, entering her consciousness, making her afraid. She could hear the cries of agony from a woman giving birth over a kilometre away, a distress call from a young girl being murdered one hundred kilometres from her house. She discovered others' pain like a water-diviner, drawing it to her breast to enhance her own heightened awareness. Pain was her aphrodisiac. It transformed the world into a place of haunting beauty.

She rarely slept more than three hours a night, but she suffered from neither hunger nor fatigue. She had learned to convert denial of pleasure into an art form.

'My love is pure,' she whispered from inside her coffin, and she held out her empty arms and pointed to her flat belly. The scars and wounds of love were invisible.

Over three centuries later, in 1950, the South American virgin 'the Lily of Ecuador' was canonized Santa Marina de Jesus Paredes y Flores.

'Santa Marina de *Hayzus*,' said Theresa Flynn, correcting the pronunciation of her younger sister Catherine. Their friend the monsignor, because of his

Spanish background and his extensive travels abroad, knew about such details as the correct pronunciation of holy words in the Romance languages and he had taught her how to say it.

'I *know* how to pronounce Jesus in Spanish. I'm not *stupid*,' snapped Catherine. Theresa always seemed to be one step ahead of her.

Already they understood the power of language. Words could wound. Heal. Transform. Transcend. Transubstantiate. Bread into flesh. Wine into blood. *Sticks and stones. Broken bones.*

St Agatha was a virgin martyr from Sicily. When she rejected the advances of a local official, he ordered that her breasts be cut off. Miraculously, her wounds healed. Soldiers rolled her naked over the ground and then killed her.

'There is such a thing as a victim mentality, you know,' said Smoking Nana. 'I read it somewhere, it's when you have something which sort of leaks out from the pores of your skin and makes other people want to hurt you.'

'That's right, blame the victims,' said Mrs Flynn.

'Is it any wonder these girls' heads are full of masochists and martyrs?' asked her mother. 'Look at yourself for once, Moira.'

'What did she mean?' wondered Theresa, and she and Catherine continued to play martyrs and virgins.

'A woman's lot is a hard one,' said Mrs Flynn. 'Pain and sorrow, trials and tribulations, and all sent to test us.'

'Mum, what's a virgin?' asked Theresa. 'You've *got* to tell us.'

'It's an unmarried woman,' replied her mother.

'I don't want to grow up,' said Theresa. 'I'll never get married either. I want to stay a virgin for ever.'

'If you're going to remain a virgin and not get married you'll end up living alone,' said Smoking

20

Nana. 'Not that I'm saying it's a bad thing. I've grown to love it. I have my own views, I do what I want. No-one bosses me around. I'm as free as a bird.'

'You'd be taking your life in your hands trying to boss you around,' commented Mr Flynn.

Grace Malone glanced at her son-in-law. 'I *love love love* living alone,' she sang to annoy him.

Mr Flynn frowned. 'Shut up you old bat!' he shouted. No he didn't, but he wanted to very much. 'Not in front of the children.' He gave his mother-in-law a meaningful look.

She chose to ignore his meaningful look. 'All this tommy-rot about martyrs,' she scoffed. 'It's a load of old cods. Why don't you girls get interested in the Beatles or Bob Dylan instead?'

'*Jesus wept,*' said Mr Flynn and strode off to take it out on the garden. He kicked the wheelbarrow a few times to relieve his feelings. '*Hell's bells and buggy wheels,*' he shouted, driving nails into a plank of wood.

'Trials and tribulations,' muttered Mrs Flynn. Her mouth was full of pins and they became like ashes, choking her. She bent over Toots on his nappy. 'Lie *still*,' she snapped and smacked two tiny disobedient thighs into submission.

Toots promptly shat all over the fresh nappy just as Mrs Flynn snapped the pin closed.

'You *haven't*,' she cried.

Toots gurgled. He gave his mother a mischievous grin.

'You can't win,' said Mrs Flynn and she raised her eyes to heaven and shook her fist, chalking up one more defeat.

'Don't look at me like *that*,' Mrs Flynn reprimanded her smiling baby. 'Life wasn't meant to be fair, as you'll soon discover.'

Toots stared at her with eyes full of love. He stretched

out his hands to his mother as if to pull her down on top of him.

Mrs Flynn collapsed onto the floor beside him and closed her eyes. She wished the world would disappear and she could be alone to sleep until all of her exhaustion had disappeared.

Toots nudged her with his head, sensing he had lost his mother's attention. She inhaled his wonderful baby scent. 'You'll be mine,' she said. 'My special one.'

Toots smiled.

'You're no use to me, you know,' complained Mrs Flynn to her eldest daughters as she vigorously stirred a pot of cabbage slush. 'With your noses in books all day or glued to mirrors, you girls are no help at all.'

'I'm a big help though, aren't I, Mummy?' said Francie.

'Crawler,' said her big sister Theresa.

'You're a good girl, Francie,' conceded her mother.

Being a good girl and pleasing Mummy was more important than anything, thought Francie and she immediately volunteered to do extra jobs around the house.

Mrs Flynn discovered Francie's love letter under her pillow when she pulled out her peach-coloured nylon nightie from under it one evening.

'Dearast daling Mummy, I love you and love you and love you the bestt motther in the hole world. Yous sincely, F.F.

xxxxxxxxxxxxxxxxxxxxxxxxxxxxxxxxxxxxxxxxx'

Mrs Flynn read the note eight times. She thought about Francie and her almost pathetic eagerness to please. She also pictured Toots, who could read her mind and though only a baby seemed to understand her in a way that was uncanny.

Perhaps after all, she decided, her life hadn't been a complete waste.

*   *   *

'I wish my hair was long enough to sit on,' said Theresa. She dreamed of hair which hung down her back in a shimmering golden curtain. Hair like a veil.

All of the saints and martyrs had long hair. Princesses had long hair, actresses and film stars: Julie Christie, Brigitte Bardot, Britt Ekland, Candice Bergen, Ursula Andress. Even Patti Boyd, wife of George Harrison, had long hair. Everybody did except Theresa and Catherine. They hated their short frizzy hair. They wished they could shave it off and wear wigs instead. Russet red like Boadicea's or brown and wavy like St Agnes's.

The girls plastered their hair down with their father's Brylcreem and every time they went to the bathroom ran a wet comb through their curls. Their efforts at straightening their hair gave it an appearance of semi-permanent dampness. They tried rubbing it with Vaseline to make it shiny and that was a disaster. Worse, they applied a household cleanser to their teeth to make them whiter and merely succeeded in removing the surface of the enamel.

'This has all got to stop,' said their mother in exasperation. 'Be satisfied with the way you are. Beauty is in the eye of the beholder. Beauty is only skin deep.'

They didn't believe her.

They went to school with dry flyaway hair and everyone called them golliwogs.

'Why does beauty matter so much?' they asked Smoking Nana.

'Pass me my smokes, will you,' she said and rolled one with a few deft movements of paper and tobacco. 'It's a way of escaping reality. Even if you were beautiful, you wouldn't be beautiful enough. There would always be something to complain about. Puffy ankles, or a fat backside. Like mine, for instance.'

23

It was small comfort.

'I have beautiful hands,' said Catherine, turning them over and examining them closely.

'What's the point of having beautiful hands if you don't have a lovely face?' taunted Theresa.

Catherine began to cry and Theresa was full of remorse and guilt. Another sin to add to her list for the next Confession.

'Who made Catherine cry?' asked their mother, looking hot and bothered from feeding Toots and the Littlies at the same time as cooking tea.

'Not me,' said Theresa immediately.

And there was another sin to add to the long list, she realized. Another lie. But was it a white lie or actually a venial sin? She inspected her tongue in the mirror. No tell-tale spots yet. Maybe it wasn't a white lie then. However, did it count because it wasn't premeditated?

How could she, Theresa Flynn, have thought herself worthy and holy enough to become a martyr? She, the worst sinner in the family.

Every night over dinner their father lectured them on the problems and disasters of the world. It was a soliloquy. No-one dared to interrupt him.

'Children should be seen and not heard,' he said. And: 'Listening is a greater virtue than talking.'

His voice scared them. It barked out orders and instructions and asked questions to which there appeared to be no answers. He told them things they didn't want to know.

He spoke of Iron Curtains. The Red Peril. The Cold War. His voice droned on. Spheres of Influence. The Communist Takeover. The Domino Theory. The Fall of the Free World. *Vietnam. Vietcong.* And: *Cultural Revolution. Red Guard.*

'*Miaw-see-tongue,*' said their father.

*   *   *

24

Theresa and Catherine made their own Iron Curtain down in the back garden out of a sheet of rusty old corrugated iron and propped it up against the fence. Theresa hid behind it and spied through a hole.

'Halt. Who goes hither? Password?' she growled.

'Red Guard,' squawked Catherine, brandishing a stick.

After several weeks Theresa and Catherine became bored with the Red Guard and pulled down the Iron Curtain. They returned to Dorothy and her father, Agnes and the Roman soldier, Maria and her rapist. Joan at the stake.

A window opened behind them. Their mother inserted her head into the gap.

'Get cracking, you girls,' she called. 'I want both of you in here to peel the spuds and chop the silver beet. Now, get a move on, or I'll be after you with the wooden spoon.'

The window snapped shut.

The girls continued to suffer in God's name. Five minutes later the window opened again.

'Or *else*,' warned their mother.

'Bloody spuds,' said Theresa.

'Shitty silver beet,' whispered Catherine.

'What was that?' called their mother, whose radar could apparently reach into the furthest corner of the back yard.

'Nothing.'

'It didn't sound like nothing to me.'

Out she came into the yard. 'Come here. This instant.'

They went, scuffing their feet, hanging their heads, taking their time.

She reached out and grabbed each of them by the ear and pulled them squealing and protesting into the house. Down the hall, into the bathroom.

Behind them the potatoes slowly boiled to slush. Meat blackened and dried on the bones.

'It's time you learnt your lesson,' she panted. 'If I've told you once . . . '

She grasped a handful of Theresa's hair and yanked her head back in one swift movement. With the other she dug into the soap with a toothbrush, swished it under the cold tap and then began to vigorously scrub her eldest daughter's teeth and gums until they bled.

'That'll teach you. Foul language – not in *my* house.'

Theresa felt as if she had slammed into a wall and fallen backwards into darkness. Her face didn't belong to her any more. It was streaked with saliva, snot and tears. Her skin tightened as the soap dried. When she had been taught the lesson her mother pushed her away.

'You next,' she said to Catherine.

Theresa refused to look at her mother. She was transformed into someone she didn't recognize. She had become a monster. And yet, mysteriously, inside the monster with the hard mouth and angry eyes was also a sweet loving mother who kissed them and made cakes. She never knew what word or action would cause her mother to change into the creature who pushed and shouted, crying they had driven her up the wall and enough was enough.

It was because they were wicked and deserved to be punished. Their father said children were like wild animals. They had to be tamed.

Catherine's head jerked up. A cry rose in her throat and was choked back. She spat. Blood had turned the soap froth pink.

After their mother left the bathroom they looked at each other without speaking.

For a full minute they assessed the damage before a triumphant smile appeared on Theresa's face.

'*Shitty, shitty, shitty,*' she whispered in her sister's ear.

'*Bloodyshittybuggerhelldamnblast,*' whispered Catherine back, without taking her eyes off Theresa.

'I don't care.'

'I don't care either then.'

'Offer it up.'

'Of course.'

Because their mother would make them martyrs.

Chapter Two

THE TALLEST MAN

A monsignor often visited the Flynns. He was the tallest man they had ever seen. He possessed a photographic memory and a prodigious appetite. He always forgot to stoop when he entered through their back door and inevitably banged his head. They waited for him to curse in Spanish, to rub the crown of his head and then give them a rueful grin. They stared at his skinny body, at the bony wrists, the long fingers, and marvelled at his height. His soutane hung in folds from his shoulders. It was too short. It looked more like a dress than a soutane. They had no idea how old he was. He wouldn't tell them. Mr Flynn said he was in his late twenties. Mrs Flynn disagreed. She said he was in his mid-thirties, maybe even older.

The monsignor brought them black olives to try. No-one liked them, but they each ate one to be polite. They would have eaten toads if he'd brought them – anything rather than offend him. And once he made *Menestra de Acelgas a la Extremeña* for them – vegetable and potato casserole. At first Mrs Flynn allowed him into her domain reluctantly. She had never known a man who could cook.

The monsignor said the dish was a meal on its own. It required only a few twists of freshly ground black pepper, a bowl of plump juicy black olives, and a salad of crisp lettuce leaves tossed with anchovies and olive oil. He brought all these ingredients with him to their house, including olive oil and garlic, which they had never used before. The olives and anchovies were precious to him. His mother sent them from Madrid.

Mr Flynn expressed his doubts about the monsignor taking over the kitchen for a night. To him it wasn't a meal if it didn't include meat.

'Are you sure you know what you're doing?' Mrs Flynn hovered, hoping to catch him out. What would a priest know about creaming butter and sugar, simmering, bringing to the boil, or basting?

The monsignor rolled up his sleeves. He heated a cup of olive oil in a pan and into it placed slices of potato. While they were cooking he boiled beans, leeks and cauliflower until they were tender and drained them. After he had carefully sautéd onion and garlic he sautéd the greens. To these he added parsley, salt and pepper and paprika. He combined the cooked potato mixture and the greens together in a casserole dish and over it poured some lightly beaten eggs. He baked the casserole until the egg formed a crisp golden crust on top. He served generous portions and when they had cleared their plates there was still some left over.

'*Algo màs?* You like more?'

Mrs Flynn paid him the ultimate compliment – she copied down the recipe. Spud and vegie casserole, she wrote in her tiny cramped handwriting in her exercise book. When she attempted the dish they all said it didn't taste as good as the monsignor's. She couldn't find olive oil and instead used the fat from the basin on the stove. She had run out of paprika too and hadn't put in any garlic.

'*Hola, buenas noches mis amigos.*'

Mrs Flynn would forget her exhaustion in her pleasure at seeing the monsignor. She hurried to put some food in front of her guest in case he should shame them by fainting in her kitchen from malnourishment. He never turned down an offer of food. He was always hungry and yet he never put on an ounce of fat.

Mrs Flynn felt sorry for him. His mother lived far

away in Madrid and his housekeeper was apparently a terrible cook.

This night they had already eaten. The monsignor appeared too tired to be interested in converting them to the culinary delights of his homeland. He wanted to be fussed over.

'Monsignor. Supper?' invited Mrs Flynn.

He hovered awkwardly wringing his big red hands.

'I did not intend to come for supper. No trouble please for me.'

He made the appropriate little play of seeming to debate the invitation.

'Oh, go on, Father.'

'Oh, well. All right then. *Gracias.*'

As if he hadn't come deliberately to cadge some supper, thought Mrs Flynn, rebuking herself at the same time for the uncharitable thought.

He flopped down on a vinyl-covered chrome chair and sighed deeply. The girls and Mrs Flynn gathered about him ready to serve.

'*Que tal?* How are things?'

'Box of birds here. Box of birds.'

'*Cómo?* You are meaning?'

Mrs Flynn smiled. 'We're fine.'

'*Muy bien. Muy bien.*'

The cake tins were full. Rolled-oat biscuits, Anzac biscuits and a Betty Crocker cake were whisked out onto plates. A lace cloth was thrown over the table and smoothed out so that it hung in neat folds over the edge. The good china was brought out – the cups with the gold rims and the blue cornflower pattern.

Theresa and Catherine stared at their mother. Why was her face so pink?

Mrs Flynn was remembering a dream she had had concerning the monsignor. He had caressed her full breasts with a slow, tender delight, in a way in which Mr Flynn never thought of doing and she had never requested of him. The monsignor moaned with

30

pleasure, whispering endearments in Spanish. Afterwards he had gone on to take her breasts into his mouth
one at a time, hungry as a child, acting as if he wanted to
devour them whole. She blushed as she recalled it.

She had awakened surprised to discover that she
had been stroking the tingling pink button between her
legs. She was rubbing her two fingers back and forth
in frantic little movements. It produced unexpectedly
pleasurable sensations. She wanted to continue, but
she soon stopped because she was afraid of losing
control.

The monsignor's long fingers now caressed the gold
rim of his china cup, rubbing against the smoothness
of the china, feeling for the little ridge at the top of
the cup. His fingers mesmerized Mrs Flynn.

He ate everything Mrs Flynn placed in front of him.
The cake tins were reopened and half a dozen date
scones produced. He ate as if he hadn't done so for
a week. When he had finished he belched quietly
behind his hand and complimented his hostess on
her baking.

The Flynns sat open-mouthed through his per-
formance, aghast at his table manners. Poor devil,
thought Mrs Flynn, he obviously had no idea. Men
could be like babies. A woman wouldn't sit there like
that and not *know*.

He had spilled tea and dropped crumbs of cake
down the front of his soutane and seemed oblivious
to the picture he presented to them. His hair stood
on end because he never combed it properly. Flakes
of dandruff clung to his shoulders. Black could be
merciless, thought Mrs Flynn.

The girls tried not to gawk. It was rude to stare.

Mrs Flynn was scarcely able to focus on his words
because she was so preoccupied with imagining how
she could improve his appearance. First she would
deal with his soutane, giving it a thorough cleaning.
Next – his teeth. How long was it since he'd been to

31

the dentist and had them professionally cleaned? And why hadn't someone pointed him in the direction of the barber? Tamed his shaggy head. Trimmed the black curls that crept over his surprisingly small ears. She wanted to ask him why he didn't care what he looked like, what sort of impression he made. Yet he liked people and seemed to expect to be liked in return.

Theresa helped herself to some white bread and honey. The honey was solid in the jar and impossible to spread evenly the way she liked it.

'Don't maul the honey,' snapped Mrs Flynn, who had eyes in the back of her head.

There was something about the monsignor, she thought, despite his many shortcomings. He was appealing and charming in his helplessness, his lack of practical sense. He lived in a more rarefied world altogether. He never made her feel ignorant – unlike Mr Flynn. She longed to do things for the monsignor.

Wherever the monsignor went women fed him. They couldn't help themselves. His neediness was irresistible to the women of St Anne's Parish where he had been loaned until another arrangement was made for a new parish priest. The women competed with each other to satisfy his terrible hunger. If he had such cravings and hunger for food, what other cravings might he have? Rumours about his housekeeper being 'no better than she ought to be', and 'taking her concept of duty to the limit and beyond it', flew regularly about the parish.

Mr Flynn dismissed the rumours. 'You'd have to be blind drunk to fancy her,' he said unkindly. 'Or just plain blind.'

Theresa and Catherine were fascinated by the tall awkward monsignor. One day he might be made a bishop and yet he visited their little house and ate their mother's cooking.

How lonely to be a priest. Never to have a wife and children. Theresa noticed that the monsignor liked women. He instinctively sought them out first in any social gathering and towered above them round-shouldered, braying at their jokes and teasing them in return.

The monsignor had travelled to Portugal, Morocco, Mexico, England, France and Italy. He was particularly fond of Mexico.

'The churches are more beautiful over there,' he enthused, gesturing wildly and almost destroying a statue. Mrs Flynn quickly rearranged the religious objects on the coffee table to avoid further mishaps.

He told them he was ashamed of the way the Spanish had treated the Indians in Mexico, but although they had committed many atrocities they had also brought beauty and elegance to the country. The churches they built were like fairytale castles and the interiors were lined with ornate gold decorations. In front of the statues there were hundreds of votive candles which burned inside little glass jars and there would be more in front of Our Lady than any other statue, even *El Corazón Sagrado* – the Sacred Heart. Often the statues were life-sized and had real hair and costumes. Tiny tin medals of arms and legs and hearts called *milagros* would be threaded with ribbon and pinned onto the garments of Our Lady and the Sacred Heart.

The monsignor told them about another Madonna, one they hadn't heard of before: *Neustra Senora de Guadalupe*, the patron of Mexico.

'On the feast of the Immaculate Conception in December 1531 the peasant Juan Diego heard a woman calling to him,' said the monsignor, settling himself into the couch.

Theresa and Catherine sat at his feet. They looked up at him expectantly.

What a beautiful picture that would make, thought

Mrs Flynn who was tempted to take a photo of the scene. But she was afraid to use the camera in case she broke it. Terrence always said she was not mechanically-minded.

'The woman revealed to him that she was actually the Mother of God,' continued the monsignor. 'She asked him to arrange to build a church up among the rocks and the cacti. Juan promised to see the bishop and give her message to him.

'But sadly, the bishop didn't believe Juan,' said the monsignor.

'Naturally,' said Mrs Flynn.

'The Virgin appeared a second time to Juan and the bishop believed him then because Juan's cloak was miraculously imprinted with the image of Our Lady of Guadalupe. A church was built and the cloak was displayed inside it. Afterwards there were many miracles.'

'What kind of miracles?' asked Theresa.

The monsignor couldn't remember. He gave Theresa and Catherine each a holy picture small enough to fit inside their prayer books. The pictures showed an olive-skinned Madonna in a green cloak patterned with stars. An enormous halo radiated out from her body and she was supported by angels.

'She's so beautiful,' said Catherine.

'She is the Queen of the Angels,' said the monsignor.

'More important than the Queen of England?'

'Many many times more powerful.'

She was an intermediary between the people and God. In this capacity, he said, her power was limitless.

Catherine decided she loved the monsignor more than her father, more than any other man she knew. Maybe the monsignor might eventually become tired of being a priest and when she grew up he would marry her. They would have children who would be tall and thin and always hungry. He would teach her how to speak and cook in Spanish.

'I'll never forget you, Monsignor,' said Theresa as she showed him to the door.

'Of course you'll forget me, Tessie.' Tears sprang into his eyes. *'Mi hija,'* he murmured. His emotions showed on his face like exposed nerves.

'You'll grow up and eventually get married and have babies. I'll be like a ship that has passed in the night. You'll see.'

'Oh, but I might not want babies,' replied Theresa. 'I haven't made up my mind yet.'

'Cómo? Dios mio. You're too young yet to know what He has planned for you,' said the monsignor.

'It's not up to you to decide,' said her mother with a tight mouth.

'Don't I have a say in the matter?'

No-one answered her.

The monsignor was already at the letter-box. He turned to wave and smile at them before loping towards his old Rover.

'Hasta luego.'

'Adiós,' called Theresa.

He turned and flashed her a radiant smile.

'Dios no se muda,' said the monsignor gently to Catherine.

It was several weeks later. They were sitting on the steps of the back porch shelling peas into a scratched green plastic bowl. Catherine loved having him to herself. The monsignor was much slower than her because when he lost himself in his stories pods slipped unnoticed from his fingers. He gestured to add emphasis to his words. A dozen different expressions might flit over his face in the span of a few moments. His face and hands were never still. Catherine knew he was like this because he was sensitive. He seemed to feel things more deeply than most other people. He anguished. He ached.

She did too. They were both sensitive, she decided.

He always understood how she felt. Long explanations were not necessary. He *knew*.

She had never seen a grown man cry until she met the monsignor. Anything could cause him to dissolve into tears. The starving millions. The plight of the lost souls. A baby born dead to one of his parishioners. A husband and wife separating. Earthquakes, floods, famine. But he always found plenty to appreciate and rejoice in as well. He delighted in the colours of nature, observed the way light fell on a leaf or flower and marvelled at its beauty. He studied the swooping dive of a bird to its prey. He saw these things as evidence of God's love for his poor creatures.

An opened pea-pod trembled between two fingers as he explained something to Catherine. He loved the Flynn children, especially their hair. It made him want to weep – Theresa and Catherine with their white hair and the rest with flame-red. All in the one family. Truly a miracle, he thought.

The monsignor had been invited to Sunday lunch and in his honour they were having roast lamb, baked potatoes, fresh peas, mint sauce and gravy followed by strawberries and cream for pudding. The strawberries had already been picked from their garden, washed and prepared earlier that morning by Theresa.

Smoking Nana was visiting again. She sat inside the house gossiping with her daughter, keeping out of the sun and fanning herself with a copy of the *Tablet*. She was deeply suspicious of nuns and priests.

'I thought it was only pagans who worshipped statues,' she taunted.

'That is very true,' agreed the patient monsignor. 'Catholics do not worship these statues. They are only reminders so we can have a picture in our minds when we pray.'

'Is that a fact? You could have fooled me, but never mind.' She sat back with folded arms. 'Here's another one then. How can your Mary be the mother of God if it was God who created her in the first place? Answer me that.'

The monsignor sighed. He took a moment to compose his thoughts before beginning to explain to her that Christ had two natures – one divine and the other human. God had assumed human nature in order to be born.

'*Comprende?* Do you understand?'

She shrugged, unwilling to concede an inch.

He had only come inside for a glass of water. He helped himself at the sink and took it outside with him.

'He hasn't convinced me,' said Smoking Nana, determined as always to have the last word.

Mrs Flynn followed the monsignor outside to apologize for her mother's rudeness.

He waved her apologies aside. 'Do not speak of it,' he said.

Catherine flicked her peas into the basin and spun the pod into an aluminium bucket alongside it. She struggled to understand the monsignor's words. *Dios no se muda. Dios . . .* God? *Dios no* – no God?

'God never changes. That's what it means.'

'Who said that?'

The monsignor was always quoting, just like her father. The difference was that the monsignor was always ready to admit when he was wrong.

'The words of a very remarkable woman. She was born early in the sixteenth century in the Castilian region of central Spain. Her name was Teresa Sánchez de Cepeda y Ahumada.'

'I've never heard of her.'

'You know her by another name. St Teresa of Avila.'

That Teresa. Catherine already loved and admired her. She too longed to converse 'not with men, but with angels'.

The monsignor told her St Teresa had experienced

years of frustration as she struggled to pray. She had been torn between worldly and spiritual concerns.

'Even the saints,' he said, 'were human.'

Catherine wondered if she would continue to struggle through her whole life to achieve perfection. Or would she remain a sinner?

The monsignor read her mind.

'Prayer is the answer to everything,' he advised. 'Have faith. Faith can move mountains.'

Chapter Three

THE VALLEY OF TEARS

Dominating the lounge from her prime position on top of the mantelpiece was a one-metre tall plaster statue of the Madonna, swathed in a protective plastic bag.

As a treat they were allowed, for two minutes at a time, to switch it on. Theresa removed the bag and pressed the small button at the base of the statue. The Madonna began slowly to rotate on her dais. The tiny light bulbs linked by wire which formed a halo around her head flashed on and off. There was a little square door in the middle of her chest. It opened and shut in time with the flashing halo. Inside the door was a plastic moulded heart with flames emerging from it. The heart contained a bulb, which glowed a dazzling red.

The children thought it the best thing in the entire house. No-one touched it without permission. Mr Flynn became annoyed if he ever caught one of his children wasting power. 'Waste not, want not,' he said on his nightly patrols around the house checking that neither hot water nor electricity were being used unnecessarily.

Flanking the Madonna were two porcelain vases formed into pairs of hands clasped in prayer. Miniature plastic roses splayed out from the china fingers. With the exception of the Italian Madonna who had been won in the last parish raffle, everything in the room had been bought second-hand through the newspaper, at auction, or from the only furniture shop the town possessed. Colours and textures screamed against each other. Swamp-coloured easy chairs were jammed alongside a mustard velour two-seater couch and a burgundy astrakhan three-seater. The carpet, already threadbare beneath the areas where furniture had been strategically positioned, was covered with heavy plastic mats. Cheap ornaments of animals, shepherdesses and saints crowded the metal shadow boxes, which were screwed to the walls safely out of reach of the smaller Flynns. The ornaments were attached to their respective shelves with plasticine in anticipation of an earthquake.

They were directly on the fault line. Mr Flynn was convinced their house lay dead centre of it. Every appliance and stick of furniture was tied firmly to sturdy hooks in the walls with nylon and wire.

They lived always under the threat of imminent disaster. Only Toots appeared unconcerned. He lay on a tartan rug in his little playpen on the floor, humming and playing with his rattle.

Mr Flynn raised a long finger and pointed to his youngest child. Toots stopped humming instantly.

His father turned his back on him.

Toots took careful aim. A small arc of vomit sprayed onto Mr Flynn's home-knitted jersey and the droplets trembled on the wool. Although everybody except Mr Flynn noticed, no-one commented. Good old Toots, they thought.

Theresa distributed the plastic rosary beads. Blue for her mother, because that was her favourite colour. Pink for Catherine. Black for her father. Red for herself and yellow, green, white and purple for Timothy, Francie, John and Andrew.

They knelt in a semi-circle in the lounge, arranging themselves around the fire. Mr Flynn stoked it up and then led his family in the recitation of the *Salve Regina*.

'Hail, holy Queen, mother of mercy; hail our life, our sweetness, and our hope! To thee do we cry, poor banished children of Eve; to thee do we send up our sighs, mourning and weeping from this valley of tears. Turn then, O most gracious advocate, thine eyes of mercy towards us, and after this our exile show unto us the blessed fruit of thy womb, Jesus: O clement, O loving, O sweet Virgin Mary.'

None of them looked at each other as they recited the familiar prayer. They were lost in their own private worlds while, outwardly at least, giving an impression of intense concentration. It was only Mr Flynn who paid any real attention to the words he spoke. His Holy Queen was both stern and maternal. He saw her also as proud, gracious and merciful. She dispensed favours to those of her subjects she considered worthy of them. She was the intermediary, the mediator.

He knew that he lived in the valley of tears. He was a senior salesman at the local branch of a store that sold electrical appliances and whiteware. That day his job had filled him with such intense feelings of boredom and frustration he wondered how he would tolerate another week of it, let alone another whole year or, worse, a lifetime.

What choice did he have? He was the breadwinner and he had no money to go out on his own, which had always been his dream. Jobs weren't easy to come by in Chatterton and he felt lucky to have one. But this did not prevent him from criticizing and ridiculing his employer when he was at home. Tom McKrill, who owned the local branch, was always the buffoon in Mr Flynn's stories.

After work he sat primly in his work clothes – white shirt pulled tautly across his scrawny chest, navy striped tie loosened, black-trousered legs crossed, square-toed black shoes shined to mirrored perfection, hair slicked back with cream.

He had temporary asylum from the hell of McKrill in the Kingdom of Flynn and here he was treated royally. They ran to obey his commands. The newspaper was brought, his slippers fetched. A cold beer. Another beer. They closed the blinds to block out the sun, which he said shone into his eyes and made it difficult to read the fine print in the newspaper.

They were afraid of him. He had his schedule and his habits. They knew his preferences, his sulking, if he didn't get what he wanted. His chair was like an altar and it was always in the same corner, away from the glare of the late afternoon sun.

The McKrill versus Flynn drama was played out late every afternoon to a captive audience. Mrs Flynn nodded and murmured at appropriate intervals. She continued to prepare tea while her husband drank his beer and read the paper.

'I could run McKrill's place with my eyes shut,' he said. 'Any fool could. He never orders enough stock. We're always running out. And delegate – pah! He wouldn't know what the word means.'

There were never enough television sets for example, to meet the growing demand for the new form of entertainment. One day, he predicted, although his boss refused to believe it, there would be a television set in every home in the country. He had read in the newspaper that there were well over one hundred and sixty million sets in the entire world already. Of course New Zealand had always lagged behind the rest of the world by a decade at least. He had shown the article to McKrill, who merely grunted, still unconvinced.

'He said to me: "But Terrence, man, what'll happen to radio?"' Mr Flynn remembered the irritating way his boss had picked his teeth with a freshly sharpened matchstick and twirled around on his high stool behind the counter. He had felt a strong desire to fling the stool and its occupant out of the front door and onto the street.

'I told him, I said: "Radios will become like dinosaurs. They've had their day. Just wait till TV starts broadcasting twenty-four hours a day and then, mark my words, no-one will want to go to work. People won't be able to tear themselves away from the set. No-one will read books any more, they'll get all their information from TV. I'm telling you, without a word of a lie, this will be our future."'

'And what did he say then Dad?'

Mr Flynn snorted.

'His mind is closed. The future is marching on past him and he can't see it. Take note. Remember what I've said. You'll see I'll be proved right. It gets on my goat, because if McKrill misses the boat and someone else in Chatterton cashes in on the TVs he'll only have himself to blame, but I'll be down the creek without a job.'

'Why don't you get your own shop, Dad?'

'Because money doesn't grow on trees, young lady.'

'How did Mr McKrill get the money to buy his shop then?'

'Family money.'

Born with a silver spoon in his mouth. Some people had all the luck, while others – they knew their father was referring to himself here – had to slave to the grave and with precious little thanks at the end of the day.

They always began the rosary kneeling upright. Within a few moments, however, they would all be slumped into the seats with their bottoms protruding, using the seats as elbow supports. It meant that none of the children could see their father. If he thought they were too slow with their responses, or mumbled, or slurred their words, they would be brought back abruptly to the task at hand by a well-timed kick to one of the row of bottoms presented to him.

'Ouch, that hurt,' the offending child would cry out.

Then they would adjust their chairs and wriggle as far away from the reach of his long arms and legs as possible.

If he was so busily keeping them under observation

43

how could he possibly be concentrating on his *own* prayers?

Their mother, who always appeared to be in agreement with their father's disciplinary measures, offered them no support. They heard her tired voice continue to murmur the responses night after night, '. . . Hail Mary full of grace . . . Holy Mary Mother of God . . . Hail Mary . . . Holy Mary . . . pray for us sinners now and at the hour of our death. Amen.'

They found it impossible to concentrate for more than a moment every night. They would slip even lower into their seats. They longed to gallop through the Rosary and reduce it from twenty minutes to ten. When they thought they had finished Mr Flynn would inevitably add on some extra prayers and requests – pleas for a pay rise, or a prayer to speed the progress of a relative on their journey from Purgatory to Heaven.

Mr Flynn would have it calculated. Old Uncle Ed who had been dead for just over a year should just about have done his time in Purgatory by now, he said.

Without looking at his watch Mr Flynn always seemed to time these extra prayers and direct negotiations with God so that they came to a neat conclusion just as the television news was about to begin.

A pine log collapsed into the flames, causing two smaller ones to fall. A shower of sparks flew out into the room. The family roused themselves, all thoughts of prayer driven from their minds. The children hurried to stamp out the live sparks with their feet while Mrs Flynn collected some large pieces with the dustpan and brush. Several sparks left a series of black marks, most likely permanent, on a section of patterned carpet not protected by a plastic mat.

'Jesus wept,' exclaimed Mr Flynn. 'You wouldn't read about it.'

Mrs Flynn wondered if she would be blamed for

44

the incident. Most of the children thought she would be. Theresa thought her mother might be lucky. They would have to distract him somehow. They always supported their mother against their father.

For the present it seemed sensible to remain silent. They made sure their faces were devoid of expression.

Mr Flynn's face was red. Was it only the firelight that warmed his face, they wondered. He frowned. His nostrils flared – not a good sign. His chest heaved. And then he cracked his knuckles and vigorously scratched his chin. They heard the scraping sound.

They let out their breath. It could go either way. They continued to watch him covertly, interpreting his gestures alternately as either benign or potentially hostile.

He ran his right hand several times through his wiry red hair, leaving the grizzled tufts standing on end.

They tried not to laugh. One wrong move at this stage and he might explode. They dreaded his anger more than anything – his quick temper which led him to cuff them with the back of his hand over their ears until they rang with a fiery pain.

Finally Mr Flynn picked up his beads again and they knew everything would be bearable for another night. They were safe. The fire would warm them. Sometimes it even seemed as if God heard them.

Mr Flynn barked out an instruction for Catherine to lead the first Decade.

'Hail Mary full of grace,' she began to recite in her timid voice.

'SPEAK UP,' bellowed Mr Flynn. 'We can't hear you. And I don't think the Man Upstairs can either.'

'THE LORD IS WITH THEE,' shouted Catherine.

'There's no need to shout now. Show some respect. Lord love us, I don't know.'

Theresa felt a flame of feeling lick up her chest and longed to cry out on her sister's behalf. Alongside, her mother shot her a warning glance.

After they had finished reciting the five Decades and the extra prayers tagged on at the end by their father, they stared hard at the television as a reminder to Mr Flynn to switch it on. He refused to let any of them touch the household appliances in case they damaged them.

Chapter Four

THE EYE OF THE NEEDLE

Catherine lay prostrate on her bed, waiting for visions. She dreamed of soaring to heaven, transcending the earthly reality of 23 Grey Street, Chatterton. She wanted to experience a trance like those of Hildegard and Teresa of Avila so badly she bit her lips until they bled. She began to skip meals, saying she was sick, convinced there must be a connection between the fasting practices of the mystics and their ability to enter trance states of ecstasy.

'*Speak* to me, Hildegard,' she begged.

'We have a nutcase on our hands,' said Mr Flynn. 'What are we going to do about it?'

'Ignore it,' answered Mrs Flynn. 'She'll grow out of it, you'll see.'

He remained unconvinced.

'The light which I see is not located, but yet is more brilliant than the sun. I cannot examine its height, length or breadth, and I name it "the cloud of living light",' said Hildegard when she was an old woman.

'You're not a twelfth-century mystic, you're a ten-and-a-half-year-old girl and I don't want you starving yourself to death,' said Mrs Flynn firmly, piling Catherine's plate high with boiled silver beet to boost her iron intake.

Teresa of Avila described her soul as a castle. Catherine saw her own soul as a locked room, one to which she lacked a vital key. She wished she could predict the future. Would her hair straighten? Would she be cursed with the stigmata? Given a vocation?

'You're a worry,' said her father. 'Why can't you be normal like everybody else?'

'Let nothing disturb you, let nothing dismay you, all things pass,' said Catherine in reply, quoting the extraordinary Teresa of Avila.

'Don't answer me back, madam,' said Mr Flynn. He boxed her over the ears, and they continued to ring for a long time afterwards.

'Mum, Catherine is cheating again. She's hiding her food in her pockets so you think she's eaten when really she hasn't.'

'Nobody likes a tell-tale,' said Mrs Flynn to Theresa. 'Why can't you be a nice girl like Catherine and Francie?'

Theresa didn't know. Their niceness made her want to throw up.

'I think the devil gets into you sometimes,' said her father. 'He's a slippery bird, there's no doubt about it. The Gentleman with Cloven Hooves can dress up the worst sin you could ever imagine and serve it up to you on a platter so that it looks like the best tucker you've seen in your life. But he's full of lies and false promises, as you'll soon discover, should you ever fall into his cunning hands. I don't need to spell it out to you – you'll see what I'm talking about soon enough.'

No matter how hard Theresa tried she never managed to be good for longer than a few hours at a time. She continued to commit sins without even trying.

Every week she went to Confession and afterwards said her penance. But the following week she returned only to confess the same sins again. Sometimes she invented new sins so she wouldn't bore the monsignor, but he never noticed.

She bowed her head. 'Bless me, Father, for I have sinned. It is one week since my last Confession and I have been rude, jealous, lying, vain, greedy and disobedient.' She scoured her conscience further. How

48

many times had she committed each sin? Once? Twice? A dozen times?

She took a deep breath.

'I'm such a bad girl,' she confided to the monsignor. She felt unhappy and unlovable.

She knelt in the dark booth, a grey cardigan draped over her head like a veil because she'd forgotten to wear her beret to school.

The monsignor smiled. Could a young girl exist who was not good and pure? Didn't all young girls have God inside them? He looked forward to the St Anne's Friday Confessions. After the tedium of the adult parishioners the girls' litanies of petty jealousies and tiny white lies were a refreshing tonic. He would have preferred to dispense the lightest of penances (a single Hail Mary?), but some of the more devout girls, like young Catherine Flynn, demanded heavier sentences.

He always knew when it was Catherine Flynn behind the grille because her long list of potential sins and imagined slights and offences inevitably included references to Hildegard of Bingen or Teresa of Avila.

'Why not play with your dolls?' the monsignor suggested. 'Don't always be worrying about self-denial and punishment. Enjoy yourself.' He refused to give her a Rosary for her penance. 'Two or three Hail Marys — that will be enough.' Catherine ignored her confessor's advice and recited an entire Rosary. Her classmates waited in the pews for her to finish, whispering and speculating about the nature of sins Catherine might have committed.

Catherine tied up her teenage doll Joan on a stake in the back yard and lit a small fire beneath it. Soon, to her dismay, little tongues of flame began to crawl along the grass. They swiftly became bigger flames which moved inexorably nearer to Toots's pram. She scurried about making futile attempts to stamp out the flames with a block of wood. John, who was standing daydreaming at the kitchen window, ran screaming to find his mother.

'Mother, bring me the stick,' commanded Mr Flynn when he arrived home that night. 'This girl has to be taught a lesson she won't forget in a hurry.'

'Don't be too hard on her, Terrence,' she begged.

'She could have burned the house down, could have killed Toots and you ask me to be lenient. Are you mad?'

'Bend over,' he said to his second eldest daughter.

Catherine obediently bent over her bed.

'Shall I pull my pants down?'

'No, that won't be necessary. You're too big for that now.'

Catherine gritted her teeth as the stick fell on her burning buttocks and calves.

She was unable to prevent herself from crying out. Mrs Flynn blocked her ears with her fingers and quickly left the room.

As soon as she opened the door a small cannonball shot through it, and the Flynn family was never the same again.

Silently Francie threw her body over her sister's.

'Francie, get *off*, will you,' said her father.

Francie shook her head. 'You'll have to *kill* me first.'

'This is *ridiculous*. You're being melodramatic. I'm not killing Catherine. I'm simply teaching her a lesson.'

Mr Flynn tried unsuccessfully to release Francie's fingers from where they clung to her sister's waist.

Francie bit his fingers hard. He shouted out and removed his hands.

'Get out of my sight!' he yelled. 'I'm warning you. You're sailing close to the wind, my girl.'

Francie continued to cling to Catherine and the two of them shivered on the bed.

Mr Flynn flung down the stick in disgust and

stormed out of the room. He was left to locate the sticking-plasters and bandage his fingers by himself.

'Next time,' he told his wife, 'you do it.'

'Of course,' agreed Mrs Flynn. She didn't meet his eyes.

'Thank you, Francie,' said Catherine.

'You'd sacrifice yourself for me too, wouldn't you Cathy?'

Francie's eyes as they looked up at Catherine were open and trusting. Seeing the faith shining out from her little sister's face gave Catherine a peculiar pain in her chest and she knew that if anything awful ever happened to Francie she would just *die*. She felt like howling except that her eyes were so red and sore that there were no tears left inside her.

'Of course,' she answered. 'You know I'd save you.'

It was the way Francie had tried to save her, she thought. No-one had ever stood up to their father like this before.

But would she save Francie? Her little sister was braver than all of them. The most pure, the most innocent. It would be Francie, rather than her or Theresa, who would become a saint.

She peered through the window into the gathering dusk. Poor Joan had melted into the blackened lawn. Too late she regretted the sacrifice.

Joan had been a good doll, providing comfort in the middle of many a dark night when Catherine woke up wondering where she was, afraid to make the journey down the hall to the toilet. On nights like this Joan had always accompanied her, leading the way, held out in front of Catherine's outstretched arms like a beacon.

'I wouldn't make a very good saint,' Catherine told the monsignor the following Friday after she had confessed setting fire to the lawn. 'I love my worldly

51

goods too much. I couldn't even sacrifice my doll for the glory of God without regretting it afterwards.'

'"If I give away all that I possess, piece by piece and even if I let them take my body to burn it, but am without love . . ."' murmured the monsignor.

Catherine was aware of the length of the queue of St Anne's girls waiting outside. This didn't stop her launching into a discussion with the monsignor on the subject of camels passing through the eyes of needles and the Church's attitude to wealth.

'It's not meant literally,' explained the monsignor. 'The camel is a metaphor, a symbol.'

'What's a metaphor?'

'It's when a word meaning one kind of idea is applied to another, to suggest a connection.'

'Yes, all right,' said Catherine impatiently, 'but why a camel?'

'There were lots of camels around in that part of the world, I suppose.'

What a pathetic answer. Priests and nuns never answered questions properly. They always went off at a tangent and then finished up by saying she had to take it all on faith. But why should she? Catherine frowned.

'And what happens to rich *women*?' she demanded to know. 'Could a very thin rich woman on a camel pass through the eye of a needle?'

Sister Mary Angela brought an abrupt end to the discussion when she flung open the velvet curtain and hissed a request for Catherine to please leave the remainder of her sins for another day.

Catherine was mortified. Trust Angles to make a scene in front of everyone. She hated her. Her teacher was ugly, fat, wheezy and red-faced. Her body smelled of lavender and mothballs and her breath of peppermint. Catherine crept past the rows of classmates. Their heads bobbed up as she passed.

As she slipped into a vacant pew she realized that

in daring to criticize Angles, even if it were only in her mind, she had sinned against charity. Her sins had been forgiven by the monsignor but her conscience was now burdened with the weight of another sin. She wished she could confess all over again so her conscience could be completely clear.

The nuns said each and every sin had to be atoned for after death. It was why souls spent so long in Purgatory. One terrible day she too would suffer in Purgatory, twisting and turning on a bed of flame, hoping that down below her family would be offering Masses and praying for her speedy release.

She bent her head. She was weak. She could not last a day without sinning.

Tears pricked her eyes. What hope did she have? One day, without thinking, she would commit not just a small venial sin but a mortal sin. A soul could be dispatched to hell because of *one* mortal sin for all eternity. Everlasting fire. Forever and ever and ever without end.

There was no time to be lost. Apparently God could call a soul to Him at any time.

The nuns said they had to suffer for their sins and offer up their suffering to God for the Poor Souls in Purgatory.

'Go to Confession regularly, tell God that you're *sincerely* sorry,' said Sister Mary Angela, 'and you'll all die with clear consciences.'

'If God knows everything we do, Sister, then why do we have to confess our sins to a priest? It's telling God what He already knows. Or have I got it wrong, Sister?' asked Catherine.

'That is not the point, Catherine Flynn. The point is that you need to *admit* your sins to God our Loving Father, so that He can *forgive* you. I would have thought even a baby knew this. Don't you want to be forgiven?'

53

'Yes, Sister.'

'Well then.' Sister continued with her lesson.

'Does everybody sin, Sister, even the nuns?' Catherine asked next.

Sister Mary Angela turned from the blackboard where she had just written the words 'MORTAL SIN' in huge capital letters and a red arrow pointing to the word 'HELL'. The piece of red chalk she was holding snapped in two between her fingers. They saw her lips move. *'Jesus, Mary and Joseph.'*

'Yes, Catherine,' she replied. 'Even nuns commit sins.' She laughed.

They laughed politely with her. *Ha, Ha!* Imagine nuns sinning. Impossible. Nuns were perfect. That's why they were nuns – already halfway along the road to becoming saints.

Salvie Catalano raised his hand. 'Excuse me, Sister, but can you tell me what type of sins nuns commit?'

Sister glared at him. 'No, Salvie Catalano, I certainly will not.'

'But Sister,' he protested.

'Not another word.' She turned her back to them and continued to write lists on the blackboard.

Salvie smirked. Soon a carefully folded wad of paper was passed along beneath the desks. It arrived on Catherine's desk. She opened it on her lap. 'Snorting,' she read. 'Farting, burping, strapping little children, being a bad-tempered ugly hag.'

A little tremor passed through Catherine. Her stomach convulsed. She couldn't control herself. She started giggling. Sister spun around to face them.

'Catherine Flynn! Stand up!'

'Yes, Sister.'

'What's going on, I demand to know.'

'I got the giggles, Sister.' And Catherine began all over again. Tears streamed from her eyes. *Snorting! Farting!*

54

'The girl's hysterical. Come to the front of the class. Now.'

Catherine tried to control herself.

'Put your hand out,' ordered Sister. Catherine stretched out her hand. She closed her eyes.

Snap! Sister's ruler cracked across her hand, leaving a path of fire behind it. Twice more her ruler came down. 'And now,' she said, red-faced from the effort, 'return to your desk and stop showing off.'

'Yes Sister,' bleated Catherine.

Sister Mary Angela gave the worst 'cuts'. Her strap was the thickest. She was the strongest, stoutest nun. The boys were always sent to her for disciplining. Even the standard-six boys were scared of her. The beefy Italian boys with their hairy footy-muscled legs and their unpredictable broken voices cowered before 'Angles'.

'I'm not as green as I'm cabbage-looking,' she told them. 'I didn't come down in the last shower. So don't come at any nonsense with me and we'll be good friends, you and I.'

'Yes, Sister,' they said meekly.

There was a telephone in the convent, but no-one actually saw the nuns listen to a radio, watch a television or even read a newspaper. They were better informed, however, than most of the parishioners who did.

'They must be mind-readers,' said Mrs Flynn. 'Don't you kids even try to put one across them, because you don't stand a chance.'

Smoking Nana encouraged them to be suspicious of the nuns. She was still mad at her daughter for converting when she married Mr Flynn.

'Converts are the worst,' she always said. 'Fanatics. Once they've *turned*, their minds are closed to any logical arguments.'

'What have you got against nuns?' asked Mrs Flynn.

'Because I don't want you passing on your prejudices to my kids.'

'My grandchildren will know the truth,' said Smoking Nana. 'They will grow up knowing there is more than one point of view on any subject.'

Their mother sniffed. 'Hymmph,' she said.

'I'll tell you why I don't like nuns,' said their grandmother. 'Because they smile far too damn much. And I don't trust anyone who is nice *all* the time.'

According to their grandmother there was a tunnel which ran between the convent and the presbytery.

'Don't have them on like that, Mum,' begged Mrs Flynn.

'Who said I was having them on?' replied Smoking Nana in a solemn voice.

'What kind of a tunnel?' asked Theresa eagerly. She looked up from the drawing she was making in Indian ink of a princess who had ringlets of hair cascading to her ankles.

'Wide enough,' said her grandmother.

'I give up,' said Mrs Flynn.

'Could it fit two people inside it?' asked Theresa. She added the jewellery last – rings on each finger, bracelets, long earrings and a crown encrusted with diamonds and precious jewels.

'Naturally.' Smoking Nana laughed. She winked at her daughter.

Theresa added a diamanté clasp to the princess's girdle. She missed the wink.

Mrs Flynn pursed her lips and then clicked her tongue in disgust and went off to attend to a mountain of washing.

Theresa titled her princess portrait, 'The Odalisque'. There, her grandmother would be impressed. She pictured a nun wriggling her way through the tunnel like a Red Indian on his tummy creeping up on an enemy. The nun crawled into the presbytery where the priest would be waiting for her. They greeted each other with a passionate kiss. Afterwards they performed a little dance through the house which involved rubbing their tummies against each other.

Theresa put her princess aside and began to draw the dance of the nun and priest. She drew them doing a tango. The nun's grin was lopsided, her eyes flashed with amusement. The priest was tall and thin like the monsignor. He too was smiling.

'Don't listen to your grandmother's nonsense,' advised Mr Flynn. 'She just can't help herself. She gets carried away.'

He shrugged his shoulders. If it were up to him his wife's mother wouldn't be allowed to set foot in the house under any circumstances. He referred to her visits as invasions. He swore each would be the last.

She visited them every six to eight weeks, travelling from Wellington. Mr Flynn said she always brought trouble with her. He said she caused difficulties between Mrs Flynn and himself by stirring up innumerable petty resentments and arguments.

'I don't want her here poisoning their minds.'

The children loved their grandmother unreservedly. They liked her hand-rolled cigarettes, appreciated her swearing and were fascinated by her smoker's hacking cough. Her body was heavy and pale. A scent of old roses mingled with the smell of tobacco on her skin. She suffered from migraines that caused her to disappear into a darkened bedroom to lie down for hours with a wet cloth over her forehead.

The children believed that it was the arguments with their father which triggered off their grandmother's terrible headaches and it turned them against him. He was aware of this and it increased his feelings of resentment towards his wife's mother.

'Terrence should have been a priest,' observed Mrs Flynn to her mother over the breakfast table one morning after Mr Flynn had departed in the car for work. 'His temperament is more suited to it, only of course he would never have tolerated it when his parishioners failed to follow his advice.'

'He's a dreadful man,' remarked Smoking Nana. 'I don't know how you cope. I hope someone runs him over or he develops a fatal disease. Not a lingering one, though, that would be too much trouble.'

'*Mum!*' Mrs Flynn's face was pink with anger. She turned her head to see if any of the children were within earshot.

They had drifted back into the room. Everything their grandmother said was of interest to them. She could transform their world with a few words.

Smoking Nana placed her hand over her mouth.

'Hush my mouth,' she said, her eyes popping in mock horror. 'I've committed a sin and I'd better run to Confession before I'm struck down by a bolt of lightning.'

'*Not* in front of the children,' snapped Mrs Flynn.

'It's about time they heard a few home truths.'

Mrs Flynn ushered them all quickly away from the table in case her mother felt the urge to divulge them.

They went, protesting vigorously, craning their necks to look back at the grandmother who wished their father dead. She had not been struck down. She had not been turned into a pillar of salt or even a column of fire. On the contrary, she had never looked in better spirits. They watched from the doorway as she pulled out the familiar yellow packet of tobacco and rolled herself a plump cigarette. She blew smoke rings in perfect circles which floated defiantly up to the ceiling where they hovered, turning the ceiling yellow.

'Jesus wept,' whispered Theresa.

She asked her friend Nicholas O'Grady, who thought he knew everything, why a priest and nun might rub tummies together.

58

His face turned beetroot red and he smirked at Theresa in a way which made her feel uncomfortable.

'They're not dancing,' he said. 'They're *rooting*.' Then he ran away.

'Gutter language,' sniffed her mother, when Theresa asked her. 'Where did you pick up that rubbish anyway?'

She told Theresa the proper word for rooting was Intercourse – something beautiful and sacred, and not to be confused with what cheap girls did with men behind hedges and in the backs of parked cars in the dark.

'Remember that,' she instructed, 'and you won't get into trouble.'

A cheap girl wasn't worth anything. No-one respected her. She *shamed* her parents.

'Listen up,' said Mrs Flynn. 'No girl of mine will grow up and go out looking like a cheap slut.'

She explained. Low-cut tops. Dresses that were too short. Too much eye make-up. Shiny fabrics. Flashy gold jewellery. Patent leather shoes. Rough language. Crude, rude, vulgar manners. No pride or self-respect. Being loud and drawing attention to themselves. Drinking. The list was endless.

'It doesn't leave much,' complained Theresa. 'How are we ever going to have any fun?'

'Goodness is more important than vanity and pleasure,' said her mother.

'Killjoy,' thought Theresa.

Nuns weren't human, decided Theresa.

'I've got them sussed,' she told her grandmother, hoping she would be impressed.

'If you knew half of what goes on in the clergy, your hair would stand on end, your mouth would fall open with amazement, down to your navel – and stay there,' replied Smoking Nana.

Theresa prayed at the foot of the Italian Madonna.

'Guard this house,' she begged, 'from nuns, intruders, devils, earthquakes and fire. We're counting on you. Amen.'

The Italian Madonna looked down with her enigmatic smile.

Was she listening?

Chapter Five

THE CLOUD IN HUMAN FORM

'Bugger God! Bugger God!' sang Theresa in the Flynns' back yard.

'Theresa!' reprimanded Catherine.

Theresa sang louder than ever to tease her sister. The words ran together: buggabuggabuggagodbugga.

The holidays were already halfway through. The day was brilliantly sunny and beckoned with possibilities. Theresa wanted to skip and dance and shout and sing but couldn't decide which to do first. Cicadas with large transparent wings shrilled from the bushes and Theresa hopped and whistled among them. Everything throbbed and shimmered in the heat.

It was the day of the Big Wash. Both clothes-lines were propped up high with wooden poles and draped with large pale forms: sheets, towels, nappies, muslin curtains, tablecloths and candlewick bedspreads. There were also altar cloths and sacred priestly garments. Mrs Flynn did the presbytery laundry to help make ends meet. The clothes were already almost dry, flapping briskly whenever the breeze caught them, as if hungry to ensnare a passing body.

The girls wove their way through this moving white sea, slapping at the fabric which whipped against their shoulders. Inside, their mother was sewing curtains. Their other brothers and sister were at the swimming baths with a neighbour. They had the garden to themselves.

They argued amicably about what they might do with this precious slice of summer freedom. Their voices were loud and cheerful as they climbed over the remains of a train constructed from wooden fruit crates.

There was a tiny flutter of movement at the far end of the garden. Something bright was beginning to materialize from out of the greenery.

Theresa saw a white light. She and Catherine ran to investigate. A beautiful woman wearing a long white dress and a sky-blue cloak and veil was levitating above the Flynns' lemon tree.

Theresa realized the identity of their visitor immediately.

Perhaps she was imagining it? She looked behind and could tell by the stunned expression on Catherine's face that she too could see the same vision. So she wasn't dreaming.

The two sisters' eyes were wide with amazement. They recognized a miracle when they saw one. There was a golden glow around the woman's head. As they drew nearer they could see there were beads of perspiration on her face, especially above her full lips. (Later, Catherine said there was a chain of beads around her neck and stars on her cloak, but Theresa could remember only the rosebuds between her toes.)

They fell to their knees. For a brief moment they were speechless. It was Theresa who found her voice first. She spoke in a garbled mixture of Mr Flynn's aphorisms and half-remembered phrases from the Loretto Litany and Antiphons of the Blessed Virgin.

'Open Door to Heaven, and Star of the Sea,' she murmured in a respectful voice, scarcely daring to raise her eyes to the dazzling apparition hovering above the lemon tree.

The apparition made no reply, but seemed to be waiting politely in case the girls had any further greetings.

'Hail Queen of Heaven, hail Mistress of the Angels,' continued Theresa bravely.

Catherine felt paralysed with shyness. Surely there

must be a correct etiquette for such an occasion. If there was, no-one had told her. Her mind went blank. Finally, an impressive-sounding salutation came to her.

'Hail Root of Jesse,' she whispered.

Neither she nor her sister had any idea who Jesse was.

'. . . Virgin most renowned and of unsurpassed beauty . . . Heavenly Ladder by which God came down . . . Mother of the Star that never sets . . . Dawn of the Mystic Day . . .'

'Hello girls,' replied the Lady in a husky voice. 'I've come to give you a message for the Pope.'

The two sisters whispered together and then Catherine spoke up in a trembling voice.

'We don't mean to be rude,' she said with bowed head.

The Lady had to crane her neck to hear.

'Haven't you landed in the wrong country? This is New Zealand, not France or Portugal,' added Theresa.

'Besides, we're just ordinary girls. Nothing special, you know,' said Catherine.

'My daughters,' said the Lady.

Just like the three children at Fatima and Bernadette Soubirous at Lourdes – it was the same. Theresa hugged herself. St Theresa Flynn – virgin martyr stigmatic.

'I have specially chosen you two to be my messengers,' continued the Lady. 'In the future your little country will be instrumental in bringing peace to the world.'

'Gosh!'

'The message is about contraception and it's very important that the Pope receives it. He might change his mind.'

Contraception? What was that?

'Shouldn't you speak to Mum first?' asked Catherine.

'The message must come from you,' the Lady replied. 'You will be the mothers of the future.' She withdrew a long white envelope from the recesses of her cloak and, leaning down, gave it to Theresa. The edges of the envelope were decorated with an ornate gold border. It was addressed to 'The Holy Father, Paul VI' in a flowing copperplate script. The envelope smelt as if it had been sprinkled with the most expensive scent in the world.

'We'll do our best.' They were overwhelmed.

After bestowing a beaming smile on them, the White Lady started gradually to disappear – feet first. Theresa was reminded of Lewis Carroll's Cheshire Cat. Finally, only the Lady's smile remained hovering in the air.

They peered up at the little tree after she had gone.

'Did we dream it all?' asked Catherine.

'No,' replied Theresa. 'Look at the leaves.'

The upper foliage had become brown and shrivelled. Later their father would bombard the tree with chemical sprays in an effort to revive it.

'Hell's teeth,' said Terrence Flynn that night in his scariest voice. 'If you girls are lying to me, there'll be big trouble. Do I make myself clear?'

Two heads bobbed nervously in response.

Their mother interrupted. 'How do you explain the fancy letter then?' she asked. 'They wouldn't know how to make that all up by themselves. How could they?'

Without Divine Intervention?

They stared at the letter with its glittering gold decoration.

Mr Flynn frowned and scratched his nose thoughtfully.

Having faith was one thing. Believing in miracles, especially miracles which had occurred in his own back garden, in Chatterton, New Zealand, was another. He didn't know what to think. Of course he believed in the visions at Fatima and Lourdes. But . . . New Zealand? What if the girls were speaking the truth?

He picked up a corner of the envelope with freshly

64

scrubbed fingers, cautiously, as if he were handling a dead cat. Then he disappeared into the bedroom to hide it in a safe place in the top drawer of the dresser while he decided what to do next.

'Why us?' complained Mrs Flynn, wishing God would take His Divine Intervention off somewhere else. 'As if we haven't got enough to worry about.'

The girls asked their mother about contraception. It might give them a clue as to the contents of the letter.

Mrs Flynn reluctantly told her daughters a few facts of life.

'Now is as good a time as any to tell you, I suppose.'

At the end of the explanation they were more confused than ever. Apparently, 'it', whatever it was, would happen to them behind hedges, or in the back of parked cars. Vaguely Theresa recalled her mother mentioning something previously, but it hadn't meant anything. She hadn't been ready to know. Now she was. She wanted to know about everything that went on between men and women. The 'something' that was 'done' to you generally involved underpants – not wearing them. And that's when she made the connection. The 'thing' that happened was something to do with down below and something being shoved up there. But shoved into what? Mysteriouser and mysteriouser, she thought.

'Now don't ever let me catch you two getting up to any of that nonsense,' said their mother quickly summing up, 'or you'll get a good hiding.'

'No Mum, we won't.'

Mrs Flynn frowned as she looked around the girls' bedroom. 'This room,' she said, 'is a disgrace. A pigsty. You ought to be ashamed of yourselves.' And she whacked them over the ears with the nearest object to hand – in this instance, a rubber sandal – to drive the message home. She swept out of the room. Theresa and Catherine pulled ugly faces at her retreating back. They decided they hated her more than anyone else in the entire world, universe, galaxy.

'They need a bomb under them,' commented Mr Flynn over breakfast, as he listened to his wife's complaints.

'Cleanliness is next to godliness,' reminded Mrs Flynn when she stuck her head in the doorway five minutes later to check on the progress of the tidy-up.

The girls moved about the room like sleepwalkers. Most of the mess belonged to Theresa. She couldn't see the point in forever cleaning up after herself. There were always far more inviting things to do.

They speculated as to what their father might do about the Lady and the letter. He had, in the meantime, sworn them to secrecy. They envisaged the envy of their classmates, the awe with which they would be regarded in future by the nuns.

'Perhaps,' suggested Theresa, 'we really *are* special. Called to be great.'

'Saints,' whispered Catherine. It was all coming true, just as she had hoped.

The nuns had told them God moved in Mysterious Ways. They wondered if it might include a trip to Rome to see the Pope and give him the letter.

'We must start learning Italian,' suggested Catherine. 'We need to be ready when we're called, don't you think?'

'Of course,' agreed Theresa. 'And we'll need new clothes as well. We can't go to Rome in our gymfrocks.'

'God will provide,' said Catherine. 'We must have faith.'

The tidying by now forgotten, the two girls sprawled on their beds and spun dreams. Fame, riches, maybe even canonization lay just around the corner.

Mrs Flynn appeared in the doorway, interrupting their fantasies. A wooden spoon waved menacingly at them. She thrust her way in through the tangle of clothes scattered about the floor.

She pointed to the largest picture on their wall, bigger even than the Sacred Heart. It showed a family on their knees together saying the Rosary. The caption underneath read: 'The family that prays together, stays together.'

'Now that's a family,' said Mrs Flynn. 'Nice little girls who are good and who don't answer back. Tidy little girls who keep their room clean.'

Mr Flynn returned home from work that night un-expectedly early and caught his wife in the act of holding the gilt-edged envelope over a steaming kettle. He snatched it from her.

'Give it back to me,' she cried. 'We've a right to know what message has been given to our daughters.'

He waved it high above his head where she could not reach it. 'I'll open it,' he said. 'I'll read it first.'

He lifted the flap carefully and pulled out the letter. He quickly scanned its handwritten contents, snorting and exclaiming with indignation as he did so.

'What does it say?' asked Mrs Flynn in a fever of curiosity.

Mr Flynn flung the letter onto the table. 'See for yourself.'

She read it. She smiled. 'Sounds all right to me,' she said, 'about time something was done. We're just weak human beings after all.'

She particularly liked the bit in the letter that men-tioned 'avoiding children for *plausible* reasons'.

'That'll be the day,' replied Mr Flynn. 'That'll be the frosty Friday.'

He put on his glasses and, after assembling all his writing things, sat down at the table when the last of the children had gone to bed to compose a new letter. He made several rough drafts before he was sat-isfied. He had to borrow a few phrases from the Lady's letter and tried to match the style of handwriting and sentence construction as closely as possible.

Education by the brothers and a lifetime of listening to Sunday sermons gave him the words for which he was searching. He wrote about upright men, conjugal acts, moral laws, the mission of generating life, God as author of that human life, and finished off with the plea to face up to the efforts needed.

'It's wrong what you're doing,' objected Mrs Flynn. 'I'll have no part of it.'

He came up to her and waved the newly-sealed letter in her face. 'You will,' he said, 'and I'll hear no more about it. I'm the head of this household.'

'What are you going to do about the letter?' the girls asked every day.

'Leave it to me,' said their father, 'I know best.'

'Have you taken it to Father Rafferty yet?'

'Not yet. But I will.'

'When?'

'Don't answer me back.'

'We're not, we're just—'

He silenced them with his worst frown.

They crept away to the sanctuary of their room. Perhaps their mother wasn't so bad. They decided they hated their father more than anyone else in the entire world, universe and galaxy.

The presbytery was gloomy and stuffy. Pieces of heavy dark furniture lined the walls, the highly polished brass handles winking at the girls like malevolent eyes watching them. The ceilings were high, panelled and spotted with mould. The rooms smelt of pipe tobacco and cats' urine. Father Rafferty was house-training two new kittens.

'Aren't they darling?' cooed the girls, their mission temporarily forgotten. 'Ooh, can't we have one, Dad?'

'No, they'd ruin the garden.'

'Please?'

'I said no.'

Mr Flynn shrugged his shoulders and raised his eyes to the ceiling. 'Girls!' he said to the priest.

The priest opened the letter.

'*Humanae Vitae?*' he said, 'can't say I've heard of it.'

Mr Flynn expressed surprise at the letter's contents. He and Father Rafferty, after much discussion, had decided to steam open the letter carefully.

Men like him didn't dare meddle in ecclesiastical matters, Mr Flynn said, but in this case, perhaps an exception might be made? Everyone knew what good Catholics the Flynns were, but they didn't want to be making fools of themselves, now did they? After all.

No, said the priest, they didn't want to be looking the fool, but in case there was a grain of truth in the story . . . the style of the envelope being what it was . . . no harm in having a look.

Mr Flynn agreed. He acted as if his daughters were not in the room with him. Speak only when spoken to, he had told them in the car.

'You've done the right thing coming to me,' said the priest. 'And now,' he went on, 'I wonder if I might not see the girls alone for a few minutes, Terrence?'

Mr Flynn wasn't enthusiastic, but in the circumstances, he felt he couldn't refuse. He waited in the hallway. They could hear him pacing and clearing his throat.

Father Rafferty got up and closed the door. 'Now girls, let's just have a little chat,' he said. 'There's nothing to worry about. But perhaps what you saw was a hallucination.' He explained what that meant. They said they understood.

'It may be that in your enthusiasm to see the Blessed Virgin and be close to her, you imagined what might happen if she were to grace us with her presence and you thought about it so hard that it began to seem real – a trick of the light. It happens.'

Theresa shook her head. She had prepared herself, knowing they would be doubted. It had happened to Bernadette and to Lucia and the children. Why would it be any different for her and Catherine? It was a test of their faith.

'No,' she replied with a solemn face. 'It wasn't a trick of the light. We didn't imagine it. We really saw her. She existed the same as you do. A cloud in human form, just as Lucia Santos described.'

Father Rafferty frowned and chewed on his lower lip.

'I see,' he said. 'So you're going to stick to your story, no matter what.'

'Yes, of course,' they said calmly.

'We're not lying,' said Catherine, 'if that's what you mean.'

'I'm sure you're very truthful girls,' the priest hastened to reassure them. 'Indeed, the nuns tell me you are. However, we must be absolutely certain that what you really saw was Our Lady and not a product of over-active imaginations.'

He couldn't stop staring at them. Their unusual fluffy white hair and the black eyes. Their confidence and steady gaze. It was impossible that what they were telling him was the truth. He didn't believe a word of it, and couldn't think how they'd managed to convince a tough nut like Terry Flynn.

And yet he was convinced they weren't lying.

It wasn't the Virgin Mary who was the apparition. Had they looked at themselves in the mirror recently?

Fey, wild, they were not altogether of this world themselves. They would have to be handled with kid gloves. Terry would be like a bull in a china shop with them. The priest shook himself.

Their fingers were long and thin like antennae, their legs brittle as sticks. The silver hairs on their legs were so fine they were almost invisible.

He forced himself to turn away. But even when he

70

had averted his eyes he found he could still see the silver, delicate as a film of gossamer, as slight and insubstantial.

He hurt inside if he stared at the legs for too long. Or at the faith glowing from their eyes. They were too vulnerable. Too human. He couldn't bear it. Sitting in a confessional hour after hour, after a while there was nothing that could surprise him any more. He'd heard everything.

Only children could shake him now. He couldn't afford to love because then the lack of it tore him up and all he could think about was a pair of arms. He dreamed of arms sheltering him, taking him in, giving him a bit of love and asking no questions. Human arms. A woman's love. What stopped him? Today it seemed too much to ask.

Yep, he wanted to say to these two harmless little fairy creatures, you can have your miracle.

But he couldn't get the words out. A lump came into his throat. He knew already what his response would have to be, even though he had diplomatically agreed to consult the other priests. He realized the girls would inevitably perceive his rejection of their story as a betrayal of trust. Dammit, his head kept getting in the way of his heart. It was why he was still in the presbytery and not out walking the streets like a beggar looking for those arms.

Outside in the hallway Mr Flynn was beginning to regret having brought his daughters here. What had he been thinking of? Some sort of crank had obviously led his daughters astray. The Blessed Mother appearing in Chatterton, New Zealand? In *his* back yard? On his *lemon* tree?

Father Rafferty promised he would talk to the other priests and that he would get back to him with their conclusions.

'Thank you for your time, Father,' said Mr Flynn.

'You've been very patient in humouring my daughters, but we won't take any more of your valuable time.'

His daughters glared at him with knives in their eyes. How very typical of their father. Perhaps he was jealous because the Virgin had preferred to reveal herself to them rather than to him. They were still protesting vigorously when Mr Flynn ushered them to the door.

'I'll sort them out,' he said in a low voice to the priest. 'I'll knock some sense back into them.'

'Now Terrence, go easy on them. They're obviously sensitive girls. You don't want to do anything . . .' the priest hesitated, before continuing. 'Anything which might cause unpleasantness and be misconstrued.'

Mr Flynn winked at him.

'Leave it to me,' he said. 'I've got my family under control.'

Chapter Six

THE TAP ON THE SHOULDER

'It's a sign,' said their father's mother, Other Nana, when the girls told her their story. To her everything was an omen predicting either God's pleasure or annoyance with the behaviour of his creatures. Omens gave an indication of unfortunate repercussions or of good things to come. Her daily routine took account of the fickle moods of 'The Old Boy', as she familiarly referred to Him. No-one for a minute assumed she meant her husband when she used this term of endearment. 'God and me, we have an understanding,' she said. 'I don't have to put on airs and graces for Him, He likes me fine just the way I am.'

'So do I,' said Grandad. He gave her a kiss on the cheek and smacked her bottom. 'This old boy likes you just fine too.'

Mrs Flynn wondered why Grandad's amorous behaviour hadn't been inherited by his son. Mr Flynn must have been the cuckoo in the nest – a mystery to himself as well as his family.

Soon after the Lady's visit Catherine discovered she had been called by God to be a nun. A little voice inside her head told her to follow His path.

'Make straight His Ways,' she whispered. Now where had she heard that before? Somewhere, she couldn't remember.

And she heard more. 'REPENT!' boomed the voice. She turned fearfully. There was nobody there. The voice went on. This time it had an accent, sort of like the monsignor's. *'Mi hija, mi hija, mi chica, mi amiga.'*

She felt shivery. She checked her feet and hands for telltale stains.

Nothing. Yet . . .

Why did she keep hearing voices? If not God's voice, then whose? Had she been called to be a nun? She would perform miracles, eventually be canonized. Only she wouldn't let them carve her body into relics when she was dead. Jesus would give her His throbbing heart aflame with love. She would take it inside herself. She would become His bride.

How would they refer to her? Catherine of the Cross? Perhaps Blessed Catherine of Chatterton, Flower of the Pacific?

Other Nana began to treat Catherine as if she were already a nun. Catherine submitted to her grandmother's hugs and kisses, embarrassed to be the focus of so much attention.

'Oh, stop it, Nana,' snapped Mrs Flynn. 'You're giving her ideas. Plenty of time yet before she commits herself to anything.'

'Ours not to reason why,' replied her mother-in-law. She drew Catherine into the lounge, away from her mother, for an intimate chat.

They sat together on the threadbare sofa. She patted Catherine's knee and then pulled out her knitting from the home-made felt bag that accompanied her wherever she went.

'Now dear,' she cooed. 'I want you to tell me everything that occurred in your vision, right from the beginning. Don't leave anything out. No little detail is too insignificant. The Old Boy operates in Mysterious Ways.'

Catherine and Theresa had repeated the story of the Lady's visit many times to their disbelieving family. During the retelling, it had inevitably acquired additional embellishments which only served to make it seem all the more authentic.

Catherine looked at her grandmother on the couch and suddenly felt disconnected from her body. In a flash of inspiration she saw Other Nana as never before. It was as if she could read her thoughts and know them in advance. She was not surprised by her heightened awareness. St Gerard Majella had been able to read consciences. Hildegard foretold the future. Everything was predestined. She was simply falling in with a plan that had been formulated long before she was born. It was meant to be.

St Catherine of Chatterton.

'Uh huh,' said Other Nana as she listened to Catherine's visions. And sometimes she would murmur: 'Mmmm . . .' or, 'Yes, go on and then what?'

One of Catherine's visions revealed her not only as a new breed of female priest but as a kind of goddess in shining white robes. In this state she wore a white veil to reflect her purity. All around her head rays of light flashed and sparkled. She floated from the altar to the communion rails, an enormous golden chalice in her hand. 'This is my body,' she said. 'This is my blood. Take. Eat.' She pulled a large white wafer from the cup and gave it to—

'Who?' interrupted Other Nana. 'Who did you give it to?'

Catherine swung around to look directly at her grandmother.

'I think . . .' she replied. 'I think I gave it to you.'

The last segment of the dream vision was a little blurred. Had she passed the wafer to her grandmother, or to Theresa? It didn't matter really. It was obviously the right thing to say because her grandmother was smiling ecstatically.

'Amazing,' she breathed and dropped a stitch. She never dropped stitches.

Catherine began to feel a little disturbed at being stared at with such loving intensity.

She asked her grandmother if she would sew her a nun's habit so that she could begin to prepare herself for her future vocation.

'I'm not wasting money on material for dress-ups,' said the ever-practical Mrs Flynn. 'Money doesn't grow on trees.'

'Now, don't worry about a thing,' soothed Other Nana. 'I'll see you get what you need, Cathy. Won't we, Dad?'

Grandad shook his head. 'Humour her if you must,' he grunted, burying himself again in his newspaper.

Catherine shot him a reproachful look. Soon he flung it down and said: 'All right, I give in, I'm only human.' He pulled his wallet out from the back pocket of his trousers and gave Catherine a handful of notes.

They were all potential nuns and priests.

The nuns said so. And nuns were never wrong. They were never wrong, but they weren't infallible. Only the Pope was infallible.

'Why shouldn't God call one of you girls to be a nun, it's not out of the question. You never know what The Old Boy is going to think of next,' Other Nana had always told them.

The church was almost empty. There were two pensioners, heads bent patiently, rosary beads dangling over a pew. A young nursing mother stared vacantly into space in a back pew. A woman emerged from the left booth. Mrs Flynn was next in line. She waited for a moment before entering the vacated booth. She pulled aside the red velvet drape and the welcome darkness closed in around her, creating the illusion of privacy. She tried not to listen to the man whispering in the booth on the other side of the priest. It was impossible

not to catch some of the words, disjointed and out of context, conveying an impression of desperate urgency. Only murder or adultery, both extracting the maximum penance and reparation, could, she thought, have produced the whispers of anxious guilt stabbing the dark a metre away from her.

Her own sins were of the more homely kind. Sins of omission, neglect, envy, malice, pride: sins so predictable she scarcely needed to catalogue them in advance. Her penances were always the same for such minor transgressions – one Our Father and two Hail Marys.

There was a scraping sound as the little door over the grille in the confessional was dragged across. Mrs Flynn saw the dark outline of the priest's head inclined towards her. Father Rafferty. She wished it had been Father O'Connor, or even the monsignor. They were easier to talk to. She squinted through the mesh. His face was in profile: a meaty nose, high domed forehead and receding chin.

It simply wasn't possible to love all of God's creatures.

'Bless me Father, for I have sinned,' she began in a low voice. 'It is two weeks since my last confession.'

She paused. The priest sat patiently.

'I hate my family,' she admitted.

'Love can often be mistaken for hate,' he murmured. 'I'm sure you don't really mean it.'

'Oh, but I do, Father.' The words had spilled out of her without thinking, but once they were said she realized they were true.

'I hate them,' she repeated. 'They give me no peace.'

She heaved an enormous sigh. A small seed that would grow into another Flynn stirred inside her. Mr Flynn had once again successfully burrowed his way into her womb.

'He has only to look at me and I'm pregnant,' she whispered.

'Sometimes sacrifices are necessary for the greater good,' said the priest in a tired voice.

She saw him cup his chin in his hands and lean his elbow against the ledge of the grille. Mrs Flynn suspected he was repeating words he had uttered a hundred times before. Was he even listening to her? She couldn't be sure.

'Another baby would kill me,' she pleaded. 'It's too much. Surely God is merciful?'

Even as she spoke she knew already what his response would be and wished she had the strength to change that which could not be changed, ever, on pain of sin.

'God never gives us more than we can bear,' he soothed.

What would he know, she thought with bitterness. How could he possibly understand what it felt like to be used-up, miserable and not even forty yet?

She refused to be soothed. 'It's not true,' she hissed. 'He gives us more than we can bear constantly. In my opinion, He never stops burdening us.'

'He works in Mysterious Ways.'

Bugger His mysterious ways, she felt tempted to shout through the grille. She wanted to rasp and scratch at the mesh with her fingernails, rip it away and pull the priest's head off.

She shook herself. She must pull herself together and finish off this farce of a confession. She wasn't sorry today. She didn't believe she deserved to be forgiven by anybody.

'My daughter,' continued the priest, 'Our Holy Father Himself has urged us not to seek artificial control of births or we will lessen the number of guests at the Banquet of Life. A beautiful sentiment, don't you agree? Try not to see things only in the short term. In the future, you won't regret you invited one more guest to the banquet.'

'What about me?' she could have shrieked. 'We've

got enough mouths to feed. I can't go on. I can't. Father, believe me.'

Father Rafferty spoke of the need for a wider vision, to be life-affirming. 'Remember,' he said. 'Abortion is murder and a mortal sin.'

Moira Flynn saw her options shrink to a narrow path through darkness. What had she expected anyway? Sympathy? She wouldn't get it here. She was on her own, in every sense. Even Terrence always took the same view as the priests.

She began to weep quietly. Her knees ached. She resented the priest for his lack of understanding.

Mea culpa. Mea culpa, mea maxima culpa.

She couldn't feel it. Couldn't say it.

'For your penance,' he said at last, 'five Hail Marys and now make a good Act of Contrition.'

He bowed his head and waited. And waited.

Words caught in her throat.

'I can't,' she croaked.

'Have you forgotten the words?'

'No, Father.'

'What is it then?'

'I don't feel sorry.'

He lit a match and she heard the sharp intake of breath as he drew on his pipe.

The bugger was smoking! The acrid smell of the tobacco and smoke wafted through the grille and made her cough.

Mrs Flynn stumbled out into the aisle, genuflected and then walked quickly out of the church, ignoring stares. At the entrance she crossed herself at the font.

She heaved a sigh of relief to be back in the fresh air. Petulant faces gazed at her from the family car, willing her to hurry up and take them all home.

'You were ages,' accused Theresa. 'You must have had hundreds of sins.'

There were days when Mrs Flynn felt there was not

79

enough oxygen in the house for her to breathe, so much of it was devoured by her husband and children. *What about me? What about me?* a tiny voice continued to nag.

She forced herself to ignore the voice. She had her Duties and Responsibilities. If there was time after that she could snatch a minute for herself.

A door slammed in the wind. A baby cried with teething pain. A plate shattered on the floor. Plates were always breaking in the Flynn household.

'Lord, give me strength,' she cried.

Theresa worried about her sister's vocation. She had imagined that if one of them were to be called it would be when they were older.

It was the first time she had felt alone within her family, separate from the daily hum of their preoccupations. Catherine and she had always been allies but now suddenly everything had changed. Catherine was unrecognizable. Her visions had given her confidence. Until now she had been obsessed with pleasing and placating, trying not to annoy or anger anybody, especially their father. Now others' opinions simply washed over her.

Theresa began to pull away and withdrew deep inside herself to brood. It had always been difficult to gain a sense of herself as separate from the rest of the family.

'Don't just sit there, *do* something,' called her mother. Mrs Flynn could never bear to see anyone idle for more than a few minutes. She never relaxed or rested. Even seated in front of the television she found ways to occupy herself with mending, knitting and ironing. Mr Flynn lounged alongside her, his hands busy with nothing more arduous than propping up the pages of the local newspaper. His wife was on the move from the minute she climbed groaning and yawning out of bed at six o'clock in the morning until she fell into bed at ten o'clock at night. She never had difficulty sleeping. On the contrary, she slept as if she were dead, sinking like a heavy stone to the bottom of a river, unaware of her dreams and remembering nothing until the alarm clock jangled her awake.

And now, to add to her burdens, she was expecting another baby.

Theresa fiercely resented her mother's pregnancy. It meant she was given even more household tasks. Her mother's belly was now as taut as a drumskin to the touch.

Monstrous, thought Theresa. *Disgusting.*

'Let me feel, let me feel it,' cried the other children when their mother announced the baby had begun to kick about inside her huge stomach.

'Tell me what you want,' Theresa asked her mother. 'A boy or a girl?'

'I don't care what it is,' replied Mrs Flynn with a weary note to her voice. She wore a floral smock over her elasticized skirt. It was already worn and fluffy with lint from being flung in the wash every other day. 'I just want to get it over with and be back to my old self again.'

'Don't you secretly hope for a girl?' Theresa couldn't understand how her mother could want another boy baby when they had so many boys in the family already.

'I'll love it no matter what it is.'

'What if it has something the matter with it? What if it's a mongoloid?'

'If that's God's will, then I'll just have to accept it,' said Mrs Flynn.

Theresa pulled away from her mother.

'Why must we always accept God's will?' she shouted. 'It's outrageous! Preposterous! Unforgivable!'

'There's no such thing as fair and no point in fighting

81

what you can't change. God knows best. You're all gifts from God.'

Mrs Flynn didn't believe a word of what she had said. Liar, she told herself. *Liar.* Mouthing a lot of empty platitudes. No wonder Theresa saw through them. She fumed, sulked, despaired. She saw her faith leaking away and disappearing like water into sand.

Theresa felt at that moment as if she had never hated anyone as much as God. She wanted to become a woman as unlike her mother as possible. She was *never* going to have children. One day she would be famous and rich enough to travel all over the world. What was the point of working as hard as her mother for so little reward, to have her belly continually full of babies? Becoming as fat as a hog. Having no energy. Feeling cross and tired every day.

Catherine could be the good little girl for both of them. Theresa tasted wickedness on her tongue, 'Jezebel,' she said. '*Fucking, bloody, shitty, trollop, hussy, baggage, witch, bitch, tart, slut.*'

This lifted her spirits enormously. She hummed.

Her father was to blame, he must be. He had done something to her mother to make it happen. He was hateful. She loathed everyone. Everything.

Shouldn't. Don't. Sin, hell, death, destruction. Punishment. Penance. Forgiveness.

Who cared? Not Theresa Mary Anne Flynn, any more.

There had been one awful moment on the first day Catherine wore her habit to school when she thought Sister Mary Patricia and Sister Mary Angela were going to send her home to change.

'And what do you think *you're* doing, girl?' barked Sister Mary Angela.

'It's my vocation, Sister,' squeaked Catherine. 'I thought I'd start practising.'

'Practising?' The nun's voice rose an octave.

'Yes Sister. Poverty, chastity and obedience. I thought it would be easier to be good if I looked like a nun.'

The nuns conferred.

The children whispered and giggled behind their hands. Catherine did her best to ignore them. Sticks and stones. She would offer it up.

Sister Mary Angela came towards her, hands tucked inside her sleeves.

'Return to your desk, Catherine Flynn. You may keep your habit on for today but you are not to be making an exhibition of yourself and getting too big for your boots. Do you understand?'

'Yes Sister.'

Catherine tried to walk back to her desk in the slow graceful way she had seen the nuns move. Unfortunately her rosary beads didn't click – they were only plastic, borrowed from home. But at least her gown made a satisfying swishing sound as she moved. She lowered her eyes, not meeting anyone's gaze directly.

'Goody goody two shoes,' whispered Salvie Catalano.

Catherine didn't deign to reply.

Theresa found Catherine sitting on top of the candlewick bedspread absorbed in reading the life of St Therese, The Little Flower.

It was only a matter of time, thought Theresa, before Catherine began to emulate her heroine's lifestyle: wearing pyjamas made out of old sacks and sleeping on nails and thorns, denying herself so that others might have eternal life, offering up her pain for the lost souls.

Catherine was a lost soul. They all were. Theresa's mood plummeted. Tears of rage pricked behind her eyelids. She was determined not to cry.

'I wish *I* could suffer like the Little Flower,' said Catherine, putting her book down.

Theresa had no intention of suffering anything in her life if she could possibly avoid it. Why suffer? It seemed crazy. Everyone in her family was crazy, except her.

She felt a strong urge to pull her sister's hair and shake her until she came to her senses.

Catherine's half of the bedroom was now a model of tidiness, highlighting Theresa's own disorder. The top surface of their dressing-table had been converted into an altar. Two candles stood in cream bottles alongside a small plastic statue of the Virgin. A crucifix rested on top of a crocheted doily in front of the statue. Vegemite jars of violets and daisies peeped out from behind the statue. Catherine had used her pocket money to buy incense from Mr Vaajani at the local vegetable shop and the room was filled with a sickly sweet scent, not unlike the incense used at Benediction.

Theresa couldn't help herself. She leaned over and pulled Catherine's hair, snatching the book from her hands and ripping out a handful of pages.

It felt good. She was tempted to rip out several more.

Catherine continued to sit passively on the bed.

'Aren't you going to say anything?' taunted Theresa, standing over her with her hands on her hips.

Catherine gave her a pitying smile. 'I forgive you.'

'I don't want your bloody forgiveness, you holy cow,' yelled Theresa.

She paused. Would Catherine resist the temptation to run to their mother and report on her? Or would she act with saintlike restraint?

Catherine got up and left the room. She returned soon with a roll of tape with which she proceeded to repair the book.

'She knows not what she does,' she murmured, as if there was a third person in the room with them.

'Half of this room is mine,' reminded Theresa. Once she had started being awful, she found it impossible to stop.

Without thinking she swept the crucifix and candles off the dresser and tossed them into the rubbish bin at the foot of the bed.

They both stared down at the tin as if at any moment a long arm might reach up from it and grab Theresa by the throat. Catherine rolled her eyes up to the heavens and began patiently to retrieve the objects from the rubbish. She calmly restored them all to their former position on the makeshift altar.

Theresa was unable immediately to think of an appropriate gesture to counter Catherine's response. She contented herself with lying on the opposite bed and humming loudly so that her pious sister might at least be distracted from her reading.

Why had they played martyrs and become impressed by the stigmatics? It was just like Smoking Nana said – a lot of tommyrot, thought Theresa. She would become an atheist like her grandmother.

'I'll pray for you,' said Catherine.

Theresa ground her teeth. Perhaps her sister might become a saint. What a nauseating thought that was. She frowned. How unfair life was.

'Bugger you, God,' she muttered.

There was no choice in the matter once you were called into God's service, the nuns said. No escape, because God always caught up with you in the end.

What if God decided to call her as well as Catherine? Two vocations from the one family. How well it would reflect on their parents. How happy everyone would be.

Impossible. She firmly put the thought out of her mind.

'God has a good sense of humour,' reminded Other Nana. 'He often picks the most unlikely candidate to do His work. Naughty boys and girls sometimes turn out to be shining examples to us all.'

What if she was right? Theresa continued to fret.

85

How would she bear it if God tapped *her* on the shoulder?

'I'd like a nice possie up in heaven,' Other Nana had told them. 'If one of you girls was called to be a nun, all the family would get ringside seats. When your mum and dad reached the Pearly Gates, St Peter would look through his list and say, "Who are you?" When they told him, he'd say, "Welcome Mr and Mrs Flynn, step inside, we've got a spot all ready for you." Wouldn't that be nice?'

'If you're chosen,' said Sister Mary Cecilia, 'He'll keep asking you. Wherever you go, He'll find you.'

Doomed, thought Theresa.

'God is a truly amazing being,' said Sister Mary Cecilia. 'He always was and always will be. He can think forwards and backwards at the same time, know everything that has happened or ever will happen. He can hold every person on earth in His consciousness at the same time. If He ever forgot about any one of you for a second, you'd be as dead as a dodo.

'You're all putty, weak human clay, just waiting to be moulded. As the tree is bent, so is the tree inclined. God knows every mean thought you have, every bad thing you do and say. You cannot hide from Him. Your life is an open book to every soul in heaven.'

Theresa had no privacy at home, and now it seemed as if she had none inside her head either. There was a crowd of people peering in, dead relatives and acquaintances as well as God, all making judgements on her, day and night.

Sister Mary Cecilia's words conjured up images of God as a spy. Retribution was implied. He was a spiritual avenger who would strike with a branding iron when her back was turned.

'If I *was* called to be a nun, and I resisted, what's the worst that God could do to me?' asked Theresa.

86

'Tell her, Mary Louise O'Reilly,' said Sister Mary Cecilia. 'Tell your friend Theresa Flynn what can happen if you go against God's will.'

'My sister Eileen was called by God to become a nun,' said Mary Louise, 'and she refused to listen to Him. She was having too much fun. Going out with boys to dances and the pictures. Buying gorgeous dresses. *She* didn't want to wear a long black dress and no make-up, and be shut up in the convent with only women for company. So she kept refusing and continued to go out and enjoy herself.'

She paused.

'Go on,' encouraged Sister Mary Cecilia.

'She came out in a *rash*,' said Mary Louise. 'The most terrible rash you ever saw and all because she wouldn't do what God asked her. It covered her whole body from top to toe. It looked awful. But still she kept refusing God. Then she became quieter and quieter, and finally she stopped going out at night and just lay around the house pining and sighing.'

Theresa pictured the pretty, vivacious Eileen lolling about the house with her inflamed skin, holding out against God with all of her puny human will. She hadn't stood a chance, and neither would Theresa if God called her to do His work on earth. The nuns said that God had given them the gift of free will, but what use was it if all of their destinies were preordained?

'One day,' continued Mary Louise, 'she upped and entered the convent. And do you know what? Her rash *completely* disappeared.'

'And is your sister a nun to this very day?' asked Sister Mary Cecilia.

'Yes, Sister.'

'And is your sister happy in her chosen vocation as a nun?'

Mary Louise hesitated. 'Yes, Sister.'

*　　*　　*

The mid-morning bell rang. Theresa surged outside with the rest of her class. Sun-warmed half-pints of milk lay waiting in crates alongside the tall macrocarpa hedges. Out in the sunshine she immediately forgot about God and His plans. She became absorbed in the present with all its pleasures. Charging into the boys in a rigorous game of bullrush. Jumping the highest in a game of elastic twist. Scoring a run in softball. Shooting a goal in netball.

God was a million miles away and that was just the way she wanted it from now on.

At first the other children teased Catherine, but after a few weeks everybody became accustomed to her new appearance and left her alone.

Mary Louise wound her finger around the side of her head.

'Loopy,' she mouthed to Theresa.

Theresa nodded. She felt ashamed of her sister for making such a spectacle of herself.

Catherine raised her eyes from her book with a pained expression as if she could read her sister's thoughts, and Theresa felt an uncomfortable twinge of guilt for her disloyalty.

'I know you're talking about me,' said Catherine, 'and I just want you to know that sticks and stones may break my bones, but names will never hurt me.'

She began to spend more time with Other Nana, who lived only a few blocks away. She asked if she could spend her weekends at her grandparents. Surprisingly, Mr and Mrs Flynn agreed.

Sometimes on a Saturday Theresa caught a glimpse of Catherine in the back of her grandparents' Morris Minor, a small dark-veiled figure with her head bowed over a book.

St Catherine, Theresa thought sourly. So why did the sight of that small patient head make her want to weep?

Theresa grew tired of having a sister who was a holy
worm. It was time to rescue her from God's clutches.
Theresa had recently adopted many of Smoking Nana's
negative attitudes towards God. But she wasn't a true
atheist, not like her grandmother. Deep down she
knew that God was lurking around out there somewhere, and she hated Him.

There was one deity, however, whom she still loved
– the Blessed Virgin and Queen of Heaven. She wondered if she should ask her for help with the problem
of her sister's vocation.

During the family's Rosary she now began to concentrate on what she was saying and to pray in earnest.

The Italian Madonna stood above them all on the
mantelpiece. She seemed to be approving of what was
going on below.

The weeks went by and Catherine showed no signs
of losing interest in the idea of becoming a nun.
She continued to practise for her future life of poverty, sacrifice and self-denial.

Mr Flynn continued with his policy of disciplining
his children during the nightly prayers and Bible read-
ings, and Theresa noticed that the Italian Madonna's
face began to assume a peevish expression. It was
almost as if she was wanting to speak to them but
was restraining herself. What would she say if she
could speak? In particular, what would she say to Mr
Flynn?

Chapter Seven

THE BLACK IRISH

Father Rafferty continued to agonize. He reread the letter several times and his doubts came flooding back. It was a wonderfully inventive story by two devout and sensitive little girls. But they had not written the letter by themselves, an adult had been involved. Who? The girls haunted him. He decided to ask them to repeat their story. This time he would question them more closely.

'What time of day was it when you first saw the Lady?' he asked, careful not to intimidate them by his manner.

Theresa and Catherine sat opposite him in the lounge, flanked by their parents. Their expressions were suspicious and anxious. Catherine was wearing a nun's habit. He noticed Theresa's knees were scraped, and there was a wart on her thumb which seemed to irritate her, for she kept rubbing it with her index finger. If she didn't stop picking at it she would soon make it bleed. He suddenly found it necessary to avert his gaze.

'Ten o'clock in the morning, I think,' answered Catherine. What did the time of day matter?

'You think, or do you *know*?'

'I remember you saying nine thirty,' corrected Mrs Flynn.

'I never did. Tell her, Theresa.'

'It was ten o'clock,' Theresa confirmed.

'Tell us again what you think you saw.'

Theresa began: white dress, blue cloak, rosebuds, a halo. Catherine chimed in: the White Lady had been tall, very beautiful, dazzling. They had seen a white light.

'All right then,' said Father Rafferty. 'How did she make her presence known to you?'

Adults were so stupid, thought Theresa. 'We've already told you.'

'Don't be cheeky. Answer the question,' barked Mr Flynn.

'We saw her. She spoke to us. We had a conversation. She gave us the letter and said that word . . . contra—'

'Contraception. Yes, go on.'

'Why would the Mother of God give it to *you*? Did you stop to ask yourselves that question?' said Mr Flynn.

'Look, we didn't ask her to come to our house,' said Theresa, becoming annoyed again. 'Why is everyone blaming us? We didn't do anything wrong.'

'You didn't do anything right, either,' interrupted her father before the priest could get a word in. 'Did it occur to you to ask Our Lady to wait while you went for your mother?'

'Yes. But she didn't *want* to speak to Mum. Only to us.'

'Funny, that,' answered their father. He crossed his arms.

'Were you frightened?' asked the priest.

'Of course not. There was nothing to be frightened of. We were so, so—'

'So *surprised*,' said Catherine.

Father Rafferty regretted he hadn't insisted on seeing the girls alone.

'Describe the fabric of the Virgin's gown.'

'It was soft, like silk,' said Theresa.

'Have you ever felt silk through your fingers?'

'No, but it's what I *imagined* silk might feel like.'

'Imagining isn't good enough,' snapped Mr Flynn. 'Father wants more than that. Stick to the facts, girl.'

Theresa burst into tears and ran from the room. Catherine followed her.

'The little devils. I'll fetch them back pronto for you, Father.'

'No, Terrence. We don't want to badger them or we'll never find out the truth.'

'We're sorry, Father,' said Mrs Flynn.

'Don't bother yourselves about it. I'll come back another time.'

'I believe them,' announced Smoking Nana, after she too had interrogated the girls.

'You do?' exclaimed Mrs Flynn. 'But you don't even believe in God, let alone the Virgin Mary.'

'You're right there. But tell me, have you ever known the girls to lie?'

'Occasionally.'

'But about something important. Other than what they call those white lies. Have you?'

'Well no, I suppose not.'

'There you are. They saw something important and outlandish that can't be explained in the normal way. I'll tell you what I think they saw. A space creature – something from a UFO.'

Mrs Flynn laughed and shook her head. 'You're as bad as they are.'

'What about the letter then?'

'I can't explain it.'

Mrs Flynn was tempted to confess to her mother what Terrence had done with the original letter, but she resisted the urge.

'Mum believes them,' said Mrs Flynn.

'So? When have I taken any notice of what the old bat thinks?' Mr Flynn yawned and stared at the television.

Theresa listened to the little movements and sounds

that were as familiar to her as her own. Catherine's preparations for sleep were elaborate. She always began by examining her conscience and followed this by a lengthy Act of Contrition. Next she would rub the relic pinned to her bodice and pray to the dead saint whose bones were inside it. She asked him to watch over her during the night. In addition to the relic Catherine's chest was crowded with Holy Communion and confirmation medals and a brown scapular.

Although Theresa also wore a relic and two holy medals on her singlet, she didn't wear a scapular.

'You'll regret it when you're on your deathbed,' predicted Catherine. 'And besides, what about St Simon?' she reminded Theresa. Our Lady had promised St Simon in the thirteenth century that whoever died wearing her brown scapular would not suffer eternal fire. Their father had told them a scapular was a kind of insurance policy. He never went anywhere without one.

Catherine also recited prayers that conferred plenary indulgences. Her favourite prayer, the Recitation of Invocations of the Holy Wounds, added up to hundreds of days off Purgatory. It made good sense to buy time now and hoard it up like money in a bank. Catherine estimated she must have stored up at least one hundred and eighty thousand days of reprieve — sufficient to save the whole family from Purgatory.

Theresa sought solace from Other Nana.

'Nana, help me. My head's in a whirl. I don't know what I believe any more.'

'You're just like your Irish forebears,' decided Other Nana. 'It explains a thing or two about your visions.'

'What does it explain?' asked Theresa. 'Are we Irish?'

'You're part Irish. Our background is bog Irish.'

'What's that?'

'You come from people who were dirt poor. They

93

didn't have a penny to bless themselves with and they weren't very well educated.'

'*Oirreland,*' chimed in Grandad, putting on a funny voice.

Theresa giggled, entranced.

'It's a land of saints and scholars, Theresa.'

'Where did we come from?'

'A place called County Kerry.'

'From the South?'

'Of course. Southern Ireland – that's the real Ireland.'

'Why did we come here?'

'To get away from the bloody Poms.'

'What are our relatives like?' persisted Theresa. 'Are there family likenesses?'

'Of course,' said Other Nana. 'You're the spitting image of my mother. She had hair like yours. It didn't come out in my generation. You and Catherine are the first two to inherit it from her. She was a big-hearted woman. She would've given you the shirt off her back if you'd asked. She always thought of others, never herself. A saint she was.'

'If you had the money, would you go to Ireland?'

'No fear. I'm quite happy to stay put until they carry me out feet first.'

Theresa asked her father about her Irish ancestry. He told her about the Black Irish.

'The Black Irish play hard,' said Mr Flynn. 'They drink hard. They have fierce tempers and handy fists. They're quick on their feet too. There's no taming them, oh my word, no. You may as well try and tell the wind not to blow or the tide not to come in. I tell you, they're a wild bunch and no mistaking it.'

They possessed silver tongues. 'They can convince you that black is white and day is night,' said Mr Flynn. 'Those jokers would put it over you soon as look at you, so watch out. Strewth.'

'Do you know any Black Irish women?'

'Oh, they're the worst kind because their tongues are so highly developed. They can slice a man into pieces with just a word. Anyway, why do you want to know?'

How could she break the news to her father that he had a Black Irish daughter?

'I want to be happy,' said Theresa.

'Well, we all want that,' replied her mother. She dished out boiled mince from a large aluminium pot.

The mince was thin and grey with little clots of gristle. It oozed over the plates like burnt porridge. Chunks of soft carrot floated in the soupy mixture. Mrs Flynn gave each of them a scoop of mashed potato. Next she served the cabbage, which had been boiled to a purée. It flowed into the mince and dribbled over the edges of the plates.

Theresa immediately felt ill.

They picked at the meal until it grew cold and then Mrs Flynn had to force them to eat it. There were tears and arguments over the mince, which Mr Flynn claimed upset his sensitive stomach. He took himself and his transistor into the lounge, leaving his food half-eaten.

Theresa observed her father's strategy. He got out of finishing his meal and they received the blame.

The sliding door between the kitchen and the lounge crashed shut behind him. 'Good riddance,' said Theresa under her breath.

'What was that?' challenged her mother in a sharp voice.

'Nothing,' muttered Theresa. A white lie. One more sin to add to the list for Father Rafferty.

Mrs Flynn carried in the dessert wearing an enormous pair of oven mitts made of cross-stitched sacking cloth. She lowered it carefully onto a kauri chopping-board near her place at the table. Mr Flynn returned to the room for dessert.

95

It was jam bake, an enormous mound of flesh-coloured greasy pastry half submerged in a moat of fruit syrup. The mood of the table dropped even further.

Mrs Flynn began to cut into the pudding. Moist slices fell away easily from the knife.

A chorus of voices started up.

'Not too much for me.'

'Just a little helping please.'

'I'm full already.'

Mrs Flynn's knife hovered in midair.

'Remember the Starving Millions,' reminded Mr Flynn. 'There are plenty of people in the world who won't be having dinner tonight. They're forced to search through the rubbish heaps for scraps. You don't realize how lucky you are.'

He looked up then, as if daring someone to challenge him.

'I don't want any pudding, thank you,' Theresa told her mother.

'You'll eat it and no nonsense from you,' barked her father.

'No.' She glared at him defiantly. *Make me.*

Everybody held their breath. Mrs Flynn bit her lip.

Theresa continued to lock eyes with her father, refusing to back down.

'EAT IT, I SAID.'

'No. I won't.'

Mr Flynn suddenly lunged forward and before Theresa realized what was happening she was cuffed over the ears.

'You'll do as you're told, my girl.'

Her ears rang. Without stopping to think she picked up her bowl and flung the contents at him.

Mrs Flynn gasped.

For what seemed like an eternity Mr Flynn didn't react. He allowed the red syrup to drip down his white shirt without appearing to pay it any attention.

Theresa was as scared as she had ever been in her

life, her stomach in knots. Bile rose in her throat at the thought of an apology. *Enough.*

In the brief moment before she slowly retreated backward out of the room without taking her eyes off her father, she hated the frozen tableau of her family.

'COME BACK HERE, THIS INSTANT!' roared her father.

Theresa ran down the hall. She snatched up her school uniform and satchel from the bedroom and raced out into the street. Fearing that her father might attempt to follow her in his car she ran down the back streets. Soon she arrived at her father's parents' house.

A quarter of an hour passed in explanations and tear-ful hugs with her grandparents. She heard the sound of her father's car pulling up in the driveway and saw the flash of the headlights as they briefly illuminated the garage door. A car door slammed and footsteps crunched on the gravel path in front of the kitchen.

Other Nana greeted him in the doorway, diminutive but determined.

Theresa heard snatches of their conversation from where she was crouching behind the dining-room table.

'She's just a child.'

'I don't care. She's got to learn to accept discipline.'

'I'll talk to her.'

'A waste of time. You're too bloody soft.'

'You're too harsh and I won't have swearing in this house.'

There was more heated discussion about discipline and interference and he soon left.

'We'll keep you here for a few days until things cool down,' said Other Nana.

Theresa was spoiled, not allowed to assist with cooking or cleaning, free to read and daydream, providing she did her schoolwork. In these surroundings it was easy to be good.

Other Nana constantly praised her. 'You're so clever,' she said.

'You're a one,' said her grandfather, who hardly ever spoke, spending all his days poring over encyclopaedias to increase his general knowledge.

The silence in the house was generally broken only by the clink of china cups on the tea tray. 'Another cup of tea?' asked Other Nana. 'Another chocolate biscuit, sweetheart?'

Sweetheart.

'Why does Dad get so angry?'

'It's the Irish in him coming out,' replied her grandmother, polishing her collection of miniature statues of saints. 'It's act now and think later. That's their way. You may as well talk to a wall once his blood is up, because he can't hear you.

'His father is the same,' her grandmother said ruefully. And, apparently, so too had been Theresa's great-grandfather. Other Nana gave St Anthony an extra rub. 'Many a time they've been known to rip the belt off their trousers and whip it across the nearest pair of legs.'

Her mild-mannered grandfather? Impossible.

Other Nana turned her attention to St Francis, using a toothpick that was covered at the tip with a scrap of cotton wool to get into the cracks between the folds of his cloak.

'What about the Flynn women?' asked Theresa. 'Does our blood rise too? Do we become out of control?'

'Don't you ever feel it burn in you like a flame until you want to explode and the only relief is to take action? What do you think it was that made you throw a bowlful of hot food at your father?'

'He deserved it.'

'Did he?' She gave Theresa such an intense look that she was obliged to turn away, ashamed and uncomfortable.

98

'Will you apologize? Violence isn't the answer to every problem. It's a bad habit to get into.'

'No, I won't apologize,' said Theresa. She raised her chin defiantly.

'I have nothing further to say,' said her grandmother. She sounded sad and disappointed.

I'm as bad as my father, thought Theresa. I don't have any self-control either once my blood rises. But instead of depressing her, the realization made her optimistic. Her temper gave her strength when she needed it. If she didn't ever become angry and act impulsively then she would be like Catherine, too timid to do anything bold.

'Hey, *I'm Irish*,' she hummed to herself back in her room. 'I'm Irish and fey and mad. Yippee!' Now there was an explanation for who she was. She was a Black Irish girl with a cloud of wild white hair like her Irish great-grandmother and no-one could take that from her.

Mrs Flynn was rushed to the hospital in the middle of the night. Theresa was recalled home. The upheaval caused by her mother's absence worked to Theresa's advantage. She was quickly absorbed back into family life and the reason for her sojourn at her grandparents' receded into the background as she was immediately required to run the house. The following day a succession of parish women arrived to roster the duties of minding the small children while Mr Flynn was at work. They came with delicious casseroles and soups. It made a welcome change from their mother's cooking. A week later Mrs Flynn was driven home by their father, carrying a tiny new Flynn whose name had not yet been decided.

After a while everyone became used to calling the little girl Bub. They forgot that the name on her baptism certificate was actually Bernadette Cecilia.

Theresa cautiously investigated this tiny Flynn morsel, which already had a light down of red fluff on its head. She lowered the white blanket which protected her baby sister.

Freed from the confining blanket, little fingers fluttered in the air. Theresa picked up a hand. Each finger was the size of a toothpick. They could be broken in an instant with one careless jerk.

The baby wriggled a fraction and gave a dainty yawn. Theresa held her breath.

Bub opened her eyes. One blue, one green. She stared long and hard at Theresa.

Theresa gulped. She'd gone and done it again. Fallen in love with another of her mother's babies. She'd been mad over Toots when he was born too.

'Aren't you a darling,' she whispered. 'Whose pet are you going to be?'

Chapter Eight

THE OVUM

'What is your honest opinion, Father?' Mr Flynn asked Father Rafferty.

Father Rafferty's voice boomed across the line. 'Terrence, my considered opinion is that we should quietly bury the whole business. The girls will soon forget about it and life will return to normal.'

'I have my doubts about that,' said Mr Flynn. 'They're pestering me every five minutes to do something. I'm in your hands, Father. I'll do whatever you suggest, but surely there wouldn't be any harm now in sending it to one of the bishops? What do you say? It'll give me some peace at home.'

'No Terrence, it simply won't do. I'd become a laughing-stock. I'm sure your girls are generally the very souls of truth and honesty. But you know what young girls are like. They can get carried away and before you know it they can't separate reality from their games and fantasies.'

'True,' agreed Mr Flynn. 'Do what you think best then, Father.'

Theresa and Catherine continued to wait for another sign of the Lady's special favour, but none came. They were forced to abandon their dreams of travelling to Rome, of learning Italian, and of becoming the focus of attention and admiration in the parish. Their back yard did not become a shrine. The lemon tree died because their father had applied the wrong kind of spray.

They heard nothing about the letter. Outwardly their lives returned to normal. There was cabbage or silver beet every night. John and Andrew practised magic tricks. Tim had become obsessed with rugby and played most nights after school. Toots kept growing and growing until he was nearly as tall as Andrew. Bub crawled after him like a shadow wherever he went. Catherine continued imitating the life of a nun.

And Theresa? She was bored. She returned to the stigmatics for solace and entertainment.

'"St Maria Maddalena de' Pazzi lived in Italy in the late sixteenth century,"' read Theresa aloud. '"As a young girl she whipped and mutilated herself with a home-made crown of thorns and a thorny belt. Her mother was disturbed by her behaviour and tried to discourage her, without success—"'

'The little madam,' said Mrs Flynn. 'She needed a damn good hiding. Her mother was obviously too soft on her. As the tree is bent, so is the tree inclined.'

'Too damn right,' said Mr Flynn. 'You've got to start from the cradle to show them who's boss. Otherwise you end up with a pack of spoilt brats.'

'"Maria was still regularly torturing herself by the time she was old enough to enter the Carmelite Convent . . ."' Theresa glanced across at her rapt audience and couldn't resist embellishing the facts. '"She proudly showed off her whipping scars to the other nuns . . ."'

Mrs Flynn's head jerked up. She frowned before lowering it again over her project. She was constructing a mat from torn strips of old clothes and remnants.

Theresa saw her mother's frown as a warning. She quickly returned to the text. '"Soon Maria was falling into trances, having catatonic fits, becoming frenzied, sexually excited over the idea of Jesus—"'

'*Pardon?* What did you say?' Mr Flynn interrupted Theresa. 'Give that book to me and be quick and lively about it.'

'Wait,' said Theresa, 'I've just got up to a soppy romantic bit.

'". . . Oh Love, you are melting and dissolving my very being," moaned Maria. "You are consuming and killing me . . . oh come, come, and love, love . . ."'

She delivered this in a high falsetto voice. The children shrieked with laughter.

'Oh love, love, love, come, *come*,' moaned Francie, parodying her big sister.

'THAT'S ENOUGH!' snapped Mr Flynn. 'I said, *give me* that book. *Now!* Where in hell's name did you get it?'

'The nuns,' said Theresa. 'It was the nuns who gave it to me.'

'Hell's teeth, they need their heads read,' retorted Mr Flynn.

'What's the matter?' asked Theresa affronted. 'It's funny.'

'I'm not entering into any further discussion on the subject, madam,' said her father, and confiscated the book.

Later, Theresa found where he had hidden it and secretly continued to read it to the other children, who were eager for more.

'"Maria started to vomit up her food. She writhed around on the floor of her room and acted as if someone was beating her. She rolled onto thorns and prickles and continued to whip herself. Her body began to resemble a road map – covered in criss-cross scars. There were scabs which were continually reopened and so failed to heal. Pus ran down her back . . ."'

'Stop!' cried Catherine, 'I can't bear it. It's too awful.' She refused to hear any more and left the room.

'Go on,' said Tim, who shared Theresa's bloodthirsty tastes.

'"Her damp cell smelt as if it contained a rotting corpse. The walls were bare save for a simple wooden cross. Her bed had no mattress. A leather thong hung from a nail on the wall. There was a candlestick on a small table by the bed. At the age of nineteen, she developed the marks of the stigmata on her hands and feet."'

The children were all familiar with the idea of punishment. If they were naughty they were smacked and slapped. But they couldn't understand why anyone would *want* to hurt themselves, or why God might require someone to deliberately cause themselves pain and suffering.

It was almost, thought Theresa, as if the stigmatics gained pleasure from the pain inflicted on them. 'Not my will, but thine.'

'It sounds like masochism to me,' said Smoking Nana when they asked her. She decided she might as well tell them about sadism too while she had their attention.

This was something new for Catherine and Theresa to puzzle over. And, although Smoking Nana couldn't remember exactly how it happened, somehow they moved onto the subjects of sodomy and bestiality as well.

The girls were more confused than ever. No-one had fully explained sex to them. Very little of what their grandmother told them made any sense. Their confusion was increased because of the words she used when describing genitals or the sexual act. Words like *willies, fannies, twats, peckers, goolies, John Thomases, intercourse, buns in the oven, up the duff, taking precautions, doing it from the rear end instead of the front.*

The front of what? Whose rear end? It sounded hideous — not something they would ever want to do, or have done to them. And certain words stood out — peculiar words that conjured up disturbing images.

'Scrotum?' they asked. 'What's that?'

'A loose bag of skin under the man's John Thomas

104

and it looks like a turkey gizzard,' replied Smoking Nana, lighting up another cigarette, her hand shaking slightly. It wasn't her responsibility, it was Moira's. What a tangle she had got herself into.

For once the girls were speechless. The information they had been given so appalled them that they wondered how they would ever be able to bring themselves to marry someone who owned a thing like a turkey gizzard hidden inside his trousers. And was this really connected to a John Thomas with a mind of its own — a feral predatory creature capable of growing to four times its usual size on sighting a naked woman?

'I will never take my clothes off when I marry,' vowed Theresa fiercely. 'Never, *never*.'

'A very sensible idea,' soothed her grandmother, afraid she had gone too far. 'Now you mustn't talk to anyone about this,' she said, 'it's our little secret. Do I have your word on that?' The girls nodded.

'Did you know, and I'm changing the subject here, that human beings shrink as they grow older? I measured myself the other day and I'm four inches shorter now than I used to be. Not only that, I think my ears have got bigger. Have a wee look, will you, dear.'

Theresa pulled back the wiry grey curls and exposed a large flabby ear. She wrinkled her nose.

'Oooh yuk,' she said. 'There's hairs growing out of it.'

'The mysteries of the human body,' replied her grandmother sagely.

Sister Mary Aquinas led the standard-five and -six girls in groups of a dozen at a time into the ablutions block to demonstrate the convent's most recent acquisition. They saw that the tip of her nose was red. It twitched. Their curiosity was now fully aroused.

They made fun of her nose behind her back. It was always a reliable barometer of her moods. The rest of her face was flour-white, her lips chapped and pleated

105

with loose skin from the cold weather. She was an imposing figure. Her authority was never questioned.

Sister Mary Aquinas had installed a white appliance in the girls' toilet block. There was a small round button at its base and a metal flap with a slot behind it.

She lifted the flap. Into the slot she dropped a mysterious long flat object wrapped in a brown paper bag. She pressed the button. There was a whirring sound and an acrid unpleasant smell filled the room.

Theresa wrinkled her nose.

Sister Mary Aquinas gave a satisfied smile and clapped her hands.

'Combustion is about to take place, girls. More hygiene, less fuss and bother. Any questions?'

Everyone averted their eyes. There were no questions.

Theresa watched and listened carefully to discover the function of the new equipment. What had been inside the package? Letters? Underpants? The white box gleamed inscrutably across the room at her. Whatever purpose it was there to serve remained as mysterious and incomprehensible to her after the demonstration as it had before she had first seen it.

The following day when she was playing netball she happened to glance over towards the girls' toilet block and saw a tell-tale plume of smoke emerging from a pipe on the roof.

On a Monday night after tea, Mr Flynn had requested a word with the two eldest girls alone. He followed them to their room and shut the door behind them. He marched over to Catherine's bed, sat down on it and patted the surface of the candlewick spread as an indication for them to be seated.

He smiled. It was not a reassuring smile. They weren't deceived by it – they were in trouble.

'Sit down both of you,' he said to them. 'It's time we had a little talk.'

They sat on the opposite bed. What had they done wrong?

'Each month,' said their father, launching immediately into the purpose of his discussion, 'your body will produce an egg. Not like a chook's egg. A wee egg that you can't see with the naked eye.'

The naked eye.

Mr Flynn crossed his arms and legs as if to hold his body together. He didn't meet their eyes as he spoke, staring fixedly at a point on the wallpaper between them. His voice was hard and raspy like sandpaper.

They didn't look directly at him. They focused instead on the rose pattern which extended in diagonal rows along the walls – anything rather than look at his neck, or his hairiness. A crucifix intersected two entwined rosebuds. A yellowing branch of macrocarpa from Palm Sunday had been tucked behind it. The drooping plastic Christ provided a morsel of comfort while their father rasped out his frightening sentences, each word falling on their ears like a hammer pounding nails into a coffin.

'What are you talking about?' asked Theresa in a tight, angry voice.

'A change is going to take place inside your bodies,' he announced in the manner of a prophet predicting doom.

'Each month your egg will ripen and the walls of your uterus will build a lining of spongy tissue loaded with blood. When a woman gets married, the egg or ovum becomes fertilized by her husband and a baby grows.'

How revolting, thought Theresa. It would be like being invaded. She wished she were a boy and didn't have to concern herself with eggs or changes. She was impatient for her father to finish and leave the room. The conversation disgusted her.

'*Tralaalaaa la la la,*' she sang inside her head to block out her father's voice. She didn't hear him

107

when he explained that if a girl's egg wasn't fertilized, the walls of the uterus, which had become engorged with blood in preparation for the egg, dissolved and released blood. This was called a *period*.

Catherine understood. Every month, for five days, instead of urinating she would bleed. It wouldn't cause much inconvenience. It didn't sound as if it would hurt. But she usually associated the appearance of blood with pain. How much blood would there be? Would it flow out of her in a rushing torrent or in slow dribbles? What if she couldn't reach the toilet in time? How would she staunch it?

'Tralalalalala,' went the voice inside Theresa's head. Inside her stomach, however, she felt a quiver of fear, a queer fluttery feeling. She wanted to stay the way she was.

'Have I made myself clear?' asked their father, still refusing to look at them.

They nodded dumbly, eyes brimming. They wouldn't cry in front of him, it would be too humiliating. They felt debased. Bodies were private. How could he possibly know what sort of mysterious activities went on inside them?

It now seemed that they were to be betrayed by the bodies they had thought they knew so intimately. Inside they were hollow. There was a wound. It was impossible to staunch it. They would bleed, stated their father, for over thirty years before the wound healed and their bodies stopped producing wee ovum seeds.

'Where's Mum?' asked Catherine.

Mr Flynn coughed and cleared his throat noisily.

'Your mother's not much good at this sort of thing,' he said.

She'd be better than you, they thought.

'I don't care,' cried Catherine. 'I want her to tell me properly.' She ran out of the room, almost colliding with her mother, who had been hovering in the

108

hallway dusting the same light switch for the past ten minutes.

'. . . Catherine?' she said in a tentative voice and reached out a hand.

Catherine pushed past her without replying. She had an instinctive desire to punish her mother.

'I'm not a good explainer,' her mother called after her.

'I don't care,' said Catherine coldly. 'It doesn't matter.'

But it did.

It was true, their mother wasn't very good at explaining. She was only marginally better than their father. Why was it, thought Theresa, that adults so rarely made sense? They always seemed to select the least relevant or the most upsetting details to include in their explanations. These details rarely conveyed the complete picture. The important bits had been forgotten or were deliberately left out.

They could tell that their mother was embarrassed to be discussing such subjects with them. Pubescence, she called it. That was the name of their disease. It wasn't fatal, but it was *lingering*.

'When your monthly arrives, everything will be different,' she promised, when she had finally been persuaded to discuss the subject.

How different? Apparently, their bodies, no longer under their control, would undergo bizarre transformations. Hairs would spring up in places that had previously been pale, hidden and private – their genitals, underarms and perhaps even the aureole, the area around their nipples.

Theresa had always believed that breasts appeared on a woman overnight. When she was about twenty – grown-up. She hadn't realized it was a slow process. And that hairs would *gradually* appear.

They had always been taught to refer to their genital

109

area as Gene. But because they had never seen the word actually written down, they had named their vaginas Jean, a friendly name. Jean was a little creature quite separate from themselves who lived 'Down There', a place they must never touch because it was a sin. They didn't know why. They had to accept it.

Their father said it was disgusting to touch Jean.

'Don't even think about it,' he said.

'But what will happen to us if we do, Daddy?'

'God doesn't like it.'

'Why not?'

'Because,' he said, 'it's filthy. FILTHY. Do you hear me?'

They nodded. Yes. Filthy, a sin. They weren't dirty. They wanted to be good, clean girls.

'Yes, and that's the way you're going to stay – good girls. There'll be no mucking about with yourselves. You must understand that I'm only telling you this for your own good.'

'Yes, Dad.'

Their father must know what was best. They obeyed him and ignored Jean. They pretended she didn't exist.

Mr Flynn found himself fascinated by the transformation of his awkward eldest daughters into coltish young women. He enquired often as to how they were feeling.

He wanted to know about any changes when they happened. He wanted to share intimate details.

The monsignor returned unexpectedly for a visit. Father Rafferty had been promoted to parish priest and was now assisted by a young Irish curate called Father Ryan. This meant the monsignor's presence was no longer required and he had been posted to a central city parish in Wellington.

'The mons is back!' Tim ran to the girls' bedroom to gleefully impart the news.

Theresa leapt from her bed, where she had been crouched over her homework, laced up her school shoes and went to meet him.

Catherine took her time. She was suddenly shy in her habit. Would he be impressed?

'Catherine . . .'

For a moment the monsignor was lost for words as he caught sight of the girl. painfully thin, dressed in her long bulky habit, her white hair protruding in feathery wisps from under her veil.

Tears came into his eyes as he clasped her hand.

The family watched him carefully.

The monsignor retained Catherine's hand in his left and patted it with his right. He shook his head.

Catherine retrieved her hand. There was an anxious lump in her throat. She tucked her hands into her sleeves the way she had observed in the nuns.

'*Mi chica*, why are you dressed like a nun?'

'I wrote to you, Monsignor. Didn't you receive my letter? God has given me a vocation.'

A little tear dripped down the monsignor's cheek and he wiped it away.

'But you are too young,' he said softly. 'Much too young. You have not experienced any of life yet.'

'God told me,' insisted Catherine stubbornly. 'I'm obeying Him.'

'We've told her not to be so silly,' said Mrs Flynn, 'but we can't budge her. Can't you drum some sense into her, Monsignor?'

'Come with me,' said the monsignor and he led Catherine out into the back yard where they were watched jealously through the windows by the other children.

'You can't change my mind, Monsignor,' said Catherine quietly.

'The religious life is a blessed one but it is not easy,' said the monsignor. He knelt down on the sack left on the grass in front of a flower bed by Mrs Flynn. She

111

had been weeding when the monsignor arrived.

He picked up a cluster of oxalis bulbs. 'Look at this weed,' he said. 'See how it spreads and how it would take over the entire garden, choking the flowers if your mother didn't take care. As a priest I too must see that the weeds do not spread and choke the good plants that are struggling to survive.'

'Yes,' answered Catherine with a hint of impatience. Why couldn't adults say what they meant without *going on*, getting off the point. She was tired of stories, bored with always being taught stuff for her own good. What did the monsignor know? Had the Virgin appeared to him or to Father Rafferty? No.

The monsignor stood up. He brushed the dirt off his soutane and waved at Theresa, who was visible at the window. He motioned for her to join them. Several of the other children ran out eagerly, but he ushered them away.

'Father Rafferty has told me of your vision,' he said gently. 'Why don't you tell me what you saw.'

Catherine began and Theresa filled in the gaps. When they had finished they asked him if he believed them.

He sighed. 'I would like to very much. But I am afraid it is impossible.'

'Why is it so hard for grown-ups to believe us?' stormed Theresa. 'It's so unfair.' She glared at the monsignor.

He shrugged and looked unhappy. 'I have no choice,' he said.

'Don't you like us any more, Monsignor?' asked Catherine.

'*Mis hijas.* You are my very special and favourite parishioners and I am more sorry than I can say to be leaving you.'

Chapter Nine

THE BLUE ARMY

A missionary came to visit their parish. A magician in a swirling blue cloak. A juggler spinning stories before a spellbound audience of three hundred children. Stories, doctrine and ideas emerged transformed in Father Thomas's low, thrilling tones. Such a deep voice for a small wiry man. His face was animated to complement the voice, his gesticulating arms cut swathes through the air, his words became birds flying way over their heads, opening windows and doors of their imaginations. *Blue Army. Fatima. The Miracle of the Sun. Our Lady of Mt Carmel.* He referred to redemption and punishment almost in the same breath. Sacrifice was required. Sincerity of intention.

I want to be perfect, thought Catherine, her lips parted, heart hammering with excitement. Her black veil quivered. Feet jiggled with nervous energy beneath the black habit. She wished she could make a sacrifice right there and then, in front of everybody, to prove her purity of intention. But she knew Angles would neither understand nor approve. Sister Mary Angela would accuse her of shameless attention-seeking.

'Do you think you are superior to everyone around you, Catherine Flynn? You've been marked out for special favours and attentions from God, is that it, girl?'

Absorbed in her usual daydreams and fantasies of imminent martyrhood and canonization, Catherine was dragged back into the present with a jolt when she became aware of a priestly finger pointing in her direction. She blushed with embarrassment and the

113

finger moved on, picking out other children, who, unable to give the missionary the response he was seeking, wilted miserably under his scrutiny.

The question was repeated.

'Tell me what the Mother of Sorrows, Our Lady of Mt Carmel, requested from us when she appeared to the little children at Fatima?'

That was easy. Catherine's right arm shot up.

Father Thomas came down off his rostrum to observe at close range the girl dressed in a nun's habit.

'What have we here, then?' he asked, his busy eyebrows operating like creatures independent of the rest of his face.

'An early vocation,' whispered Sister Mary Aquinas. She prodded Catherine. 'Stand up, girl.'

Father Thomas stroked his chin. His mouth twitched with barely suppressed amusement. The nuns tittered.

'Do you know the answer, little Sister?'

'Our Lady asked us to say the Rosary every day,' replied Catherine.

'She did indeed,' exulted the priest, and his cloak rippled behind him as he made his way back to the rostrum. 'And do we all say the Rosary *every* day?'

Half of the children raised their hands in response.

'Only *half* of you?' he groaned.

The missionary buried his head in his hands for a couple of minutes. They wondered if he would recover.

He lifted his head briefly before staring mournfully down at the microphone again. The children waited, not knowing how to share his pain.

Catherine felt smug. *They* said the Rosary *every* night.

Theresa wondered at the connection between the Rosary and the mysterious Blue Army for which he was seeking fresh recruits. Would they have to leave home and visit Portugal? Travel to Fatima and visit the shrine? Nobody would ever know she and Catherine had their own shrine at the base of the dead lemon tree in the back of their garden.

'Our Lady has begged us to stop offending God. Her own heart, encircled with thorns, is constantly wounded by ungrateful men with their blasphemies and sins.'

Theresa tried to imagine what it would be like to have a heart like a pincushion. And although Father Thomas said it was *men* who flung darts into the pincushion, she knew that she herself was just as much to blame. She pictured the Madonna wincing every time she said 'damn' or 'shit', the expression of outrage that must crease Our Lady's brow whenever her mother said 'Hell's bells and buggy wheels', or her father shouted 'Jesus wept', when things went wrong, which they seemed to, all the time. And she realized that it was not possible for any of them to become perfect. She would continue to fail, to cause offence, no matter how hard she tried.

So why even try to be perfect? To make sacrifices for the greater good when the graces deriving from these sacrifices and struggles were immediately bound to be cancelled out by 'blasphemies and ingratitudes'.

Father Thomas invited them to join the Blue Army of Fatima. To fulfil the requests of Our Lady of Mt Carmel, which were to receive Communion and attend Confession on the First Saturday of five consecutive months, to say the Rosary every day without exception, and to make sacrifices in reparation for sins.

The nuns nodded and murmured agreement, black veils bobbing in unison, a flotilla arriving in safe harbour.

But why a *Blue* Army, wondered Theresa and Catherine, seated at opposite ends of the packed little hall with their respective classmates.

115

Because blue was the Madonna's colour, said the missionary.

Above the hall door, like eyes watching them, were two framed black and white photos, one of the founder, Sister Mary Ignatius, and the other of the incumbent pope, Paul VI. The hall smelled of floor polish and beeswax. In one corner an old black piano was draped with a white embroidered cloth.

The missionary roused himself to new heights of oratorial brilliance.

'CONSOLE THE BLESSED VIRGIN!' he roared, thumping the rostrum with his fist.

They sat up straighter in their seats. Even the nuns, with their ramrod backs, sat taller. Sister Aquinas's nose glowed a troubling red.

He began to tell them about The Miracle of the Sun.

'In the year nineteen hundred and seventeen, nearly one thousand people at Fatima witnessed a ball of fire whirl above the earth for twelve whole minutes. Imagine. And while they watched – what did they see?' He paused and looked up at the ceiling.

No-one answered him. They too looked up. There was nothing there, only the wood-panelled ceiling desperately in need of a paint.

'The ball of fire began to plunge towards the earth. People were terrified. They thought it was the end of the world. But at the last minute they were saved. The ball of fire shot back up into the sky and merged with the sun. A miracle.

'But that's not all of the story. Our Lady showed the children a vision. A sea of fire. Inside the flames, writhing in agony, were the lost souls. *Burnt to a crisp.* They screamed in pain and despair. And there were devils too, hundreds of devils and other terrifying creatures.' Father Thomas rolled his eyes expressively. '*Hundreds of devils.*

'Make reparations for sins. Only then will the tide turn.' He gave them a piercing look. 'We're not talking

116

about flesh and blood matters here. What we're talking about is the *rulers of the world of darkness*.'

They nodded. Satan and his works.

'Our Lady said: "When you see a night that is lit by a strange and unknown light, you will know it is a sign that God is about to punish the world with another war." But if Her wishes are fulfilled, Russia will be converted.

'*Russia converted*. No more communists. Peace in the world. We can sleep safely in our beds at night without fretting about what the Ruskies might be up to.'

He said the world was at a crossroads. They could make the difference, but only if they joined the Blue Army.

'Yes, Father,' they chorused. Priests were always right. They must know. It was what their parents wanted too.

He showed them a brown scapular. Any child who didn't already wear one was to file up to the stage and receive one from him. Every time they kissed their scapular they would receive a partial indulgence, he reminded them. Anyone who wore a scapular would not suffer in the flames of hell. 'And that is a promise,' he said. There were other ways they could accrue indulgences. Reciting the Rosary in a group bestowed a plenary indulgence.

Theresa was in a daze. She found herself following the rest of her classmates up to the stage to receive a scapular from the priest.

'*Kiss it*,' he urged and his breath smelt of old socks. His thin lips pressed lightly on the coarse fabric before he gave the scapular to Theresa. She placed her lips on the exact place on the fabric already touched by the priest's mouth.

She returned with the others to her classroom and for the remainder of the day found it impossible to concentrate on her lessons. Instead, graphic images of the lost souls, frying in agony, reduced to cinders, ran continuously in her head like an endless repeat of a horror film. Anxieties and fears surged around and around in her stomach like dirty laundry in a machine. She felt nauseous. Her head hurt, she was close to tears. What was the matter with her?

Inside the cubicle in the girls' toilet she was shocked to discover dark stains on her underpants.

She had been punished for becoming an atheist and a Jezebel. Under the influence of Father Thomas she had reconsidered her position. Perhaps she had been too hasty in rejecting God. She had accepted a scapular, agreed to join the Blue Army. It seemed, however, that she had left her decision too late. God had lost patience with her.

'I'm so sorry, God,' prayed Theresa. 'I'll be very very good from now on. I'll never offend you again. I'll do anything. Even become a nun, if it's what you really *really* want.'

At home that night she changed her underpants three times. Each time fresh stains appeared. And every time she checked they were still there.

The stain of sin.

Was the Virgin referred to by Father Thomas the same as the White Lady she had seen with Catherine? The White Lady had made no mention of Russia. They had not been given a vision of Hell. They had not been terrorized by their vision. On the contrary, seeing the White Lady had been the most exciting thing she had ever experienced. No-one had succeeded in making her doubt the truth of what she had been shown – a bright light, a shimmering incandescent figure, a woman with a low musical voice, a radiant smile. The monsignor had said the White Lady was a figment of their over-wrought imaginations, of religious fervour carried to excess. He said he was concerned for them.

He had betrayed them.

We'll show all of them, vowed Theresa. She knew with certainty that one day the White Lady, Star of the Sea, must return, this time bringing proof of her visit. No-one would dare to doubt them again. And then – St Theresa Flynn, the stigmatic virgin of Chatterton, would be in all the papers. She pictured fountains of blood pouring from her hands and feet. Journalists would be queuing to interview her and to hear her predictions for the future. Mr Holyoake, the prime minister, would visit 23 Grey Street. They would lift the plastic mats from the carpet in honour of his visit. He would ask her advice just as so many popes and kings had sought wisdom from Hildegard.

The family grouped around the statue of the Italian Madonna. This time they were reciting the Litany of Loreto, another of Mr Flynn's impromptu additions to the Rosary. There was still a spare five minutes before the news was due on the television. Why waste it when they could be putting the time to good use, said Mr Flynn.

'Virgin most powerful,' he thundered. He never worried about getting the sequence right and sometimes favourite phrases were repeated.

'Cause of our Joy,' murmured Mrs Flynn stifling a yawn.

'Vessel of Honour,' added Catherine as they went around the circle clockwise.

'Refuge of Sinners,' contributed Theresa.

'Queen of Virgins,' piped up Tim.

On and on it went around the circle – Virgin most Venerable – Mystical Rose – Morning Star – House of Gold – Tower of Ivory – Mirror of Justice.

Please God, please Mystical Rose, begged Theresa, her thighs damp with blood and perspiration. *Please*.

119

Chapter Ten

THE BLEEDING HEART

Theresa discovered the reason for her mysterious bleeding. So God hadn't punished her after all. She could become an atheist again. She removed her scapular and hid it at the back of a drawer. Smoking Nana said she was a woman now that she had her period.

'Is it nice to be a woman?' Theresa asked.

'No,' said her mother. 'I wish I had been born a man.'

'But why?'

'You ask too many questions for a little girl. You'll find out soon enough. Enjoy your freedom while you can.'

'What freedom?' replied Theresa. 'You tell me what I can do and what I'm not allowed. I don't have any say. When can I do what I want? How old do I have to be?'

'When you leave home,' said her mother. 'That's the day you can choose. And I hope you remember what you've been taught.'

In the meantime there appeared to be nothing to look forward to. However, now that Father Rafferty had decided to ignore the letter the Virgin had given them, they were no longer sworn to secrecy on the matter by their father. They were free to divulge their secret to anyone they chose.

Theresa told Mary Louise.

'You're pulling my leg,' said Mary Louise. 'Next you'll be telling me you've been called to be a nun too.'

'Are you saying you don't believe me either?' said Theresa with a quivering lip.

'Why would Our Lady visit Chatterton? It's the biggest dump on earth.'

'She brought a letter about contraception.'

'I know what that is,' smirked Mary Louise.

'What is it, smarty-pants?'

'Mum takes her temperature every day. Does your mother?'

'I don't know.'

'Don't you know anything?'

'No.'

'Mum takes her temperature every morning at the same time. She uses a special thermometer and leaves it in her mouth for ages.'

'How long?'

'I s'pose about five minutes.'

'Why does she take her temperature? What does it have to do with contraception?'

'Something. She uses graph paper. It's very scientific.'

'I don't get it.'

'You're so dumb.'

'You don't know either.'

'I do so.'

Theresa was puzzled. What did the Virgin's visit have to do with thermometers?

Mrs Flynn had a double chin, which she fiercely resented. She tried to disguise what she saw as her greatest defect by raising it with an odd little bobbing motion when she spoke. This disconcerted people when they first met her. Moira Flynn's teeth were perfect, but this didn't make up for the sight of the despised chin every morning in the mirror.

Her children thought she was beautiful – but very old. They loved her permed red hair and the peculiar green eyes that came originally from their grandmother and which only Francie had inherited.

She was thirty-five years old. She woke every morning unable to believe this was her life, that this really was *it*, as good as it got.

What would her life have been like if . . . if she hadn't

met Terrence? If she hadn't become a Catholic? If only she had listened to her mother.

'We've got a lot to be grateful for,' she told her daughters. If she said it often enough she might come to believe it.

'What have we got to be grateful for?' asked Theresa, swooping hawk-like to snatch up her mother's words.

'A roof over our heads. Terrence's weekly pay packet. A happy home. All of you kids. One day if you're lucky, you and Catherine and Francie will find good husbands and you'll have the same.'

'We will?'

'Yes. You'll know when Mr Right turns up.' His arrival was apparently only a matter of time. As Theresa was eleven and Catherine ten, she predicted he'd probably arrive in about ten years' time. If they were lucky.

If they weren't they might get left on the shelf, out in the cold with the other lonely unhappy spinsters. Spinsters were always lonely, always unhappy. Finding Mr Right, said Mrs Flynn, was the only way for a woman to attain true happiness.

'But Mum, how will we recognize him when we meet him?' asked Theresa. Her mother's words conjured up images of a Jesus-like apparition, a reward for being a good girl, something guaranteed.

'You'll know,' she replied, 'beyond the shadow of a doubt.'

The shadow of a doubt.

'When you meet Mr Right,' continued their mother, 'all you want to do is get married and have babies. The love inside you grows so big it has to have an outlet. It comes out as a dear wee baby.'

She gave them a knowing smile.

Her daughters looked anxious. From where would the dear wee baby come? Your mouth, your armpit? Your tummy button?

An expression came over their mother's face they

had never seen before. They didn't know what to make of it. Suddenly she seemed a stranger. It disconcerted them. She represented everything that was safe and familiar in their world. She always told the truth. They believed everything she said.

They wanted to know more about babies and love and Mr Rights, but after giving them a few tantalizing hints their mother refused to reveal any further information.

Moira Flynn failed to understand why people made such a fuss about sex. She didn't enjoy it, nor did most of her friends, even though they cracked bawdy jokes that would have shocked Mr Flynn if he'd known. Naturally she never admitted her marriage wasn't all that it seemed.

Smoking Nana had plenty to say on the subject.

'Tell him to tie a knot in it,' she told her daughter. 'You've got enough children. Why risk another?'

'Mum!'

'You've got to laugh or you die,' cackled her mother. 'Why don't you have a hizzy and put your mind at rest?'

'I've already had enough ops to last me a lifetime.'

'True,' said her mother. 'After I had my hysterectomy I swelled up like a balloon.'

Moira Flynn pulled her brows together. Her mother thought she resembled a mule, but she knew better than to say so.

'All I want,' cried Moira, 'is for everyone to be happy.'

'Happiness doesn't come cheap,' replied her mother. 'Everything has its price.'

Father Rafferty promised that God would reward them in the end, that all the pain and suffering would not have been in vain.

I want my reward now, thought Mrs Flynn. I don't want to wait until I'm dead.

Terrence always entered her well before she was ready for him. He became impatient if she took too long to become aroused. Foreplay was dealt with in a perfunctory manner – a kiss on the lips, a tickle of the nipples, followed by a quick stroking of her thighs. He generally wanted her to touch his penis then, but it might just as well have been the rubber hose on the washing-machine as far as she was concerned. It meant nothing to her. Then before she knew it he was in, expecting her to be ready for him. Almost immediately he began to complain about how dry she was. It was easier to let him do what he wanted and get it over with.

Her mind roamed freely while he was inside her. She listened to his grunting and heaving as he toiled above her and planned the school lunches or worked out the week's budget. Occasionally she emitted a low moan – the walls were paper thin – other than this she barely participated. Sometimes she didn't utter a sound and he didn't seem to notice. He always came too quickly, long before she was ready.

'I've lost my hard-on in the time it takes you to decide if you're interested or not,' he said, if she dallied.

She heard the recriminatory note in his voice. *Her fault.* Wasn't he entitled to sex when it was safe? Was it too much to ask, for her to lie there while he made love to her? Even if there was nothing in it for her, asked a tiny voice deep inside her. A treacherous little voice because it prevented her from being happy.

But how did she know what she wanted, if she didn't *feel* anything, she thought. She was tired of pretending. She longed for intimacy but never experienced it.

Why couldn't he touch her for once without it having to automatically lead to sex? She especially needed him to caress her during the times when it was unsafe to have sex, but if he couldn't enter her he lost interest altogether, rolled over and immediately fell asleep.

She closed her eyes and dreamed of a love full of passion and tenderness that did not involve Terrence thrusting his insatiable organ inside her for two and a half minutes and then immediately afterwards losing interest in her, pulling out, rolling off and falling asleep.

Her dream man would give her wonderful presents. She would be discovered, opened up like a flower and lovingly caressed. Words which normally remained locked up in her chest would tumble out and be listened to.

'Sweetheart,' the man, not Terrence Flynn, would say. And . . . 'darling'. He would take her away and they would live happily ever after. She would begin again, the past and her children fading into the distance behind her, as if they were merely the headlights of passing cars and she had her life to begin again – young, slim and preferably without her double chin.

'What if Mr Right turns out to be a Miss Right?' asked Catherine in her quiet little voice. She had just learned a new word beginning with 'L' which Mr Flynn had explained was a woman with a sick mind.

Catherine's voice was so soft and tentative that no-one paid any attention.

Miss Right, indeed, thought Mrs Flynn, who could hear a pin drop three rooms away.

Miss Right would have a voice the sound of which was like having honey trickle into your ear, thought Catherine. Her skin would smell of almonds and aniseed, roses and geraniums. She wouldn't be much good at sport and she'd prefer reading books all day to doing almost anything else. Miss Right would play the piano and sing like an angel. Catherine could imagine herself having fun with a Miss Right for ever.

'My Mr Right will be like John Lennon,' announced Theresa, who had clipped from newspapers and magazines every article she could find on the Fab Four. 'He will be a poet and we'll write stories together every day and sing songs.'

Mrs Flynn uttered a scornful laugh. Her daughters were shocked at the sound. Its mocking echo continued to reverberate long after she had taken herself back to the kitchen. She placed a sack on the floor, knelt on it and began to scrub the kitchen lino.

'She cleaned the floor only yesterday,' whispered Catherine. 'Why is she doing it again so soon?'

They peered around the doorway and spied on their mother. She was scrubbing vigorously, both hands gripping the brush, whipping up a lather all around her. As she scrubbed she was removing the pattern on the lino. Beneath the familiar diamond design another grid began to emerge – rows and rows of hearts.

They leaned closer. Around each heart was a crown of thorns.

Mrs Flynn emptied her bucket of grey water and poured some fresh. As she ran her mop up and down the length of the floor the pattern of hearts began to fade, leaving it a dull red.

'I gave you my heart and you gave me a child,' sang Mrs Flynn out of tune. 'I gave you my life and you spent it . . . Oh woe, woe, woe is the day I gave you my heart, because now I have only a stone. Woe . . . woe . . . woe . . . '

'I can't *bear* that song,' said Catherine, putting her hands over her ears and running back down the hallway.

On the wall above her bed the Sacred Heart gazed down reproachfully at her. Blood from the flaming heart held in his right hand trickled down over his fingers. She had never noticed before the way the heart resembled a slab of raw steak. Even the thorns around the middle of it were oozing blood.

'I gave you my heart,' hummed Theresa, bursting into the room and then stopping when she caught a glimpse of her sister's face.

'Oh, why is everything so *sad*?' said Catherine. She knew her mother was unhappy and the knowledge of it pierced as deeply as if it were her own heart that was crowned with thorns. She felt powerless to help.

Full of despair she picked up *Good Wives*. But she knew that she would find no comfort there. Beth was about to die.

'Here, cherished like a household saint in its shrine, sat Beth, tranquil and busy as ever; for nothing could change the sweet unselfish nature, and even while preparing to leave life, she tried to make it happier for those who should remain behind.'

Tears pricked Catherine's eyes when she read of 'the dark hour before the dawn' . . . and, 'she quietly drew her last, with no farewell but one loving look, one little sigh'.

She flung her head down on her pillow and began to cry in earnest. Her mother's voice wound its way around and around in her head like a snake, 'Oh woe, woe, woe.'

I will not be sad, Theresa told herself sternly, and she too turned to her books for comfort. The stigmatics always cheered her up. She quickly found her favourite story, that of Blessed Clare of the Cross. When she had died the nuns opened up Blessed Clare's heart with a razor and discovered all kinds of objects inside made of muscle and body tissue – a miniature cross, nails, a crown of thorns, a spear.

Theresa went over to the bed where Catherine lay crying. She began to run her hand through her sister's wiry curls.

'Don't,' said Catherine, preferring to wallow in her misery, although as soon as she snapped at her sister she regretted it.

'Please yourself,' replied Theresa. Catherine of Siena was far more interesting with her extreme self-denial. She had been known to eat the pus from lepers' sores.

Jesus had pierced the saint, creating an opening in her right side and placing his own glowing heart inside. It was a human heart, a throbbing, swollen organ of muscle engorged with blood and on fire with love.

Theresa felt an odd little stirring between her thighs as she read this and because it felt nice, peculiarly nice, she read the passage again. Then suddenly she stopped reading about throbbing hearts being swapped about because it occurred to her that she was probably committing a sin. According to Sister Mary Angela you could sin in thought as well as deed.

St Catherine had first experienced the stigmata in 1373, when a crown of thorns seemed to be squeezing her head. The nuns claimed the saint had refused all food from the age of twenty. Yet mysteriously she had lived for another thirteen years.

St Margaret Mary was as perverse as Catherine of Siena. She possessed great powers of healing, but she also had a fondness for devouring all kinds of bodily secretions: sweat, pus, vomit. She described them as delicacies. She had even been reported as having devoured the diarrhoea of her patients. Despite her thirst for tales of blood and gore, Theresa began to feel nauseous after contemplating the ecstatic excesses of Margaret Mary.

'Hey, Catherine,' Theresa called to her sister. 'Do you want to hear something *really* disgusting?'

Catherine looked across at Theresa's flushed face and bright eyes.

'No.'

Theresa hesitated. She could sense the presence of the devil tempting her. *Tell her anyway . . . go on.*
The devil won.
'How would you like to eat lepers' pus? Or vomit?'
Catherine blocked her ears and ran from the room.

Chapter Eleven

KEEPING UP APPEARANCES

1968

'Mary Louise says her mother takes her temperature every day,' said Theresa.

'Is that a fact?' Mrs Flynn banged the iron over her husband's shirt.

'Do you take your temperature every morning?'

'I do.'

'Do you? Why?'

'So that I can work out when I ovulate.'

'Why do you need to know?'

'It's nothing that need concern you, my girl.'

'You haven't told me what I wanted to know.'

'I never said I would.'

'I've found out why our mothers take their temperatures,' said Mary Louise.

'Who told you?'

'Patricia.' Mary Louise's education had been considerably augmented by exposure to the opinions of her older brothers and sisters. They were always either falling in love or out of it, and a distorted version of the more salacious details of their liaisons was relayed daily to an astonished and impressed Theresa. There were ten children and they lived squeezed together in a house that had been renovated and extended to such a degree, all without permits, that entering it made Theresa feel she was in a rabbit warren of little passages and mezzanines from which one or other of the O'Reilly mob could inevitably be heard either sobbing, shouting or screaming with laughter. She was overwhelmed by her friend's family. Her natural ebullience completely vanished in the presence of the voluble O'Reillys, all of whom teased her unmercifully. There were bunks tucked into every available nook and cranny. Little alcoves, scarcely more than walk-in cupboards, had been curtained off to allow Louise's older siblings the privacy they demanded. The parents had long since abandoned any attempt at maintaining order.

'What did Patricia say?' Patricia was seventeen. She wore daringly short skirts and a great deal of black eyeliner. She had a voice like a foghorn and a laugh that sounded to Theresa like water running down a drain. Mrs Flynn called Patricia a slovenly trollop. Theresa admired her enormously.

'Patricia said our mothers need to know when their egg is made so they can avoid having sex.'

'I still don't get it.'

'Your mother doesn't want your father's sperm to find her egg 'cos then she'll have a baby.'

'Is this really true? You're not making it up?'

'Cross my heart and hope to die. Your mother isn't a saint, you know. She has sex with your father. Don't you *know* how babies are made?' cried Mary Louise, her eyes shiny with delight.

'Sort of,' admitted Theresa. 'Not really.'

'I'll tell you. It's like this. Your mother rubs your father's penis until it grows a foot long. Then he pokes it inside her hole and wiggles it around in there until it swells up and squirts out seeds like a pop gun. Patricia says it feels ticklish and nice and once you've started you can't stop wiggling. So there.'

'I don't believe you. You're lying.' Theresa burst into tears. She remembered what Smoking Nana had told them. *John Thomases. Turkey-gizzard scrotums.* It must be true.

'You want to know what else Patricia said?'

Theresa was uncertain.

'Whatever our mothers are doing, Patricia says it's not working because they keep having babies. Did you know my mum is having another one?'

'But you've already got ten kids. When is she going to stop? You'll run out of room.'

What was it that wasn't working? What were their mothers doing wrong? Theresa knew she teetered on the precipice of discovering a dark and terrible secret.

'Mum, did you read the letter the Virgin gave us?' asked Theresa.

'Yes dear.'

'What did it say?'

Her mother hesitated. 'The letter said women had the right to limit the size of their families for plausible reasons. It said that the marriage act was beautiful and natural and it didn't always have to lead to procreation.'

Theresa was confused. 'What is a marriage act?'

'You'll find out when you're older,' said her mother.

'I am older, I just started college, remember?'

Theresa sought out Father Rafferty. This time she would discover the truth.

'Mum told me what was in Our Lady's letter,' she began.

'Theresa, I thought we had agreed to put all of that behind us, to forget it.'

'Father, I can't forget it. I'm tormented. The letter said women didn't have to have big families if they didn't want to, they have a choice.'

'No,' said the priest, 'the letter conveyed the exact opposite.'

'It did?'

'Yes.' The priest rubbed his jaw. Something didn't add up. He would have to get on the phone to Moira. Theresa sat in front of him draped in her gym frock. Her little breasts created a bump where the pleats began. She wasn't a little girl any more. Her ankle socks had been replaced by darned pantihose. The gym frock was too big for her. It was obviously a hand-me-down. Her nails were bitten. There was a pimple on her chin. She seemed to be changing in front of his eyes. He wanted to hug her but restrained himself.

'Moira, Tim Rafferty here. I had a visit from your Tess today.'

'Yes,' said Mrs Flynn cautiously.

'She came with a far-fetched story she said you had told her. I'm referring here to the contents of the letter they say was given to them by Our Lady.'

'Oh . . . that.'

'According to Theresa, you told her it promoted the idea of birth control.'

'Oh no, Father.' Mrs Flynn gave a nervous giggle. 'She must have got the wrong end of the stick. You know what children are like — they hear only what they want to hear.'

'Let me put it another way. Would you not say that the concept was rather mature for an innocent girl of thirteen like Theresa?'

'Is it?'

'What I'm getting at is, does your daughter understand the ramifications of birth control, Moira?'

'Girls these days, they certainly know a lot more than we did in my day.'

'Moira, I'm concerned about your girls.'

'That makes two of us, Father. Look, I really appreciate your call, letting me know. I'll have a word with her.'

Smoking Nana told Theresa that her face had character. This was more important than beauty, she said.

'Are you trying to tell me I'm ugly?' demanded Theresa.

'You're putting words into my mouth,' replied her

grandmother. 'I never said that. All I meant was, a lively personality is more captivating than good looks alone.'

'I want both,' said Theresa.

She sulked for the rest of the evening and covered up the bedroom mirror with a cloth so that she wouldn't have to look at her characterful face framed by hateful frizzy blond hair.

'You're sailing close to the wind, my girl,' warned Mrs Flynn.

'Theresa is going through an anti-everything phase,' she told Smoking Nana. 'She's anti-God, anti-me, won't speak to her father, won't talk properly. She's going to the dogs. I wash my hands of her.'

'Leave her be,' advised Smoking Nana.

Theresa began deliberately to leave off the ends of her words, speaking in a slovenly manner, saying 'doin'', 'thinkin'', 'gonna' and 'eh'.

Mrs Flynn ignored her mother's advice and invariably corrected Theresa's pronunciation.

'How do you expect to get anywhere in this world,' she said, 'if you can't speak properly?'

'Who wants to *get* somewhere?' sneered Theresa, fully aware that she was behaving badly, and unable to stop herself. 'Who wants to talk all *la-di-dah*?'

'You do,' replied her mother. 'You're an ambitious little madam. And don't try to tell me you're not behaving like this deliberately to aggravate me, because you're succeeding, my girl.'

Mrs Flynn cuffed Theresa over the ear with the back of her hand. 'Get out of my sight for at least two hours,' she warned. Theresa fled.

'I hate you, I hate you, *I hate you*,' she muttered all the way down the hall.

Her mother came after her and stood in the doorway of the bedroom, legs astride, hands on hips, fire in her eyes.

'I just want to tell you, Theresa Flynn,' she said, 'that I heard every word you said, and I think you're a mean and selfish girl. What's got into you?'

'Nothing,' said Theresa. Her face was tight and her lips were pinched together like a vice in an effort not to cry. She hated not only her mother but herself as well and almost everybody else she could think of.

Mrs Flynn continued to stare with an expression of weary frustration.

'Don't frown,' she said finally, 'or your face will stay like that and nobody will ever love you, because you'll look so bitter and twisted.'

'I don't care,' replied Theresa defiantly, between clenched teeth. But she did.

Her mother shrugged her shoulders and left the room, having instructed Theresa to stay there and not to come out until she was in a better mood.

As soon as her mother had gone Theresa leapt off the bed, crossed the room and slammed the door. She collapsed onto her bed and cried.

Catherine sat quietly on the opposite bed nibbling a rolled-oat biscuit, sipping orange cordial and reading *Wuthering Heights* for the third time.

She glanced over at her sister's heaving shoulders and at the frizzy head which was buried face down on a pillow. She knew she would get her head bitten off if she said anything.

'I hate *everyone*,' murmured Theresa five minutes later when the sobbing had subsided. She hiccoughed.

'It's nothing to do with me,' replied Catherine in an even tone. She took another swallow and read for the dozenth time her favourite passage.

'The intense horror of nightmare came over me: I tried to draw back my arm, but the hand clung to it, and a most melancholy voice sobbed, "Let me in – Let me in!" . . .'

'I hate everyone, including you!' intruded Theresa's

voice. '*You're* too perfect as well. I'm surrounded by perfect people and it's enough to drive anyone mad.'

'Yes, it's true, you are mad,' agreed Catherine without looking up, her finger marking the passage.

'. . . *Yet the instant I listened again, there was the doleful cry moaning on! "Begone!" I shouted, "I'll never let you in, not if you beg for twenty years."*

'*"It is twenty years," mourned the voice: "Twenty years. I've been a waif for twenty years!"*'

One day a man would love her the way Heathcliff loved Cathy – in a doomed wild fit of passion.

Catherine bit into her biscuit and sighed. *Heathcliff* . . . Dark. Mysterious. Strong-willed. *Bad.*

Catherine and Heathcliff were held *asunder.* Heathcliff's breast heaved *convulsively.* They were locked in an embrace from which it seemed they would never be released alive.

Heathcliff foamed like a *mad dog.*

He gathered Catherine to him with *greedy jealousy.*

He covered Catherine with *frantic kisses.*

He was Catherine's *soul.*

Catherine drifted into a fantasy about what it would be like to be swept off her feet. But she found that after the first passionate kiss from her swarthy hero, the fantasy tended to become fuzzy and lost. What would happen next? Perhaps this was the stage at which they were supposed to take each other's clothes off. But then what? It was all so embarrassing. Why couldn't people simply write masses of passionate letters to each other, or else kiss and leave it at that?

She wanted to give her soul to someone for safe-keeping and to feel like dying if her love wasn't reciprocated. Then it would be true love. Only how could she be dreaming of being held asunder and kissed greedily when she had been called to be a nun?

Or had she?

Why shouldn't she dream about mad-dog men if she wanted? It wasn't as if she had taken her vows yet. She stared down at her nun's habit as if she were seeing it for the first time. It had become very hot and prickly over the long summer.

Hoping Theresa would be too self-absorbed in her misery to notice her, Catherine quietly got up and removed her habit until she was standing only in her knickers. She twirled about the room, enjoying the freedom of movement without cloth dragging about her ankles. She'd forgotten how it felt to have the full movement of her legs.

She looked at herself in the mirror on the back of the wardrobe door. It was quite a nice body really, even though she was too skinny. She was very pale because she hadn't exposed it to the sun all summer. The others hadn't even been able to persuade her in for a swim because she had refused to take off her habit.

What a waste of a summer. For the first time she regretted the swims she might have had, all the sunbathing and playing she might have enjoyed if only she hadn't been trying to be a nun.

Theresa watched every move her sister made with narrowed, suspicious eyes. In her curiosity over what Catherine might be up to she completely forgot why she had felt full of hatred towards everyone only moments previously.

'Changed your mind?' she taunted.

Catherine swung around with a flushed face. 'Course not. Don't be silly.'

But the seed of an idea had begun to take root in her mind. Gradually, over the next few weeks, she couldn't stop wondering if perhaps she had made a mistake. It was most embarrassing. How could she back down now?

She wished someone would make the decision for her because she no longer felt any pleasure when she put on her habit each morning. Instead she kept remembering what it was like to feel the warmth of the sun on her bare skin, the joy of running around a court playing netball or tennis.

But how would the nuns respond if she admitted she might have made a mistake?

Theresa stomped off to school hating everyone. She thought about death and then she thought about hell. She would probably wind up there because it was all she deserved. Catherine followed behind in her habit, daydreaming and humming to herself.

'Bitchbitchbitch,' muttered Theresa thinking of her mother. What did she have to look forward to? Nothing.

'Fuckfuckfuckfuck,' she added experimentally. This was a new word. She wasn't entirely sure what it meant.

'Bitchfuckbitchfuck . . .' And she almost missed it, which would have served her right. Considering everything.

There was the White Lady. Stuck on the roof of the local dairy. Waving frantically.

'Holy cow,' gasped Catherine.

The veil caught on the chimney and ripped beyond repair. The Virgin slid down the corrugated roof.

'Crikey dick.' Theresa ran. Catherine ran. 'Hold on.'

Chapter Twelve

THE ROSE WITHOUT THORNS

It was the first time they realized that only they could see the Lady. Women strolled past accompanying their small children to school and ignored them.

The Lady slithered about the roof desperately trying to gain a foothold. She tumbled over the edge and just in time grabbed the drainpipe. She swung from it like a tattered rag doll stained with green slime and dirt.

'Jump!' suggested Theresa.

The Lady closed her eyes, took a deep breath and plunged. She landed on Catherine who broke her fall. They rolled over and Theresa helped them up and brushed them down. Fortunately neither suffered more than minor cuts and grazes.

She bled. She was human. She perspired. They could smell it.

'I've been looking for you two,' said the Lady.

'You were?' Glimpses of human frailty didn't prevent them being awestruck all over again at her presence.

'Nobody believed us.' There were tears in Catherine's eyes. 'They called us liars. Can you give us proof?' She remembered the monsignor's story of Juan in the cactus field. A cloak miraculously emblazoned.

'All in good time. Everything went sadly astray. I arrived at the wrong house. But here we are.' She beamed at them.

What were they to do with her? She needed to be given dry clothes, maybe even a meal. And they were already late for school.

They decided to take her to Other Nana's. Their grandparents were away on holiday, but they knew where the key was hidden.

They passed neat squares of lawn shaved bald, and gardens trimmed to regimental symmetry. Letter-boxes painted white with chrome numbers. Giant wooden butterflies hovered on pastel weatherboard walls. Generous concreted driveways were lined with annuals. Dogs dreamed, chained to their kennels, plump cats baked on the warm paths. It was so familiar and safe. The woman in the long white silky dress, her torn blue veil fluttering in the wind like a kite, stared with enormous fascination at swans carved from tyres, gnomes fishing by the goldfish ponds.

'I'm hungry,' she said.

They gave her Weet-bix and powdered milk.

'What is this?'

'It's what people have for breakfast nowadays. Tastes delicious. Try some.' They added brown sugar and preserved peaches.

The Virgin encircled the plate with one arm and pulled it closer to her. She gobbled up the cereal as if she hadn't eaten for days.

After the Virgin had finished her second helping, Theresa gave her instructions on how to flush the toilet and operate the stove, television and radio.

They found some coins in their grandfather's change jar. With these they bought a loaf and a bottle of milk. When they returned they demonstrated how to make tea, coffee and toast.

They sidled into their respective classrooms after morning break with forged notes from their mother and all day they thought of nothing but the Virgin. Would she still be at their grandparents' when they returned from school?

'What is this?' asked the Virgin, holding up the iron. Every electrical appliance in the house seemed to be whirring or boiling. She exclaimed over everything. The cartoons on television. The voice on the radio. The excitement of boiling water quickly in a kettle. The wonder of using the stove for heating the canned foods. She had already opened Watties peas, corn, baked beans and spaghetti. Something else for them to have to explain to their grandparents.

The Virgin had run herself a bath and washed her hair with soap. They had never seen her without a veil before.

Days passed. The Virgin and the girls settled into a routine. They smuggled slices of bread and wedges of cheese into their satchels, along with sachets of instant pudding and Maggi soups. They spent as much time as possible talking to her after classes.

Finally they had the opportunity to study her close up. She was beautiful, but not like a film star, although she had the same star-like qualities. They couldn't stop staring at the flawless features, marvelling that such an angelic creature had deigned to visit two unworthy Flynns. Her eyes were like sparkling jewels. Her olive skin was unblemished and wrinkle-free. She possessed long elegant fingers and toes. Her voice was musical, soothing as a lullaby, promising warmth, security and comfort. They couldn't imagine the Virgin ever yelling or screaming or arguing. She had perfect control, perfect pitch, perfect manners. All of this only served to highlight their own faults and failings.

'Why is she here?' asked Catherine. 'I don't understand it. Do you think she might be stuck, unable to return to heaven?'

'Don't be silly,' replied Theresa. 'It's all part of a master plan. She's just biding her time, learning about Earth, waiting to see what she'll be called to do next.'

'Maybe she's come back for the same reason as last time,' suggested Catherine, 'only this time she's going to do it differently, as no-one believed us before.'

'Are we part of the plan?'

'Yes, we are.'

'Our Lady, the Virgin Mary and mother of Jesus Christ Our Lord, is the perfect woman,' said Father Rafferty in his Friday catechism class. 'She was also the perfect wife and mother and she gave without counting the cost. I hope you girls will strive to be like her in your own lives.'

'What do we do if she's unable to ever return to heaven?' asked Catherine. Theresa couldn't decide whether it was an advantage or a problem that nobody but she and her sister could actually *see* the Virgin.

They couldn't hide her at Other Nana's for much longer because she and their grandfather were due back from their holiday in a few days.

'How many languages can you speak?' asked Theresa one day when they visited the Virgin to check if she had enough food.

'I have always been able to make myself understood by anyone I chose to speak with. It hasn't been difficult.'

'How do you know what to say?' asked Catherine. Was there no end to the talents the Virgin possessed?

'God fills my heart and guides my words. I am merely Her Handmaiden.'

'You mean He's not really an old man with a beard?' asked Catherine, struggling to understand.

'Exactly. She is not male or female in the sense you comprehend it,' said the Virgin. 'Neither is She young or old. She simply *is*. She always was. What I am saying is the truth, but it is up to you whether you choose to believe it or not.'

She?

'Can you prove it?' asked Theresa. Up to them? Choice? They were being expected to believe in the most amazing ideas. Was this what the nuns referred to as a mystical experience?

Once they had become accustomed to being in the company of this dazzling creature they had relaxed back into the slovenly ways for which Mrs Flynn was constantly berating them – interrupting, biting fingernails, sprawling on chairs instead of sitting upright.

The Virgin, however, was always a model of decorum. During the day she read her way through Other Nana's back issues of the *New Zealand Woman's Weekly*. She made copious notes as she read. They were consumed with curiosity about the content of her notes. She mysteriously referred to them as her 'Research'. In the late afternoon and evening she watched television until it went off the air. She appeared mesmerized, moving only occasionally to flick minute and invisible specks of dust from her robe or to add to the pile of notes which were always placed beside her.

Theresa made a folder for the research. On the front she stuck a glittery Nativity scene retrieved from an old Christmas card. She peeked at the research when the Virgin left the room to go to the bathroom. She was disappointed to discover that the notes were made up of indecipherable scribbles and symbols.

The Virgin coughed discreetly behind her hand, a signal the girls had come to recognize as an indication that she had something important to say to them.

She wasn't normally very talkative. If she wasn't imparting messages from God it seemed that she didn't actually have a great deal to say. She rarely spoke unless spoken to first. She was too busy doing her research and making notes. 'Don't interrupt me,' she begged, 'I'm thinking.' The sisters were obliged to spend hours in her company often completely silent, a torment to them both. However, they did manage to complete vast amounts of homework in the studious atmosphere surrounding the Virgin and this earned them merit points at home with their mother.

The Virgin coughed again to attract their attention. 'I have a small favour to ask of you,' she murmured.

The girls angled their bodies towards her. *Anything.*

'There is the small matter of my robe,' said the Virgin. For the first time in their acquaintance she appeared to be vaguely embarrassed. 'Due to my awkward predicament, I have no alternative garments to wear,' she explained.

Of course. How could they have been so insensitive?

'In the normal course of events I would not be requiring garments, but I have regained my earthly form in order to facilitate communication with you.'

'You wouldn't fit into anything of Mum's,' said Theresa.

'You're much slimmer,' observed Catherine. 'Other Nana's clothes will be too small and so . . .'

Her voice trailed off into silence. How were they supposed to find robes and veils suitable for the Virgin Mary in Chatterton? It was an impossible task.

'Sheets?' suggested Catherine.

Theresa shook her head. Not good enough. Besides, how would they gain access to the sewing-machine without attracting the attention of their mother?

'If I were to wear modern-day clothing,' said the Virgin, 'I would be able to mix with other people. It's time I stopped being invisible to everyone but you two. I want to be able to understand the lives of the ordinary women around me.'

This was all very well, thought the girls, but didn't the Virgin realize that she emanated golden light, a haze of brightness around her, which had been very disconcerting until they became accustomed to it. Or maybe she had it within her power to dim this light and become more like an ordinary person.

It was Catherine who thought of borrowing money from their grandfather's small-change jar, going to the

St Vincent de Paul's opportunity shop and buying second-hand clothing.

The Chatterton St Vincent de Paul shop smelt of dishcloths and mothballs. A tiny old woman waved her tea cup at them from her stool beside the counter. There was a pile of socks and stockings which she had obviously been in the process of sorting and mending. She poured herself another cup of tea from her Thermos and apologized for not being able to offer them one too. She poured milk into the cup out of an old tomato-sauce bottle.

There was nothing remotely resembling the garments the Virgin normally wore. They found a black turtle-necked jersey, a cream crêpe de Chine blouse, a narrow knee-length skirt and a full red ballerina-style skirt with a border of black horses around the bottom.

In a crumpled carton at the back of the shop they also discovered several unopened Cellophane packets containing silk underpants, a cotton singlet, a lace petticoat and a pair of sheer black stockings with an apricot lace suspender belt.

'Deceased estate,' commented the dwarf woman, peering over their shoulders.

Catherine made a face at Theresa. 'She'll never know,' said Theresa, sweeping it all into a bundle.

Catherine enquired how much it would all come to.

'How much have you got?' asked the woman shrewdly.

'Five dollars and seventy-two cents.'

'How much is that in pounds? Oh it doesn't matter. That'll do.'

Theresa pulled out the brown paper bag from her school satchel and the coins spilled out over the counter. The woman swept the money into a battered shoe box.

*   *   *

The Virgin didn't know what to do with the clothes when they presented them to her. She held the underpants up in front of her with a puzzled expression. When she discovered the stockings she began to laugh.

They had never heard her laugh before and it made her seem a different person. Usually she acted a little bit like a nun, but they thought she was too beautiful to be a nun. She had the reserved manner of someone accustomed to living on her own, like their Aunty Violet. Although she was called the Mother of God, she didn't resemble a mother. There was no category into which they could fit her, and that was another reason why they weren't quite sure how to treat her.

Theresa often felt as if she were the mother in the relationship, and that didn't make sense because she was just a girl. The Virgin was too delicate and refined to cope with the real world. She needed to be protected from harm.

'What have you given me?' asked the Virgin when she had thoroughly examined all the garments.

Didn't she know what to do with the clothes? They could scarcely offer to help her dress. The Virgin explained. Apparently she didn't wear underpants. She had no idea what a bra was.

The girls were amazed. Was it possible that the Virgin never actually looked at her body? If she was so holy and mystical how could she have produced a baby? The more the girls thought about it, the more unlikely it seemed. Had she closed her eyes while her Son was born and simply pretended it wasn't happening to her?

According to their mother, giving birth was a painful and bloody business involving stitches, the shaving of pubic hair and much panting, groaning and swearing. Mrs Flynn, who liked to think that she was a good Catholic no matter how fraught her circumstances, did attempt to restrict herself to 'damn', 'blast' and 'hell's bells' when things went wrong. Mr Flynn had confided that their mother invariably swore profusely every time she gave birth. She said 'shit', 'bloody' and 'bugger'. Naturally, Mrs Flynn denied any such thing.

After receiving instructions from the two girls, the Virgin disappeared into their grandmother's bedroom to experiment with the clothes and underwear.

She emerged wearing the black jersey and the straight skirt. The outline of her breasts could be clearly seen beneath the tight jersey. Even the shape of her buttocks in the narrow skirt showed prominently. Her brown hair hung like a shining brown veil down the length of her back. It was long enough to sit on, observed the girls, full of envy. The Virgin's legs proved to be long and shapely and were further enhanced by the sheer black stockings.

The stockings soon slipped down her thighs – she hadn't understood the function of a suspender belt.

'You look gorgeous,' said Catherine. She looked like a model from a magazine.

She could have been any age. Her face was completely unlined, although according to Catherine's calculations the Virgin should have been at least fifty when her son died. She also hadn't aged a bit since being assumed up into heaven almost twenty centuries ago.

When they mentioned this to the Virgin it led to a very complicated discussion which she referred to as 'metaphysical' and which they only partly understood. Apparently, she didn't really exist at all as a physical being, she was simply a projection of Divine Energy which was so powerful that it *seemed* as if she existed, whereas in fact her spirit was mostly away in another plane with God. Or to put it another way – it was a particular concentration of power and goodness manifesting itself as God.

'God loves you,' the Virgin said in an uncharacteristically sharp voice, 'but She doesn't *need* you. Remember that.'

It sounded like a threat. They didn't know how to reply to her. Was she right? It wasn't what they had been taught.

'Why do you call me the Virgin when you refer to me?' she wanted to know. 'That is not my name,' she said.

'What is your name then?'

'I am called Mary.'

'Were you a Virgin, like they say?'

Mary paused before replying, choosing her words with care. She told them, without elaborating on the details, that it was impossible for a woman to have a baby without the assistance of a man.

'The union between a man and a woman,' said Mary, 'is a wonderful thing. It has been very misunderstood. As an expression of love, rather than of power over a woman by a man, sexuality can become a gateway. A place of passage.'

What did she mean? A gateway to where? What sort of passage? It was yet another example of the maddening way adults contained their world in code instead of speaking in plain English. Would it always be like this? When they were older would the secrets which adults disguised inside a tight web of mysterious words open up and reveal the truth to them? But how could they go on from day to day feeling confused like this, knowing that understanding was only a hair's breadth away?

Their bodies and minds yearned towards the Virgin. She knew truths denied to them.

They tried to explain to themselves the nature of the fascination which the Virgin exerted over them. At the beginning of their acquaintance it had been her beauty and perfection which had entranced them. It was as if they had been visited by a fairytale princess. More recently, this fascination had been overlaid with something else. More complicated feelings. Powerful longings which remained as yet unexpressed. They had reached the limits of their knowledge of language and could not find the words to describe her. They only knew they could scarcely bear to be out of her sight.

They realized she would be with them for only a short while. There was a sense of urgency. They couldn't waste a moment of precious time with her.

The Virgin Mary paced up and down their grandparents' small lounge like a caged animal.

'I would like to walk and explore,' she said. 'Please take me with you.'

Didn't the Virgin understand what their lives were like? Even though they longed to spend every waking moment in her company, the reality was they simply weren't free to come and go as they pleased without making up excuses to explain their absences. There was school and, afterwards, homework. This didn't include all the numerous jobs which their mother piled upon them at every opportunity.

It wasn't until they were out on the street and the Virgin began to receive admiring looks from women for her hair and from men for her lovely slender figure that they realized she could now be seen by other people. The removal of her spiritual garments had obviously brought about a change in her earthly form.

She no longer glowed. She resembled a contemporary woman. And what set her apart at first glance was her stunning physical beauty.

An old man approached them leading a yapping Pekinese. He doffed his black felt hat. 'Madame,' he said, and bowed.

The Virgin nodded and smiled. 'Can we keep walking?' she asked. She was in excellent humour. 'I like meeting new people.'

They had thought her shy. They had been mistaken. They could overhear comments from housewives who were out shopping. 'She's a looker all right.' 'Where d'you think she sprang from?'

149

A boy rode along the footpath on his bicycle. He swerved and came towards them, then leaned down and pulled Theresa's hair. It was Nicholas O'Grady. 'Ouch,' yelped Theresa.

'Crikey dick!' whistled Nicholas. 'Is she a film star or somephink?'

'Go away!' snapped Theresa. 'Who said you could join us?'

Nicholas O'Grady grinned. 'Catholic dogs,' he hummed. 'Stink like frogs.'

'Who do you think *you* are then?'

Theresa could see endless problems and practical difficulties stretching out before them as they attempted to carry out their responsibilities to the Virgin without attracting too much attention. Before nightfall half of Chatterton would have heard the Flynn sisters had been seen in the company of a film star.

The Virgin walked slowly, gracious as a queen.

Soon they found themselves standing outside the popular new Love Bite Coffee Bar at the end of High Street. Their father called it a den of iniquity. A sinful place where people could lose their souls if they weren't careful. Mr Flynn's disapproval of it meant they were automatically drawn to the place.

Through the windows they could see that it was full of long-haired students who had returned home for the summer holidays. The inhabitants of the café had stopped drinking their coffee and were all staring out through the window at the girl in her nun's habit standing alongside the tall beautiful woman accompanied by a schoolgirl with an extraordinary cloud of white hair.

'We can't go in,' said Catherine anxiously, pulling at Theresa's arm to restrain her. 'We haven't got any money.'

'No, let's,' said Theresa. 'The Virgin wants to see the real world. She said she wants to meet young women. Here's her chance.'

Chapter Thirteen

THE DEN OF INIQUITY

The owner of the Love Bite leaned over the table and grasped a handful of the Virgin's soft brown hair. She ran her fingers lightly through it.

'You've got gorgeous hair,' enthused Maureen to the Virgin. 'It's long enough to sit on.'

And then, with what seemed to Theresa and Catherine a shockingly personal gesture, Maureen lifted the hair to her nose.

'Mmmmm,' she sniffed. 'It smells lovely. What sort of shampoo do you use?'

The Virgin blushed, overcome by the attention. 'What is shampoo?' she asked. She used soap to wash her hair.

'What? You're having me on, aren't you love?' Maureen patted the Virgin's hand and winked at Theresa and Catherine. 'Your friend's a card,' she said.

Customers began to trickle in for lunch and Maureen got to her feet to attend to them.

'All right,' she smiled. 'When can you start?'

'Immediately,' replied Theresa.

The Virgin nodded. Theresa wondered if she understood that she had just obtained her first paying job.

'I want to live the life of an ordinary woman,' said the Virgin on the way home.

But how could she ever be ordinary? How could anyone fail to recognize immediately how special and different she was, wondered the girls.

She had been obsessive about the subject over the

past few days, interrupting her research to speculate on what form this ordinary life might assume. The girls felt ill-equipped to advise her. They knew of few callings for women – mother, nun, film star or martyr. She was already a mother and her Son was dead. How could the Virgin Mary become a nun? Martyrdom was out of the question – she was already immortal.

'Why don't you become a film star?' suggested Theresa.

'I would like to reach ordinary women,' mused the Virgin. 'Perhaps I could appear on television, on radio, in the *Weekly*. Why not?'

'What's heaven like?' asked Catherine later as she brushed the Virgin's hair with long sweeping strokes. It was the first time either of them had touched her, and Catherine felt oddly thrilled by it.

'Let me have a turn,' said Theresa jealously. 'You've been doing it for ages.'

As they spent more time in the Virgin's company, however, their feelings of awe and shyness were gradually being replaced by something else – affection.

I love her, thought Theresa with surprise. She stopped brushing the Virgin's hair while she marvelled at this realization.

Uncharacteristically the Virgin relaxed her posture. She allowed herself to lean against the back of the chair, soothed by Theresa's stroking. When Theresa had finished Catherine took over again and massaged her scalp. Theresa manicured her nails. They both wanted to keep touching her.

'Heaven,' murmured the Virgin. 'It is a state of being and not a place. To reach heaven is to have every longing satisfied, to be surrounded by a love so all-encompassing and tender no human being on his or her own could ever attain it without God's help.'

For a moment Theresa was distracted and forgot to buff the Virgin's exquisite nails. 'That's not what they tell us. If it's not a place and only a state of being why are you still here with us?'

'God moves in mysterious ways,' the Virgin replied. 'I am here only in order to carry out Her wishes.'

Theresa smiled to herself. What would her father say?

'She is both male and female. There is no word to describe Her magnificence.'

The night before her grandparents returned from their extended holiday Theresa had asked the Virgin what her plans were. Where would she live? Would she remain in Chatterton for a long time or was she simply passing through on her way to another secret destination to deliver other messages?

'Maureen has offered me a room in her house, after that only God knows,' answered the Virgin. 'But my time here is limited. She has plans for me. I have much work to do while I wait.'

'What kind of work? Tell us. Can we help?'

The Virgin shook her head and mentioned the word contraception again. Her first attempt at conveying her message had failed and she was preparing to go out into the world to deliver it herself.

Theresa wondered how the Virgin could soil herself over such a grubby business. *Jean. Fannies. Eggs. Scrotums. Taking temperatures. Yuk.*

The girls were concerned for the Virgin. They were convinced she would not recognize evil when she was confronted with it. The world outside Chatterton was vast and unknown. Dangerous.

'Be careful,' they warned her. Anything could happen. 'Don't speak to strange men.'

The Virgin wrapped her paltry possessions in a bundle inside her old robe and abandoned the sisters to start her new job.

The Virgin worked as a waitress for two months then

153

disappeared up north. Maureen was put out, the Virgin had been a great attraction at the coffee bar. The girls had occasionally managed to see her briefly after school if business was slow. Before she left town she arranged to meet them at the park to say goodbye.

'Take us with you,' pleaded Theresa.

'Your place is with your family.'

The Virgin remained firm in her resolve to leave them behind. Realizing she could not be persuaded otherwise, Theresa did the unthinkable and clung to the Virgin's new skirt. She vaguely recalled the story of reformed sinners who believed they could be saved if only they could touch the hem of His garment. Perhaps it was the same with the Virgin.

Her little ploy was unsuccessful. Both girls cried. They didn't believe they would ever see her again. They remembered all the questions they hadn't yet asked.

The Virgin gently disengaged her hands from theirs, picked up her small bag and walked away from them and out of their lives.

In the weeks that followed they went over and over the details of her visit. They remembered most clearly of all their impressions of her as she was leaving.

'She seemed like a stranger all of a sudden,' said Theresa.

'She was very keen to get away from us. Do you think we'll ever see her again?'

'Of course we will. She loves us.'

'How do you know?'

'I just know.'

Catherine's doubts about her vocation continued to plague her. Both girls had become quieter and more thoughtful since the Virgin's departure. They pined for her without understanding what it was they missed.

Mrs Flynn noticed changes. The girls had perfect

154

manners. They spoke beautifully and performed routine household tasks without being asked. But they seemed reluctant to attend Mass and had to be bullied into it by their father. 'No girl of mine . . . ' they heard every Sunday.

One day Theresa arrived home from school bearing a letter from Reverend Mother addressed to her parents. When their father came home from work, Mrs Flynn led him to the bedroom where they could be heard talking in low voices behind the closed door. No-one in the household was surprised when after half an hour Catherine was summoned to join them.

Later that evening Catherine appeared at the dining-table wearing an ordinary skirt and blouse. No-one made any comment, sensing from Catherine's red-rimmed eyes that she preferred to be left alone.

Theresa realized later, to her great surprise, that Catherine was actually considerably relieved the burden of her self-imposed vocation had been lifted and the decision made for her. Within a few weeks it seemed incredible to the family that Catherine had ever worn a nun's habit and once believed herself to be called by God to be one of His Brides.

Theresa never forgot. And it was she who discovered the remnants of a nun's habit in the bottom of the incinerator in the back yard when she went there to burn the household rubbish.

Catherine could hear a little bird of happiness singing in her chest. Life opened out before her like a box of treasures. She could be anything she wanted to. But not a nun, or a saint. The Virgin had made suggestions when she finished her research and was about to depart. Perhaps a writer, she advised. Or a teacher. A social worker. A psychologist even. Why not?

Chapter Fourteen

THE HAIRDRESSER

Saturday. Mr Flynn was listening to the news on the transistor radio. Mrs Flynn was loading a wash. Bub wailed in the background. Toots could be heard soothing her. The machine whirred into action. Theresa and Catherine were trying to escape Mrs Flynn's vigilant eye and avoid household chores.

Tim was daydreaming over the dishes when he broke a plate.

'Butterfingers,' chided Mrs Flynn as she passed by with a bucket of washing in one hand and a child attached to the other.

Tim tried to be as inconspicuous as possible as he bent down to pick up the broken fragments off the floor. He wrapped them quickly in a newspaper.

'You clumsy galoot!' cried Mr Flynn. 'Why can't you ever keep your mind on the job?' He clouted Tim over the ears, sending him flying halfway across the room.

The unusual sound of a motorbike roaring down his driveway distracted Mr Flynn. They heard it screech to a halt by the back door.

Mr Flynn rushed to the door and flung it open. He was ready to shout at whoever had entered his property without his permission. In his experience, motorbikes meant one thing – trouble. Two small children trailed Mr Flynn to the door. Visitors were a rare occurrence.

'Get out from under my feet,' he snapped, pushing them away. They took no notice and scurried out in front of him to greet the stranger.

They watched the man remove his helmet, tie it to the handlebars and saunter over.

'What can we do for you?' asked Mr Flynn in a quiet voice.

The children recognized the tone. He had told them that motorcyclists were a pest and an abomination on the face of society.

'Get inside, all of you,' said Mr Flynn to the children. 'I'll deal with this lot.'

The children stood their ground, their curiosity fully aroused.

The young man with the long wavy dark hair and leather boots unclipped his trouser legs. He laughed in a disrespectful manner. Mr Flynn glared at him. The young man took the bulging khaki duffle bag from his shoulders and the carrybag from his side saddle and placed them carefully on the porch. He dug his hands deep into the pockets of his black leather jacket. His crushed velvet trousers strained at the seams all the way down to his knees where they billowed out into flares. He wore an Indian silk scarf around his neck and an earring in his ear. There were fine silver bangles on both wrists. His boots had built-up heels and were scuffed with dust and grime from his journey.

'Don't you recognize me, Uncle Terry?' he asked.

Mr Flynn took a step backward. He squinted at the creature calling himself family.

'No,' he answered crisply. 'I don't. Should I?'

Mrs Flynn returned from the clothes-line. The children gathered by the back door, silent with awe.

'I'm Neil, Nancy's son,' he said. 'Of course you haven't clapped eyes on me for yonks, but, well . . . here I am.' He flung his hands out in an awkward gesture. 'Are you going to ask me in?'

They gawked at him, trying to see some resemblance to Mrs Flynn's older sister Nancy. She and her husband were both short and dumpy. Neither of them possessed much hair.

Mr Flynn sniffed. He took his time stepping aside

to usher his nephew through the door.

Mrs Flynn moved in to soften the impression her husband had created. 'You'd better come inside so we can all have a good look at you.'

'Nancy's boy,' mused Mrs Flynn. Poor Nancy.

Mr Flynn sat down at the head of the green Formica table as if he were about to conduct a meeting.

His nephew sat as far away from him as possible, at the opposite end. Mrs Flynn served them each a cup of tea. A plate of coconut rocks divided the space between them.

Too shy to speak, the children gathered around the table to observe their cousin. John reached out and tentatively felt the sleeve of the leather jacket. Mrs Flynn swiftly slapped his hand away.

'Don't touch,' she said.

'It doesn't matter.' Neil smiled at John who, after stealing a glance at his father to see if it was allowed, cautiously returned the smile.

'It's the real stuff,' added Neil with pride. 'You wouldn't catch me wearing vinyl.'

Nice for some, thought Mrs Flynn, whose purses and bags were all made of the cheap stuff.

'I'm on holiday,' Neil explained, chomping through four coconut rocks and six slices of toast. Mrs Flynn handed them to him in a trance. She could have dispensed toast all day and her nephew, to be polite, would have kept eating.

'It's a shame we can't offer you a room,' said Mr Flynn. 'As you can see, we're full to capacity here.'

'Be cool, man,' replied Neil. 'I've brought a sleeping-bag. I can sleep on the floor. Don't give up your beds for me.' Mr Flynn decided to let that one pass.

'So what do you do for a crust, lad?' he asked, leaning back with his arms folded.

'I'm a hairdresser.' Neil seemed determined to remain in good humour. 'I could set your hair if you like,' he offered to Mrs Flynn.

158

'I'd like that,' she replied. 'Hair-sets are a luxury I can't usually afford.'

Neil looked around the table at his cousins. 'You could all do with a bit of styling in the hair department,' he said.

'Likewise,' muttered Mr Flynn.

'Pardon?' Neil switched on a megawatt smile.

Mr Flynn glared at the charmer. He wondered if he was dealing with a poofter. His nephew resembled a girl in his paisley shirt and neck scarf. He might own a leather jacket and a motorbike, but Mr Flynn felt that even so he was looking at a fairy. It went some way towards explaining Nancy and Dick's absence from recent family gatherings. They were probably too ashamed.

He's like Heathcliff, thought Theresa, only not at all moody.

He's like Mr Rochester, thought Catherine, only younger.

He could do with a good feed, observed Mrs Flynn.

'How long are you planning to stop here?' asked Mr Flynn, fearing the worst.

'Not long,' replied Neil. 'I'll see how it goes, man. You'll hardly notice I'm here before . . .' He snapped his fingers. 'I'm off. Like the proverbial ship in the night – that's me. It's only a hullo–goodbye trip this time I'm afraid.'

Mr Flynn winced. A fairy, all right. You could spot them a mile off.

'What do you believe in, Neil? What's important to you in this life?' he asked.

Neil grinned at his uncle. 'Only got one life, Uncle Terry, and this is it. Unless of course you believe in reincarnation. I assume you don't, being a Catholic and all?'

'Certainly not.'

'I believe in peace,' said Neil. 'Love and peace. Not war. Freedom of the individual . . . yeah. I like rock music. I like to hang around with my friends and talk all night. That's me in a nutshell, Daddyo.'

Mr Flynn shuddered. It was worse than he'd suspected.

'You're not a *hippy*, are you?' He spat the word out. 'A flower child or some other such weirdo? A drop-out?'

'Hell no. And I'm not a bum. I work hard and play hard.'

Mr Flynn said he despised the modern age. He loathed Pop Art. The Permissive Society. Drop-outs. So-called Psycho . . . psycha . . .

'Psychedelia?' supplied Neil helpfully. 'Whatever turns you *on*, Uncle Terry,' he said shrugging, his voice full of sarcasm.

The girls gaped.

Mr Flynn gave a mirthless laugh. 'Ha funny ha ha,' he said. His voice rose to a shout. 'Well, I don't believe in that rot, not a word of it. D'you hear me?

'And now tell me, Neil,' he continued aggressively. 'What's your opinion on this Vietnam business?'

Mrs Flynn sighed. Not politics again. How could she divert her husband to protect Neil?

Neil hesitated for a moment before plunging in. 'I'm utterly opposed to the war. As a matter of fact, I was one of the protesters who paraded up Queen Street in Auckland last month to present a petition to the mayor. I had a placard . . . yeah.'

'I see.'

'Terrence . . . I don't think . . .' said Mrs Flynn.

Her husband ignored her.

He began to explain to his nephew his opinion on the 'Domino Theory'. How a Red Curtain would descend on the Free World. When Laos and Cambodia went that would be it. The Commos would sweep down

160

through Asia and, before you knew it, Australia and New Zealand would be mown down along with the rest of them and then – goodbye freedom. He reached out for the pepper and salt shakers and with the aid of some knives and forks began to move them around the table to demonstrate just how this would come about. The salt became Laos. The pepper was Cambodia. The cutlery was called into service to represent the other at-risk areas.

Neil opened his mouth several times during this monologue, but his uncle was always too quick for him.

'How would you like to have all your personal liberties stripped from you in a flash? Eh?' demanded Mr Flynn, sticking his head out over the table so that it was almost thrust in Neil's face.

It was a rhetorical question. Mr Flynn managed to talk for another fifteen minutes on the subject of communism while his family sat yawning in their seats, ignored by their father and yet trapped at the table until he had finished.

He banged the table with his fist. The cutlery jumped in response. His children woke up, blinking, afraid. But Neil was there. Their father wouldn't . . .

Laos went for a tumble and Cambodia did a little jig before righting itself.

Neil's face reddened with the effort of keeping his temper. He sat frowning and wriggling in his seat. The only way he could insert a sentence into the relentless flow of words was to talk over his uncle. It didn't achieve anything other than making Mr Flynn almost apoplectic. Neil's arguments were dismissed out of hand before he had a chance to properly develop them.

'And what about poor old Czechoslovakia?' interjected Mr Flynn. His mouth was flecked with spittle. Tanks surged across the cragged terrain of his face.

'What – *about* – it?' snapped Neil, clipping his

words so they stacked up across the table like knives ready to carve up his uncle.

'The Commos will take over the world if they get half a chance.'

'I already said I believe in freedom of the individual – in peace. I supported Dubcek.'

Mr Flynn snorted in disbelief. 'Empty words,' he sneered. 'You're full of so-called high ideals but you and your lot aren't prepared to *do* anything about the situation. You're cowards, all you draft-dodgers. You leave it all to someone else every time. That's the story isn't it? . . . Eh? Tell me if I'm wrong. Go on.'

He sat back again with his arms folded across his chest. Prove yourself, said the arms. You're not a man, said the eyes. A wimp, said the curl of the mouth. You're nothing – not a worthy opponent.

In desperation Neil excused himself to go to the bathroom. He took his time, calming his nerves by sitting on the toilet to have a cigarette. When he had finished he flushed the butt away and opened the window to get rid of the smell.

Without his adult male audience Mr Flynn finally, to his family's enormous relief, ground to a halt. He contented himself with muttering dire predictions for the future while he explored his teeth with a wooden toothpick.

'Crikey,' said Neil to the girls later when his uncle was out of earshot, 'does he always go on like that? What a pain in the neck.'

'Everything on the radio makes him mad,' said Theresa.

'I feel like the Pied Piper,' commented Neil as the children followed him into the lounge. He turned abruptly.

'Boo!' he said, and giggled in a high-pitched voice. 'Boo!'

Theresa and Catherine giggled back, entranced.

'I don't think I can stomach three days of that gadfly's giggling,' hissed Mr Flynn to his wife.

She shushed him. 'I think he's a lovely boy. Please . . .' she begged. 'For Nancy's sake.'

Everything contained in Neil's duffle bags was available to whoever wanted to try it on, read, smell or taste it. Jacket, teasing comb, hair curlers, cologne, chewing-gum, books and *Playdate* magazines. He assumed in return that everything in the Flynn household was equally available to him, being family. The only possession they weren't allowed to touch was his special professional haircutting scissors.

'You'd faint if I told you how much these little beauties cost,' he said.

Mr Flynn's transistor radio was lifted out of its protective plastic bag. Knobs and dials which formerly had responded only to Mr Flynn's fingers were casually rearranged. Dials which had never moved beyond the National Station now discovered pop songs.

Neil knew all the words to every Beatles song. He also sang along to Engelbert Humperdinck and Mr Lee Grant, to Ray Columbus and The Chicks.

'What a gas, eh?' said Neil.

He found the Madonna in the lounge, lifted off the plastic bag and set her revolving.

'This is really cool,' he said. 'I can't believe it.' He exclaimed over the fridge, washing-machine and stove being tied to the walls. 'What's this for?' he asked, pointing to the white card taped over them.

'To protect everything, of course,' replied Catherine. Couldn't he see how important it was to preserve the surfaces of things?

'And this?' Fortunately neither Mr nor Mrs Flynn were present while their nephew catalogued their house. Neil scraped his feet on the sturdy plastic mats which protected the long strip of carpet down the hallway.

Didn't Neil understand anything? Theresa explained. 'If things aren't covered up they get ruined.'

'But that's life,' said Neil. 'Things become old and used-up. That's natural. Then you go out and buy new things. It's simple.'

'We can't afford it,' answered Catherine primly. 'Besides, we all dent and break things without even trying.' The fridge represented their father's sweat and blood, as did the washing-machine and everything in the house. They owed everything to him. Without his job at the electrical shop there would be nothing. They would all go hungry. They were grateful.

Neil explored every corner of the house. Infected by his enthusiasm, for no-one had ever put their home under a microscope before, Theresa and Catherine began to see their environment with fresh eyes.

Neil's family was not Catholic. Only the children's mother had converted from her side of the family.

'Is Grandma still wild about it?' he asked the girls. They nodded.

'She told me once that your father was a fanatic,' said Neil.

They were shocked. 'Oh no.' They denied it vehemently. Whatever they might privately think, they would never allow an outsider to criticize him. Besides, how could they tell if he was a fanatic or not?

Neil continued to probe and explore. 'Fascinating,' he would say, or 'mesmerizing'. It was only his uncle he refused to listen to. Mrs Flynn was flattered. She had never been listened to with such open-minded enthusiasm before.

'You poor thing,' Neil murmured as Mrs Flynn told her stories and listed her complaints.

'Do you have a girlfriend, Neil?' asked Theresa.

'Not *exactly*,' replied Neil.

'I'm sure you'll find someone,' consoled Theresa.

'I don't want to settle down,' said Neil. 'I want to travel.'

'Of course,' said Theresa and Catherine, immediately deciding not ever to settle down and to travel instead.

'Girls, there's a groovy big world out there and you know what, I'm heading off into it. London, here I come. Whooah!'

Neil began a cushion fight with the children which carried on through every room in the house, ending finally with everyone in a heap on the floor.

'What a gas,' said Tim.

'Yeah, cool man,' gasped Theresa, ready to follow her new idol to the ends of the earth.

'*What's* going on?' Mr Flynn demanded to know when he arrived home from work.

Everything was going on. His house was being turned upside down. They all had new hairstyles, even Mrs Flynn, whose hair had been teased up at the back. She ran to the mirror to admire it a dozen times a day. Neil had advised her to grow out her perm. 'Get with it,' he said.

'I'm too old to keep up with fashion,' she told him.

'You're not old,' he said. 'You're not even forty. Not even middle-aged.'

'I'm not?'

'Course not.'

The girls pestered their mother to buy them new clothes.

'Can't afford it, I'm sorry.'

'We can't ever afford anything,' they moaned.

'Not with eight children,' said Mrs Flynn.

Theresa and Catherine already had crushes on Neil, even though he was their cousin. Now that they had

165

read his magazines they knew who he was. *Donovan*.

'You're the spitting image,' drooled Theresa.

'I don't know what's got into you two girls,' said their mother. 'You're mooning about the house like a couple of ninnies.'

'The sooner the gadfly is out of our hair the better,' said Mr Flynn. If Neil had been a different kind of nephew he might have enjoyed sitting down with him and having a few beers. As it was . . .

He could hear the familiar giggling from the girls' bedroom.

There they were, the girls bright-eyed and enthusiastic. Theresa was having her hair backcombed on one bed. Neil was creating the Afro look on her. The littlies and Tim were sprawled over the other. Neil was cross-legged on the bed telling them about *Hair*, the new musical. He said there were naked people on stage.

They shrieked. In *public*, they chorused in disbelief. Fancy that.

Mr Flynn caught the tail-end of the conversation. *Nude bodies*, he heard. He noticed all three girls were wearing scarlet nail polish. He had never seen Francie so animated. Not trusting himself to speak, he backed out of the room. In the kitchen he noticed his precious transistor was out of its bag.

'I don't remember giving anyone permission to touch it,' he said. Tenderly he wrapped the transistor in its bag again and, after checking with his watch, switched on the news. Instead he was treated to the sound of the Beatles at top volume.

'What's this *rubbish*?' bellowed Mr Flynn, observing that the dial had been moved off its regular station.

'My patience is wearing very thin,' he warned the transistor, in his nephew's absence. 'He's sailing very close to the wind, my word, he is.'

In the three days of Neil's visit *Jane Eyre* and *Wuthering Heights* had been consigned to storage. Theresa and Catherine's bedroom walls were now papered with pictures of the Beatles torn from Neil's magazines.

'PIN MARKS!' yelled Mr Flynn when he saw them. 'You've *ruined* the walls.'

Mrs Flynn patted his shoulder and made shushing noises. He brushed off her hands as if they were stray insects.

'Hey, be cool, man,' said Neil, trying to be helpful.

Mr Flynn turned on him and gave him a filthy look. 'I don't remember asking for your opinion,' he said.

'What's the problem?' asked Neil.

'You're *the* problem,' Mr Flynn suddenly decided. 'I think it's about time you were on your way again.'

A wail of protest broke out from his wife and children. 'Don't be mean. That's not fair.'

'That's *enough*. I don't want to hear another word about it.'

'I was planning to head off tomorrow anyway,' said Neil with dignity, 'and I wouldn't dream of staying where I wasn't welcome.'

The children were more impressed with him than ever. Fancy Neil standing up to their father like that.

'You *are* welcome,' whispered Theresa and Catherine afterwards. 'We love you, don't we kids?' All the children nodded.

Neil packed quickly, stuffing his possessions back into his duffle bags. He gave his magazines to Theresa and Catherine.

'Will you come back and see us again?' asked Theresa.

'That depends on your old man, doesn't it? He treats me like a dead rat the cat dragged in.'

Theresa saw her mother's mouth tighten in the characteristic expression she adopted whenever something annoyed her or made her angry. It was as if an invisible hand were sewing up her lips to prevent words from escaping that would give voice to her true feelings. While Neil had stayed with them this expression had rarely been in evidence.

Neil gave each of them a turn sitting on his BSA motorbike.

The world was reduced to its customary grey hue when he had gone. But things were not entirely the same. Into their narrow lives, stifled by Mr Flynn's opinions and punishments, a small chink of light had appeared. A tiny ray of hope.

It was better than nothing.

No-one knew Francie's dreams. She had become a solitary child. She rang Other Nana every day and they had long conversations which gave them both enormous pleasure and baffled the rest of the family.

'They don't *say* anything,' remarked Theresa.

Francie didn't offer any explanations. It was the language of love she spoke. She and her grandmother talked in code. Every word was imbued with meaning. The most humble enquiry into the details of the other's day was correctly interpreted by both to demonstrate in a hundred different ways how much they cared for each other.

'She has an old head on her shoulders, that one,' said Other Nana to Grandad. 'She's an old soul.' How else to explain the things Francie seemed to know almost by instinct? She could enter another person's body and feel their pain.

'I would walk over hot coals for her,' said Other Nana. None of her own children had affected her like this.

Chapter Fifteen

HUMANAE VITAE

'*Roma locuta est; causa finita est,*' said Father Rafferty. 'Rome has spoken, the matter is settled,' he read from his typed sermon. 'Our Holy Father, Pope Paul the Sixth, has finally come to a decision concerning the subject of human life and conjugal morality.

'Some of the younger women from this parish have expressed doubts over Our Holy Father's latest pronouncements,' he added. 'However, all that He is doing is trying to preserve the *sanctity* of human life.'

His eye roamed about the congregation. His parishioners stirred uncomfortably in their seats.

'God never said that following His laws was going to be *easy*, that it wasn't going to involve a little bit of *sacrifice*.'

Mrs Flynn kicked at the kneeler in front of her. Sacrifice indeed! What did he think they all were? Breeding mares?

She watched Father Rafferty's mouth moving up and down, the gobs of spittle bobbing about on the edge of his lower lip. Terrence leaned forward, his legs crossed, nodding as if he agreed with every word. She felt sick with anger towards him. There would be changes. She had never rebelled before, but the blatant unfairness of *Humanae Vitae* took her breath away.

Her husband glanced at her to gauge her response. She felt his eyes on her and refused to turn and look at him.

As was his custom, the priest waited on the front porch after Mass to greet his parishioners. Mrs Flynn left by a side door to avoid confronting him. She was wary of her anger. How did she express it without driving people away, and losing their love?

But right now she felt her anger so strongly she didn't trust herself to speak. Let anyone try and tell her that *Humanae Vitae* was for her own good.

Mr Flynn knew he would never dare to go against the Pope's decisions. Nevertheless, he allowed his mind to wander for a moment and daydream about the alternative, what might have been possible if the Pope's decision had only gone the other way – if he hadn't altered the girls' heavenly letter. If indeed that was what it had been. He still couldn't be sure if Father Rafferty had even forwarded it on.

Someone had put the girls up to it. Must have, because they'd gone very quiet on the subject. He knew how easily they were led astray.

None of the children listened to the priest. Theresa could not see how *Humanae Vitae* had any connection with her life. She had no opinions on the subject, and didn't follow what Father Rafferty was referring to. The Pope's decision sailed over her head.

Catherine's response was similar. Rome was so far away. The Pope was from another world. Sometimes it was difficult to imagine anything existed beyond New Zealand.

Outside the church a row had broken out, an argument between the liberals like the Schwartzes and the Calvinos led by a feisty woman called Carrie Hoop, and the conservatives and moderates led by the Gargulios and the van der Winkles. Mrs Flynn stood on the sideline.

Father Rafferty strode over to intervene before people became reckless and said things that were unforgivable and unretractable. The women ushered the children away to play so they could talk to the priest uninterrupted.

'There is a time and a place,' murmured the priest. No-one took any notice.

Theresa and Catherine hovered on the fringe of the group, determined not to miss out on the excitement.

'The encyclical demonstrates a negative attitude towards love and marriage,' said Carrie Hoop. 'How would a bunch of celibate men over in Rome know what it's like for women? They wouldn't have a damn clue.'

Among the group of women in Crimplene dresses and unflattering coats, hats and mantillas, bright sparks like Carrie and Clara Schwartz stood out like exotic parrots amongst a flock of sparrows.

'We want change,' said Carrie Hoop. 'I'm fed up with having the same old excuses served up over and over again. It's 1968, not 1900. You've got to move with the times.'

'The Church is not a barometer of fashion,' rebuked Father Rafferty. 'It has stood the test of time.'

'And what does *that* mean?' demanded Clara Schwartz. 'Nothing. Just words. Empty words. Who does the Pope think he is fooling?' She stood with legs astride.

Like a man, Catherine thought.

Clara's hands were on her hips and a red leather handbag swung like a flag from her right wrist. She wore a short navy dress edged in white piping and a white straw hat. She was an accomplished dressmaker and the most stylish woman in the parish.

Maria van der Winkle bustled over to confront Clara. 'Women like us need to take the lead in the community,' she said in a stern voice. 'We should be leading by example, not making an exhibition of ourselves in front of our children.'

'I'll think about setting an example,' retorted Clara,

171

'when we live in a reasonable world with fair rules and regulations. What if the Pope is wrong? Have you considered that possibility? That he might not always know what's best for everybody?'

Theresa was fascinated. No-one ever had arguments at church. It was unheard of to criticize the priests in public. She drew closer.

A little group advanced on the priest and Father Rafferty flushed and retreated a couple of steps. He shuffled his feet unhappily.

He coughed behind his hand. 'Ours is not to reason why,' he said. 'The powers that be have decided and we must obey or leave Mother Church.'

'It's not my *damn mother*,' shouted Carrie Hoop, in what several people on the outer fringes considered an excessive display of feeling. 'A mother would not say no to the pill.'

'Our Holy Father has sought the advice of men wiser than us in this area of conjugal morality,' said Father Rafferty.

Carrie Hoop looked as if she was about to spit.

'That's *exactly* what I'm talking about,' she said. 'Men have decided. Women haven't had any say in the matter. *Conjugal morality*? What would priests know about the subject for heaven's sake? The rhythm method isn't reliable. You can stick it.'

Several other mothers muttered agreement. Father Rafferty looked dismayed.

Catherine and Theresa stared at their mother to see how she was responding. Mrs Flynn scarcely ever smiled. She always gave the impression she carried the weight of the world on her shoulders. Now Theresa caught a glimpse of a different person. Her mother smiled, her green eyes gleamed and her red hair shone in the sunlight.

Theresa was excited and curious. Her mother had a secret and she wanted to discover what it was.

*   *   *

172

Everything kept changing. Even the nuns.

When Theresa and Catherine went to the convent and sat down in their respective classrooms they were shocked to see that the nuns had dramatically altered their appearances over the weekend. The stiff white bands on their foreheads had disappeared. Their newly-dyed hair waved and curled cheekily from under the new shortened veils.

The nuns had legs after all. Their hems had been shortened to mid-calf length. They looked self-conscious and slightly ridiculous.

But it wasn't just the garments which had changed. The nuns seemed to the girls to be more feminine. Now they were no longer mysterious – they were human.

The nuns made no comment on their altered appearances and, taking their cue from this, nor did the girls. Inside the classrooms they acted as if nothing out of the ordinary had occurred. Outside, the girls talked of nothing else.

After a week it seemed unbelievable that the nuns had ever covered up most of their foreheads, necks and legs. One young nun, Sister Mary Claire, went even further than the others. She wore a simple cross pinned to her breast and a white blouse and cardigan with a skirt raised to the knee. But two days later she appeared in a skirt which was mid-calf length like those of the other nuns.

The girls grinned. Sister Mary Aquinas on the warpath again. Where would it all end?

Mr Flynn predicted the worst. 'Today short skirts and veils and hair showing. Tomorrow – goodbye convent. Look at what's beginning to happen in the States – priests and nuns falling away like flies, fleeing in droves. Thinking they know better than the Pope. I don't know what the world's coming to. I don't like it. My word, I don't. Strewth.'

'Well I *do*. It's a good thing they're modernizing,' commented Mrs Flynn. 'About time, I say.'

*　　*　　*

' "Nonetheless the Church . . . teaches that each and every marriage act must remain open to the transmission of life" . . . I think the Holy Father makes himself abundantly clear on this point,' said Father Rafferty, looking around for response from the Chatterton Catholic Women's League. It was a thankless task he had been given. He feared for the future of the Church in the face of the anger he saw around him. The Church was in crisis and it didn't seem to realize it. Over in Europe there must be thousands of Carrie Hoops and Clara Schwartzes.

Mrs Flynn continued to fume. Anger slowly burned. It was a permanent state of mind these days. Pope Paul was as bad as his namesake.

Carrie Hoop spoke up and she expressed exactly what was in Mrs Flynn's mind.

'I still don't *understand*,' said Carrie. 'I know the Pope has put his foot down, but can you tell me, Father, what it is exactly that he objects to? What's *wrong* with contraception?'

'Allow me to quote,' replied Father Rafferty. He put on his glasses and picked up his folder of papers again. ' "It is to be feared that the man, growing used to the employment of anti-contraceptive practices, may finally lose respect for the woman and, no longer caring for her physical and psychological equilibrium, may come to the point of considering her as a mere instrument of selfish enjoyment, and no longer as his respected and beloved companion." '

He took off his glasses again and blinked at them.

'Hogwash!' snorted Carrie Hoop. 'The Pope and I are going to part company on this one. As far as I'm concerned he's punishing us for being women. He's a complete misogynist. Otherwise how could he possibly do this to us?'

She got up and left the meeting. No-one spoke until they heard the door swing shut behind her.

174

An excited babble of conversation broke out. The priest raised his hand for silence.

Mrs Flynn longed to run after Carrie Hoop. What made her so bold and headstrong, able to stand up to anyone in authority? She seemed to have no fear. It struck her then that Theresa would probably be like Carrie when she grew up. Already her eldest daughter demanded an explanation for everything. She wanted proven facts and became angry if she didn't get them. Mrs Flynn didn't know what to do with her.

'How do you define contraception, then?' asked Clara Schwartz.

'It's simple,' replied Father Rafferty. 'Contraception prevents conception taking place, by stopping fertilization or implantation.'

Clara nudged Mrs Flynn. 'No more sinking the sausage for the boys,' she whispered.

Mrs Flynn reddened. Some things shouldn't be talked about.

'Why is a man telling us this?' Clara whispered again while the priest was speaking. 'Why a priest and not a nun?'

'What use either of them?' whispered back Mrs Flynn, surprising herself with her daring. There, she had finally expressed an opinion.

'Don't we have any say in what happens to our bodies?' asked Clara. 'Are we supposed to keep breeding till we collapse from exhaustion? Is that what the Pope wants? That's very nice, isn't it?'

Father Rafferty looked wretched. He didn't answer. Slowly the women drifted out of the hall and he was left alone clutching his papers.

'How about it then?' Terrence Flynn asked his wife later as she lay with her back to him. He placed his arm around her waist. She didn't respond. His hand dropped lower to feel underneath her nightie.

'I've got a headache,' she replied. Mother of God, *no*.

'You ought to do something about these headaches of yours,' he said in a disgruntled voice. 'They're a liability.'

She was being tortured on a rack. The priest and the Pope's words ran together. '. . . *Love that is faithful and exclusive until death . . . The love is fecund . . . destined to continue, raising up new lives . . . Each and every marriage act.*'

She had already approached Father Rafferty in the confessional on the subject of sex. 'I can't satisfy my husband's desires,' she had confessed.

'Keep trying,' the priest had advised. 'God so loves a trier.'

She knew Terrence didn't see her as a 'mere instrument of his selfish enjoyment', so why did she feel sinful if she didn't want sex?

The subject of contraception remained on Mrs Flynn's mind. The priest had said natural family planning was still acceptable. The trouble was, accidents happened. Her cycle wasn't regular. She was prepared to give up sex with Terrence, but she knew she couldn't hold him off for ever. He felt entitled to it when it was safe. But it was never safe. Abstinence was the only solution. *Exclusive, faithful unto death.* It was a sentence she had been given by the Pope, not a reprieve.

Leaving the children in the care of Theresa and Catherine one day, she went to the library. She wanted to know when life began. At the moment of fertilization? When the fertilized egg reached the uterus?

Poring over diagrams in the library, Mrs Flynn discovered her little pleasure button was a clitoris. It was hidden beneath a hood. She saw diagrams of female genitals undergoing dramatic changes as the woman

176

became aroused and later climaxed. It amazed her. All this mysterious activity going on inside her. She studied a vagina which had ballooned at the end. Above it, raised in the air like a dancer, was the uterus. She saw a picture of muscles contracting. A diagram of orgasm, the uterus contracting. And yet somehow none of it had anything to do with *her*. Did her uterus contract? Had she ever experienced spasms of pulsing – a gallop at the end? She doubted it.

She saw Fallopian tubes in a diagram waving like flower heads. It was all rather pretty.

The next big event was Smoking Nana's sixtieth birthday. The family held a party for her. Mr Flynn mellowed sufficiently to give his mother-in-law a big hug and a kiss.

'Speech, speech,' they all cried after the toast.

'I always thought I'd be a withered old bird when I got to sixty, but I'm not,' said Smoking Nana.

Mr Flynn looked as if he was about to comment. Theresa stared him down and he took another piece of cake instead. Theresa went over to stand by her grandmother. She put her arm around her. '*I* think you're beautiful,' she said.

'It's nice of you to say so, dear. Time goes so fast. You have your thirtieth birthday and you think it's a disaster and then the next thing you know you're forty and it's nothing. You're so busy in your twenties with kids you don't have time to stop and then one day you do. You look in the mirror and you go – God, is that me?'

'I know what you mean,' said Mrs Flynn, 'I need another shandy.'

'Women!' said Mr Flynn. 'Always worrying about their faces.'

He smacked his wife lightly on her bottom with the

back of his hand as he walked past her on the way to the kitchen to top up the drinks.

She pulled away, annoyed. 'Don't do that.'

'I'll do what I like in my own home,' he said defiantly.

'That's what you think,' said Moira Flynn.

Chapter Sixteen

THE CRUSH

1970

The television was on in the lounge. Theresa gasped as a familiar figure with a long mane of hair came into frame and disappeared again. She turned to check if Catherine had noticed. They signalled each other discreetly.

'It was her,' said Theresa later in their room. 'I know it was.'

'How can you be so sure it was the Virgin? She can't still be in New Zealand. Not after all this time.'

'She's in Auckland,' insisted Theresa. 'How can we find out where she is? We must track her down.'

'You must be joking. How can we find someone in a city as big as Auckland? All right, so she might have been the woman in the background in the news item. And then again, she might not. We can't know for certain.'

Theresa was optimistic. They would see the Virgin again in the future.

Mrs Flynn slapped Toots hard across the back of his legs.

For nothing, thought Theresa, at least nothing important. And he was her mother's favourite too.

She pulled her mother away from Toots, who was crying loudly. It hurt her to hear Toots wailing like that. Sometimes she didn't know whom she loved best. Most of the time it was Francie because it was impossible not to love her. She was so good and kind.

She loved Catherine the way she loved herself, so that didn't count. They were two halves of a whole. But Toots had a special place in her heart.

She gave him a cuddle and when he had finally stopped crying sent him outside again to play.

'Don't hit Toots,' she said to her mother. She was angry. 'He didn't deserve it. Why do you lash out like that?'

Mrs Flynn slumped in a chair. She looked exhausted. 'I don't know.'

Her mother suffered in the heat. There were damp stains on the underarms of her dress, already soiled by Bub's sticky fingers.

'I get so frustrated,' said her mother in a flat voice, not at all her own. Fat tears dripped down her face and she didn't even bother to mop them up.

'I don't understand you,' said Theresa.

Her mother stared at her with dull uncomprehending eyes. She took her time replying. 'I don't understand you either.'

Catherine could hear her mother calling her in the distance, but she didn't bother to reply. Her book was too absorbing. But her concentration had already been broken, and soon the words on the page began to run together. She read the same sentence three times without taking in the sense of it. Her eyes focused on the pattern of roses opposite. She stared and stared until the petals separated, fell away and dissolved, and then her eyes glazed over. Her mother's voice sounded in the far distance.

Mrs Flynn continued to call from the kitchen, the tone of her voice rising several notes. Words repeated themselves in her mind like a song on an old familiar record. *Lazy. Thoughtless. Rude. Selfish*. They rushed into her head like a fountain of blood.

She flung open Catherine's door and discovered her sprawled out on her bed with books scattered untidily around her. Catherine's eyes were open, but they weren't focused on her mother. Mrs Flynn had captured her daughter in a moment of deep solitude. Her hair was now long (grown against Mrs Flynn's wishes) and floated against the pillow like dandelion fluff.

Messy, impossible hair, thought Mrs Flynn. The sight of her daughter filled her with a burning, uncontrollable rage. She grabbed Catherine by the hair and screamed at her.

Catherine's senses came ricocheting back in a flash as she was picked up and shaken. Her hair felt as if it were being pulled out by the roots.

She began to scream. And was appalled to discover she had wet her pants in her fright.

Francie was now eleven. Her hair was straight, red and long enough to sit on. She heard the screaming and after quickly adjusting the elements under every pot on the stove and lifting their lids to prevent their contents from boiling over, she wiped her hands on a tea-towel. Sighing deeply, and feeling a terrible tightness in her chest, she went into the bedroom and pulled her mother off her sister. She then propelled her mother out of the room, firmly pushing her towards the door. Mrs Flynn went like a lamb, flopping limply against Francie. Behind them, Catherine continued to wail.

In the kitchen Francie and her mother completed the dinner preparations. They manoeuvred around each other with practised ease. Both were pleased Theresa had not yet arrived home. Her presence would have inflamed an already volatile situation. Francie saw no point in discussing what had happened. It wasn't the first time her mother had lashed out at Catherine.

Theresa and Catherine would both be gone within a few years. It would be awful without them, but at the same time it would relieve the pressure. There was

181

not enough room to breathe. They lived on top of each other like sardines in a can.

She often felt sad. Everything seemed hopeless. It was difficult to believe anything in their lives would ever improve. I must be even stronger, Francie told herself. I must be so strong nothing can ever hurt me.

For Catherine, life in Chatterton began to take on the form of a nightmare. Increasingly she retreated to the solace of her inner world. Her fantasies began to seem more real than the events at 23 Grey Street.

She made an effort over Francie, but it wasn't easy to be close to her. Her younger sister had become withdrawn and uncommunicative. And, of greater concern, she had simply stopped developing physically. While her classmates grew, Francie remained the same size. She had only one friend, who was called Dorothy, with whom she had conducted a restrained and dignified friendship for the past five years. Francie was a solitary child and took everything seriously. Catherine worried about her. She was so quiet that sometimes she seemed to blend into the furniture.

Every afternoon Francie helped Andrew and John with their spelling and their multiplication tables. They had become her responsibility while her mother attended to Bub and Toots. John drew pictures of himself flying a topdressing plane. He showed clouds of poison descending on the house like a veil, burying them. 'You're a worry,' said Francie. 'You wouldn't bury your pal Francie, would you Johnnie?'

John snatched back his drawing. He began to sketch and colour frantically. He showed her the modified drawing. The plane was bigger now. There was a girl sitting alongside the pilot. Her long red hair flew out behind her and disappeared into the clouds. Francie frowned.

'And Bub? Would you save Bub and Toots?' she asked. John gave her a horrified glance and put his

182

hand over his mouth. He picked up his drawing and ran from the room.

At five Toots had the most confidence of any of them. His independent and boisterous nature seemed never to be crushed other than momentarily by any reprimand or blow.

'How many more years are you going to be the boss of me?' he demanded to know from his father. 'Three years? Four years? Tell me, how many?'

His father laughed. He liked Toots's sense of humour.

Toots's spiky red hair stuck up in tufts. His legs were always covered in cuts and bruises.

Bub adored him. The little girl followed him everywhere and he showed endless patience towards her, lifting her on and off the swing, picking her up and cuddling her when she fell over and hurt herself, reading her stories at bedtime, making up the words he didn't know and figuring out the story by studying the pictures.

Mr Flynn was treated with a wary respect and avoided. He made a few attempts to involve Tim and the younger boys in his workshop tasks, but they soon gave up when he became annoyed at their slowness.

Mrs Flynn and Francie had an understanding. Theresa and Catherine had always been a team. Tim and Francie supported John and Andrew. Toots was devoted to Bub. Everyone knew this. There was no need to discuss it.

Catherine survived with her inner life intact. It had existed for her as a strong undercurrent flowing through her childhood, connecting her to life as far back as she could remember. Now she scarcely ever thought of Teresa of Avila's interior castle and no longer tried to model herself on the Spanish mystic. Through her fantasy life she had discovered her own escape route.

She had learned to protect this inner world. It

existed inside her head like a cave she could retreat into. She could even leave her body behind her as if it were merely a shell. Theresa was the only other human being who had ever been allowed to penetrate as far as the cave entrance.

It was like this until Catherine met Linda Harrison at the Chatterton Public Library.

Catherine was researching Egyptian burial customs for a project when a tall skinny girl flung a striped shoulder bag onto the floor, put down a huge pile of books and sat opposite her at the study table. She opened a book on Greek myths.

The girl chewed the end of her thick black plait as she read. She was a fast reader — as fast as Catherine. Soon she stopped to take some notes. Catherine peeked at the large looped writing.

Catherine studied the girl. At first glance she was physically unremarkable. Her eyes were a little too close together. She had an upturned nose and a wide thin-lipped mouth.

The girl looked up suddenly and Catherine blushed.

'It's rude to stare, you know,' she said in a sharp voice.

'I didn't mean to.'

'Yes, you did. So what's the verdict? Am I beautiful, or plain with a few redeeming features?'

Catherine wasn't sure how to respond. Should she tell her the truth or invent something?

'You look intriguing.'

'That'll do.' It was the girl's turn to stare at Catherine.

'I've never seen hair like yours before,' she said. 'Have you done something to it or is it natural?'

'It's natural.'

'You're lucky.'

'Daphne is my favourite,' said Catherine. She had delved into Greek myths the previous summer holidays.

'I know who Daphne is,' said the girl, 'she's the woman who was transformed into a tree.'

184

'I like women who change into other things. Into fish or birds.'

'Or women who have nests of snakes in their hair.' The girl stood up to reach for another book and Catherine realized they were the same height.

'What's your name?' asked Catherine.

'Linda, after my grandmother.'

'I'm Catherine and I go to St Cath's.'

'I can see that from your uniform.'

'Do you go to the state school?'

Linda laughed. 'Is that what you lot call it? *We* call it the Chatterton Dump.'

There was a silence while Catherine tried to think of something witty to say in reply. She wanted to impress the girl so that they could meet again.

'Do you come to the library much?'

'Often. I've seen you before. My mother's the librarian.'

'She's your mother?'

Catherine hadn't imagined the librarian was any-body's mother. Linda's mother wore ankle-length skirts, Indian shirts, red Roman sandals and long swinging beads. She had long hair and wore little round glasses.

'She's an anachronism for Chatterton,' said Linda.

'Oh, quite,' agreed Catherine. She made a mental note to check her dictionary later. And how could she arrange to see Linda again?

'I don't know any convent girls,' remarked Linda.

'I don't know any state-school girls.'

'I come here most days after college to wait for Mum, except for Thursdays when I have music.'

'Why don't you go home?'

'There's no-one there. I don't have any brothers or sisters.'

'What does your father do?' Catherine was sure Linda's father would be something interesting like a teacher or an artist.

185

'My dad ran off with someone else ages ago. It's just me and Mum. I like it.'

'Do you see him?'

'Hardly ever.'

'I'm the second eldest of eight kids. I never get any privacy at home, and we can't afford to buy books. That's why I come here.'

'I'll see you around then.'

Catherine grinned. 'Yes, all right.'

Linda possessed a bubbling sense of humour and her face was often creased with laughter. Catherine began to laugh more. She learned how it felt to laugh until she ached.

They worked their way through the small library's limited resources, swooping on anything that seemed obscure, bizarre or unfathomable. For the first time Catherine had discovered a peer who could match her reading level, a girl her own age who could challenge her, a different kind of best friend. They shared their treasures. Linda had read about bird women and snake goddesses. Catherine had read about the persecution of witches in the Middle Ages. She told the sceptical and amused Linda about Hildegard and about Teresa's visions, about Margaret Mary, who ate vomit and diarrhoea. And because Linda was hungry for more 'weird Catholic stuff', she told her about relics, scapulars, novenas and plenary indulgences.

'It sounds fucking nuts,' pronounced Linda.

'It is,' sang Catherine. 'Fucking fucking *fucking* nuts. You are absolutely one hundred per cent right. Fuck relics! Fuck scapulars! Fuck plenary fucking indulgences.'

And she laughed until she thought she would snap in half. She gasped. Snot flowed from her nose and she didn't bother to wipe it away.

'It's fucking awful, if you want to know,' she said solemnly, staring across at Linda, 'and that really is the truth.' She waited for Linda to turn on her heel and walk out on her. She waited for the earth to swallow her up.

Linda continued to sit perfectly still. There was a concerned expression on her face.

She reached out a freckled hand. 'It's going to be OK,' she said.

'Is it?' asked Catherine. 'How do you know? How does anyone?'

'Because nothing stays the same for ever.'

And even though Catherine didn't believe her, the peculiar tight feeling that often twisted her chest stopped hurting.

She was happy.

She sang around the house and everyone remarked on the change in her.

'What's up with Cathy?'

Theresa suspected, but she kept her thoughts to herself. She was surprised, yet because she knew Catherine better than anybody else on earth, she realized that what she was thinking must be true. Catherine had a crush.

But Catherine didn't want to expose Linda to her family. She wanted to have something of her own. The friendship with Linda was too fragile, too new and too precious to be trampled underfoot or, worse, forbidden.

Fucking. Fucking nuts.

'You swear a lot,' said Catherine.

'And it feels *great*. I bet you don't even know what fucking means.'

'I do so.'

'Fornication. Fucking fornication.'

'Do you despise Catholics?'

'No, but I think they're pretty weird. How can you go along with it and not rebel?'

'We're not allowed to rebel.'

Linda hooted with laughter. 'You're priceless,' she said.

'And do you have to ask permission to breathe?'

As well as her job as a librarian, Linda's mother was a part-time writer working on a teenage novel. She could discuss the novels of Jane Austen and the Brontës in depth and yet be equally at home talking about the latest Margaret Drabble or Doris Lessing, and Catherine became a devoted fan. She swore too, and she didn't seem to mind or notice when her daughter did likewise.

'Your mother is amazing,' said Catherine. 'You could ask her anything and she wouldn't be shocked. You're so lucky.'

'Am I?' Linda took her mother for granted. 'You wouldn't really want her for a mother,' she said, 'because she's too nosy. She wants to know every-thing. And I mean *everything*.'

'What sort of everything?'

'She's an emotional vampire. She wants to hear about all my feelings and responses in minute detail so she can analyse them. I feel as if I'm always under a magnifying glass. I have no privacy. Sometimes I make stuff up just to keep her going. She thrives on it. You'll see what I mean, because she'll probably start on you next. I expect I'm in her novel as a character going through some terrible sort of crisis while a marvellous mother sweeps in to rescue me.'

'Better that than a prince on a white charger doing the job,' said Catherine. They giggled.

'When can I meet your family?' asked Linda several times. She always received the same vague reply.

'Soon.'

'How soon? I don't believe you have a family. Are you hiding them from me? You're not ashamed of them, are you?'

'Course not.'

'Well then, prove it.'

Catherine knew she couldn't hold off her friend for ever. She decided to introduce Linda gradually, letting her name crop up in conversation casually until her mother expressed an interest in meeting her. She would bring Linda home when her father was out.

'I hope you can drum some sense into my daughter,' said Mrs Flynn when she finally met Linda. 'She's got her head in the clouds most of the time.'

'The sign of a genius, I would say,' retorted Linda.

Catherine grinned. She took Linda to the room she shared with Theresa. She had cleaned up that morning in preparation for the visit, but of course Theresa had untidied the room as soon as she arrived home. There were library books scattered about, and clothes lay in a heap on the floor.

Theresa was sitting on her bed in her cotton bra and knickers eating a slice of toast and reading a book. Her hair, recently brushed, crackled with electricity and floated in a halo about her head. Her mouth was smeared with jam.

Linda was startled. She looked from one to the other.

'Yes, I know,' said Catherine grumpily. 'We look like twins, but we're not.'

'Thank *God*,' said Theresa in her poshest voice.

Catherine wanted to strangle her.

Linda leaned over the bed to get a closer look at the Sacred Heart. Catherine waited for her response. Nothing – just polite and curious interest. Linda went over to the holy-water font at the doorway. She dipped her fingers. 'Show me how you do it,' she said.

Catherine demonstrated the sign of the cross.

'What else have you got to show me?' asked Linda. 'I want to see everything. Relics. Rosary beads. Medals. Statues. Haul it out so I can inspect it.'

Chapter Seventeen

THE BELL JAR

With jealous eyes Mr Flynn watched his daughters grow up. He waited for disaster. He wished he could lock them up – they were too beautiful to be let loose. Someone would claim them, leave grubby paw-prints all over their delicate white necks and run dirty fingers through their white dandelion-fluff hair.

'Your bodies are Temples of the Holy Spirit,' he told them. 'Abuse them and you abuse God who lives inside them.'

'Yes, Dad.'

He wanted to grab them by their thin heartbreaking necks. Let any man dare to leave bites there. He was in charge. But he saw his girls toss their superior heads and smile their superior smiles, acting as if they owned the world.

They didn't. He'd prove it. He'd show them.

'Come here,' he demanded.

They came.

'Yes, Dad?'

'It doesn't matter.'

He smiled. They came when they were called. He was in charge and they knew it.

'I want you to keep yourselves clean,' said Mr Flynn. 'And I don't mean hygiene. I'm talking about modesty and purity. Keeping yourself pure for your husbands so they respect you. No man likes second-hand goods. Don't you dare let any Tom, Dick or Harry slip in through the back door. Do it through the front door, with marriage. I don't want to see either of you end up shacked up with a bloke like some cheap tart who should know better.'

'No, Dad.'

'It's up to you girls to set the standards, and for the boys to fall into line. If you dress modestly and don't go about looking cheap, you'll attract the right sort of boy.'

'Yes, Dad.'

'The main point I want to make is that you're not to let any boy touch you down there.' He pointed in the general direction of their genital area and their eyes flickered uncomfortably.

'I know what boys are like. They've only got one thing in their filthy minds. I'm warning you. Don't lead them on past the point of no return. Let them boil with lust. That's their problem. Keep your wits about you at all times.'

'Why is it us who have to be pure? Why do we have to set the limits?' raged Theresa out of earshot of her father.

'Boys don't have any will-power or self-control,' replied Catherine. 'You know that. Dad said so.'

'Maybe he's wrong,' suggested Theresa. 'Have you thought about that?'

'How do you know what to do with a man when you finally get married?' asked Theresa.

'Love finds a way,' replied their mother gloomily.

Catherine pictured The Way as a dark mysterious cave. It was entered by a monster of a man whose wild uncontrollable thoughts had led him to violent action. Penetration. Ejaculation. A man who didn't care if having his way led to his sperm swimming to the top of the vagina, up into the uterus and over to the Fallopian tubes. And according to her biology book, the bit about human reproduction, it was all to fertilize an unsuspecting little egg that waited patiently above the spongy, blood-lined tunnel of the uterus.

They would have nothing to do with boys. It was safer. Their mother referred darkly to 'buns in the oven', of girls being 'up the duff'. At school the girls knew who was a slut, a slag, a mole. They were the girls who 'went all the way'. And there were men who didn't use a joey, a Frenchie, a rubber.

It was all very well. But what was a joey – a type of underpants?

They learnt the language, but it didn't mean anything. Naming the parts of the body, describing the act – what did any of it have to do with romance?

'It's time you girls thought about jobs.'

Jobs? The girls were outraged. They wanted to study, go on to university.

'We'll see,' said Mrs Flynn. 'Don't take anything for granted.'

Why should they? She and Terrence had never had a chance to do what they really wanted. Both had been forced to leave school at sixteen to help bring money into their households. She wanted the best for her daughters, for them to have a different life from hers, but at the same time she found herself feeling jealous. They would have the opportunities she had been denied.

'If you behave yourselves,' said Mr Flynn, 'we *might* just consider letting you go.'

His tone of voice was a red rag fluttering in front of Theresa's vision. He couldn't prevent her studying and later having an exciting career. She was determined to escape Chatterton. 'You can't stop me,' she snapped.

'Really?' he said, eyebrows bristling.

Theresa caught the train to Wellington to spend her August holidays with Smoking Nana. She vented her frustrations over her future as soon as she arrived.

192

'I don't care what Dad says. He can't really stop me, can he?'

'It's important to be true to yourself,' said her grandmother, 'and to follow your destiny, no matter what. Leave your father to me, I'll deal with him, don't you fret.'

Theresa began to cry.

'What is it?' asked her grandmother, bending over her. Theresa didn't know.

'I want to be me,' she said.

'You can be whatever you want to be these days.'

'Can I really?'

'Yes. It's different now. Look at my life, I was forced to leave school at fourteen and go out to work. I didn't have a choice – but you do. I've had to educate myself by reading everything I could get hold of. But you've got brains, girl, and you owe it to yourself to make the most of what you have.'

'But you're happy, aren't you?' Theresa hadn't given much thought before now as to whether adults in her life were happy or not.

'I'm content with my lot. I've got used to being on my own and I like not having any man around telling me what to do. That's freedom, all right. Sometimes I wonder what my life would have been like if I'd had more education. I regret we weren't able to keep your mother at school longer, but I did my best and that's all anybody can do.'

Smoking Nana lived in a shabby 1920s wooden bungalow. It had a red corrugated-iron roof and a large pear tree in the back yard. The fence behind it had long ago collapsed, and children and stray dogs used her property as a thoroughfare. It didn't bother Smoking Nana. She welcomed the company. Sometimes she gave the children biscuits – shop-bought ones. She didn't like baking.

She had never been able to afford to maintain the house in a good state of repair, not on the wage she received as a clerical worker for the Education Department. Now that she was coming up towards retirement she would be living on even less. Paint peeled off the outside walls. Inside, the stained timber had become blackened and sticky with age and neglect. Every surface was crammed with bargains acquired at auctions and sales over the years. Sets of linen bought up to twenty years ago still lay in their original Cellophane wrappers in her cupboards. She had enough fine bone-china tea sets to have served tea to at least fifty people, along with similar quantities of sherry glasses, dinner sets and toby jugs. She attended the Wellington auctions once a week.

'What do you need all this stuff for?' asked Theresa. On her annual visits she always liked to explore. The kitchen cupboards were crammed with tins and packets of food, enough to last her grandmother several months if necessary.

'You never know when it'll come in handy,' said Smoking Nana. 'I don't like to be caught short.'

Waist-high bundles of newspapers tied with string lined the hallway. Smoking Nana intended to dispose of them, but like so many other tasks waiting to be done in her house she simply never got around to it. There were shoe-boxes of old Christmas cards and birthday cards, cartons crammed with photos which spilled out of curled-up, black-paged albums.

'The only way I'm leaving here is head first,' said Smoking Nana. 'I'm never going into an old folk's home. You'd have to shoot me first.'

'What are you talking about?' asked Theresa, alarmed. 'You're not going to die, are you?'

'No-one lives for ever. My bones aren't what they were. I'm disintegrating as we speak.'

'You're not.'

'I am too. My eyesight's going. My hearing is starting to pack it in. My hip's been playing up.'

Smoking Nana poured herself a shot of neat whisky.

'I want a drink too,' decided Theresa.

'Help yourself.'

Theresa pulled out a bottle of Cointreau.

'Is this nice?'

'Marvellous. Try a small glass first and see how you like it. I'll finish what you leave behind.'

The Cointreau was thick but clear like water. It tasted sharp, sweet and warm as it slipped easily down her throat.

'It *is* marvellous.'

They lounged on the long sofa and sipped in companionable silence. The huge dark clock in the hallway chimed the hour in muffled tones.

'Can I have another one?' asked Theresa. 'Will it make me drunk, do you think?'

'Maybe. Just don't throw up on the furniture, will you.'

Smoking Nana's bedroom overflowed with treasures. Clothes which didn't fit into the crammed wardrobe hung from hooks on the wall. Two drawers of the Scotch chest had lost their handles and were left permanently half open. Sepia-toned prints of nymphs and cherubs in round varnished wood frames dominated the room. It was all auction loot. Bundles of the *New Zealand Woman's Weekly* leaned against one wall, next to a smaller stack of *Thursday* magazines which went back as far as 1968.

'Can I read them?' asked Theresa. A recent issue contained a feature article on the new women's liberation movement. A photo immediately caught her eye. 'Mary Blessed: It's time for women to have their say.' It was her. Mary Blessed was the Virgin! Three years had passed since she disappeared. Should she reveal Mary Blessed's true identity to her grandmother? Would she scoff?

'You're very interested in that article,' observed Smoking Nana. 'Not thinking of becoming a women's libber like your grandmother, are you? You know, Theresa, they're only repeating what I've been saying for years, only no-one would listen to me. I was years ahead of my time, even if your father thought I was mad.'

It was Theresa who poured the next whisky for her grandmother.

'How many will it take to get you drunk?'

'Three to four.'

'Good.' Theresa had some tricky questions to put to her grandmother.

'What was it like for you the first time with a man?' she asked after Smoking Nana had drunk three whiskies.

'You're being very personal, young lady,' said her grandmother, but she didn't sound annoyed. 'People always imagine that the first time will be terrific — like in your daydreams. But it's not like that. I didn't enjoy sex the first time — it hurt. That was a surprise. I didn't know what to do and neither did Tom. It was very embarrassing at first. It was a long time before I got anything out of it and that only happened when I realized I couldn't totally rely on him — I had to make it happen for myself.'

Theresa blinked. Her grandmother's words were shocking and confusing, but she had absolutely no doubt they were true. She could still remember her grandfather clearly. He had been a quiet sensitive man, inclined to moodiness and depression.

'What do you mean? What was it you did for yourself?'

'It's called masturbating — so you can have an orgasm. If you waited around for a man to bring you one you'd be waiting till Christmas.'

What did she mean? Touching yourself down there? But that was wrong. Or was it? Unlike her father, her grandmother didn't think it sinful or disgusting.

'Even if you love someone a lot the sex always changes. At first it's tense, exciting, nerve-racking.

196

After six months, a year, maybe two years, it becomes comfortable and easy. Later it can become a chore, or then again it may not. It depends.'

'On what?' asked Theresa, almost afraid to breathe in case her grandmother stopped talking.

'The time of day. How you feel. Having children around. It's impossible to have sex in the morning if children are likely to rush in at any moment. At nights you're often too tired. You don't always want to when you have your period, although for some women that's when they get the most aroused.'

'That doesn't seem fair.'

'Of course not.'

Smoking Nana put her cigarette down for a minute. She clasped Theresa by the shoulders and stared intently into her eyes. Theresa saw how she was loved. 'I want you to promise me something,' her grandmother said, 'that you never, *never* have sex with someone if you don't want to, or do anything that makes you feel bad. Don't let any man put pressure on you.'

Theresa was puzzled. 'Of course I'm not going to have sex with someone if I don't want to. Why would I? I'm not stupid.' She chewed a fingernail. What else did she want to know while her grandmother was in the mood for confidences?

'Did you ever go off sex completely?'

'Yes. It's not unusual. You can't expect to feel the same way about someone for ever.'

'I want to know if you ever had sex with anyone besides Grandad?'

Her grandmother paused.

'Go on,' urged Theresa. 'Tell me the truth.'

'All right then. I had a lover for years called Sam.'

'Is this true? You're tricking me.' Theresa bounced up and down on the bed. Suddenly a thought struck her.

'What about Grandad? Did he know?'

'Yes. He knew all along.'

'Why didn't he divorce you?'

'We still loved each other. In those days divorce wasn't so common. Eventually Tom believed that I could love both him and Sam.'

'I don't understand. How can a woman love two men at once?'

'It's possible, believe me.'

'Did Mum know about Sam?'

'Yes.'

'Did you ever go off Sam?'

'I never stopped loving him, but that doesn't mean that I always wanted to have sex with him. Sometimes we didn't speak for months.'

'What happened to Sam if you never stopped loving him?'

'He died a year before your grandfather.'

'Were you sad?'

'I wanted to die.'

'I can't imagine Mum ever having sex or being passionately in love. And yet I suppose she must have done it at least eight times. Uggh.'

'Your mother has always resisted me,' said Smoking Nana. 'There are a lot of things we don't see eye to eye on, but all the same we have an understanding and she knows I would do anything to help her.'

'She knows that?'

'Of course.'

Theresa was surprised.

'Do you think you might be like Catherine?' asked Smoking Nana. 'Someone who falls in love with other girls?'

Theresa sat up abruptly, holding the blankets up over her chest to keep warm. 'How did you know?'

'I'm not blind. I could see what was going on under your mother's nose. It's all right, I'm sure she doesn't know. She's an innocent.'

'I think I've had enough truth,' said Theresa and to their mutual astonishment she promptly burst into tears.

Her grandmother passed her a handkerchief and gave her a hug.

True Love. The real thing. How did you know, wondered Theresa. *Really* know.

The True Love's touch was like no other's. It burned. He became your destiny. It was fate. You had no say in the matter. You followed him to the ends of the earth. Whither thou goest there go I. But what if you didn't want to? Why didn't it apply to the man? Theresa an explorer, and the True Love trailing behind moaning, 'Oh hell, not another desert, not another wretched pyramid. I want to go home and do the dishes, or make a bed.'

Because men weren't like that? Because they always wanted to be in charge, as her grandmother warned? But what if your True Love was also your best friend? And you had equal say in everything?

A man and woman in true love lived happily ever after. They had to. If Catholics got divorced they couldn't get married again. It meant living in sin unless you wanted to live on your own.

How was she going to meet her true love in Chatterton?

Chapter Eighteen

LOVE AND DESTINY

Theresa was in love. Peter van der Vossen was the best-looking boy at Chatterton Boys High and he had noticed her. Already he was lending her books from his parents' well-stocked home library.

She had met him through an inter-college debating team competition two years previously. He had stood out, appearing much more confident than the other boys. He was funny too. She had liked the way he made everyone else laugh with his droll witticisms.

'How do you know it's *love*?' asked Francie.

'Because my heart is going pit-a-pat,' answered Theresa. She chased Francie from the room.

'Perhaps I've romanticized him into someone he's not,' Theresa anguished to Catherine. She couldn't stop talking about him. Sometimes it was enough simply to speak his name.

'I want to kiss him. I want to touch him. I want to hold his hand,' whispered Theresa.

'Do you?' breathed Catherine. 'Do you really? What else do you want to do?'

'That's as far as I'd go . . . I think. But what if I can't control myself?'

Catherine had no doubt what would happen. 'You'd be up the duff.'

'Not me. I wouldn't be so dumb.'

Astonishingly, her father had agreed to let her go to the pictures with Peter, providing she was brought home immediately afterwards by Peter in his father's car.

'No mucking around afterwards,' ordered her father.
'Oh no, Dad. I'll be straight home. Promise.'
He tweaked her nose.
She scowled.
'See you are, my girl.'

Theresa sat in Peter's father's car. She held Peter's hand. He squeezed it. She returned the pressure. He squeezed it again.

Theresa glanced towards the house. 'I should go,' she murmured. 'Dad wanted me home early.'

'You are home early,' said Peter. 'He'll know you've arrived.'

'If he knows I'm outside the house, he'll be wondering what I'm doing. You don't know what he's like.'

'Relax. We're just talking.'

Theresa kept silent. She didn't want to make a fuss. They continued to talk.

She didn't hear her father until the car door swung open.

'About time you were inside, girl. You've been outside here long enough.'

Her father pulled her out of the car, and dragged her down the driveway after him. Her knees grazed the gravel.

Behind her Theresa heard the sound of a car quickly pulling away.

Peter would now ignore her. He would tell all his friends. She would be a laughing-stock.

'I don't like your tone of voice, my girl,' said Mr Flynn. He pulled at each of his finger joints one at a time until they cracked. Theresa flinched at each hateful little snap, hoping his fingers would break off. He must know it repelled her.

Theresa believed he could see deep inside her mind and read the contradictory thoughts and emotions

201

surging through it better than she could herself. She hated the idea of him knowing and felt powerless under his gaze.

Beneath her lowered eyelids resentment burned, and plans brewed. She couldn't let him realize this if she were to get her own way. He was able to see into her head only if her eyes were open. He said eyes were the windows of the soul. Theresa made sure she kept the blinds drawn. She was determined to get her own way for once.

'I don't like *your* tone of voice either,' she longed to say. She tried to modulate her voice into a honeyed tone to soften him up. She focused on her goal.

'I'm very sorry, Daddy,' she said in a gentle voice. 'I'd appreciate it if I could go out with Peter tonight. I promise I won't be late.'

'It's out of the question.' His voice rose. 'No girl of mine—'

'WHY NOT?' she shouted back at him. She forgot she had dared to think she might persuade him with guile. There was no reasoning with him once he was in this mood.

A raw little creature sprang out of her with claws exposed, limbs flailing, desperate to bite, scratch — and draw blood. It was a creature whose existence she was only vaguely aware of. It frightened her with its rage.

Her anger stormed from her in full flood. It was part of her, yet separate, something ugly, bloody and down-right bad. This feral creature leapt into action without prior warning, ready to devour whatever was in its path. It transformed her into someone she couldn't recognize.

She could tell her father was excited by her anger. His eyes glistened. She was disgusted by the latticework of fine red veins in the whites of his eyes. His hair was greasy with his awful hair cream. There were flecks of dandruff on his collar. How loathsome.

'Not another word,' he said, holding up his hand for silence.

He was like a traffic warden, controlling her flow of words, her every movement. *Do this. Don't do that.* It was intolerable.

The atmosphere between them was electric. Theresa stepped back. A passive hand held in the air could swiftly be transformed into a violent hand, raised to strike.

She swallowed hard. Now she was older, seventeen, these battles of will between them seemed to her to have undergone a subtle shift. A new element had crept into their tussles. It made her feel uncomfortable.

'Boys have only one thing on their filthy minds,' he said in a thick voice.

She breathed again. Finally, the real issues were out in the open. Her body was the territory in dispute. It was about whether some young 'whippersnapper' could go anywhere near it without her father's permission.

'I'LL SEE WHO I WANT, YOU CAN'T STOP ME,' she yelled.

'CAN'T I JUST?' he yelled back.

They were in the section of hallway closest to the kitchen. Theresa could hear the muffled roar of canned laughter from the lounge.

Her father's hand was raised again. This time, as she'd feared, it quivered with barely suppressed anger. It was a hand poised not to warn but this time to strike.

She fled to the bathroom. Trembling, she jammed a chair up under the door handle and sat on the toilet seat.

Her father bashed on the door a couple of times. She could hear him breathing. Soon he gave up. She heard his heavy footsteps retreating slowly down the hallway.

When she stopped shaking she began to run a

shower. She ran it as hot as she could stand it, drowning out the sound of her sobs.

The knocking started up again as she was drying herself quickly with a threadbare towel.

'I won't be long,' she called out.

She hastily pulled on her knickers, but not quickly enough. His rattling on the door knob dislodged the chair, which fell to the lino with a crash.

Her father burst in. She had one foot in and one out of her knickers and clutched the skimpy towel to her breasts. He strode over to where she was cowering against the shower door and wrenched the towel from her. It happened so fast she felt winded by it. She wrapped her arm protectively over her chest and stared at him, shaking with fear. He had never gone this far before. She couldn't speak. There was an awful silence which stretched on and on while she continued to shiver, dry-mouthed in front of him.

'I'm your father. I can look at you if I want to. You've got nothing to hide. Nothing I haven't seen before.'

He flicked at her breasts with two fingers. He then turned on his heel and walked out.

She was too shocked to cry. She moved like a sleepwalker, gathering her clothes and putting them on. She went to her room and undressed again. She switched off the light, climbed into bed and tried to control her shaking body.

Half an hour passed. No-one came to find her. How could her strength and resolve be stripped from her so easily, leaving her humiliated and degraded?

She remembered Hildegard, who had advised kings and popes. She must have possessed a powerful inner strength which had sustained her through her long life. Unlike her, wavering, doubting, often feeling scared and then not being able to find the words to explain it to anybody. Who would she explain it to anyway? Where was *she* to get her strength from . . . God? She hadn't been able to find Him. He didn't exist.

*   *   *

'He's unspeakable,' said Catherine. 'You should have called me.'

'What could you have done?' asked Theresa.

'Why didn't you find me?' asked Catherine. 'Together we might have stood up to him.'

Theresa tried to remember why she hadn't asked for help. Why hadn't she called for her mother? But what if her mother hadn't believed her? Was she making a fuss over nothing? Did her father have the right to do as he pleased? If he kicked her out, where would she live? How would she support herself?

'I felt crushed by him,' she said. 'I didn't realize anyone could help me.'

Chapter Nineteen

THE SERPENT

Theresa learned from the latest encounter with her father that it didn't pay to be truthful. She began to invent assignations with girl-friends and enlisted their support in deceiving him. She continued to see Peter in secret.

Peter's family were Dutch and had immigrated to New Zealand in the mid-fifties. He wasn't a Catholic, which only increased his appeal for her. His father was a doctor and his mother a teacher at Chatterton College. Peter didn't have any brothers and had only one sister, older than him by two years and already at university, where she was studying law.

There appeared to be no shortage of money in the household and Peter was given a generous amount of pocket money each week which he spent on books and records rather than saving. He seemed confident his parents could put him through university.

His house had been designed by an architect. It was surrounded by native trees. Their hallway was lined with books, half of them in Dutch. Everything in the house matched and seemed new. There were long beams with no paint on them. No carpets on the floors, instead thick striped mats that Peter said had been woven by hand. The cushions didn't even have flowers, they were in plain bright colours, also in a coarsely woven fabric. There was no statues, no Sacred Hearts or crucifixes. The walls were white and covered with paintings that had no figures in them, only patterns and textures. The sofas were huge, big enough to sleep in. Leading off the back door was a glassed-in room paved with various shaped stones. Large broad-leafed plants flourished in this area. Peter called it 'the patio'.

Theresa turned to Peter. 'Are you very rich?'

He laughed. 'No, of course not. What's so special about this place?' He gestured to embrace the room.

He obviously took it all for granted. It was so *civilized*. You could *breathe* in a house like this. You could spread out, feel creative, make things. She had always believed, without any evidence to back it up, that there had to be another way of living.

'Do you like it?'

'I *love* it. The house is utterly beautiful. I wish I lived here. I wish I was you.'

He told her she could look around if she wanted. Like a cat sniffing out its territory she wanted to smell and touch everything.

'Coffee?' asked Peter, switching on a foreign-looking electric bean-grinder.

Her reply was lost in the whirring noise that followed. She nodded. She had never drunk anything other than instant before.

It was Saturday. Theresa was supposed to be studying at a friend's. Peter's parents were away for the day visiting a relative. They had the house to themselves.

Peter wanted to discuss *Brighton Rock*. He was asking her about the Catholic stuff in it, references he didn't understand. Like her he was mad about reading.

They were in the lounge listening to Leonard Cohen. Peter didn't like the singer — too mournful, he said. Theresa liked him a lot. His voice seemed to express the melancholy which sometimes overwhelmed her, for no obvious reason.

They had been hugging and kissing for an hour already and were both hot and sticky. Outside, the cicadas throbbed and a refreshing breeze blew in from an open window.

Peter stroked her breasts through her tee-shirt. She breathed quickly. He went to lift up her top, but she gently pushed his hands down.

'What's the matter?' he asked, 'don't be so uptight. You're not frigid, are you?'

She pulled away, her face aflame. And then she felt angry. She remembered what her grandmother had said and for once her advice overwhelmed her father's messages.

'You don't ever have to do anything that makes you feel uncomfortable.'

'Don't worry, I won't hurt you. It'll be fun. You'll like it, I promise. Come on, relax.'

How could she relax? Her ankle was jammed under his, but she was too embarrassed to tell him. She had pins and needles in her foot. Her face still felt hot. Did she have B.O.? Was her lipstick all kissed off, or smeared unflatteringly over her face? She should have stayed at home.

Boys are only after one thing.

Was it true? Did Peter only want sex and nothing else? What if he dropped her afterwards?

An easy lay. Her mother's voice penetrated her now. Why wouldn't they leave her alone? The three of them were like consciences hanging on a chain around her neck.

She hesitated. 'I'm not sure,' she said. 'I don't know if it's what I want.'

Peter acted as if he hadn't heard her. He undid his zip, unpeeled his jeans.

She watched him without saying a word, unable to tear her eyes away. She didn't stop him. She waited to see what he would do next. He kept his eyes on hers. They were very bright and excited.

His jeans were discarded and tossed onto the floor.

Peter's penis was astonishing. She saw veins, blood vessels. It was monstrously enlarged. It waved at her from his curly blond pubic hair.

Theresa leaned over and, still without saying anything, poked it cautiously with one finger. It wobbled obligingly, springing back into position when she withdrew her hand.

Leonard Cohen's laments became an etched backdrop, an integral part of what she would remember later. It was nothing at all like she had expected.

She batted the thing back and forth with three fingers, treating it like a toy.

Leonard Cohen knew what she felt, what she wanted to feel, the sad romantic yearning that linked up with her fantasy life and yet bore no relation to the veined helmeted alien she was *actually* touching.

'Ouch!' he said and pushed her fingers away.

She laughed.

'What's so funny?'

She laughed again, a mixture of hysteria and embarrassment.

'It's so . . . so . . .'

'So . . . *what*? Tell me,' he demanded, offended.

Theresa found the word she was looking for. It was so *ridiculous*. And now, more amazingly, the thing had wilted under her curious and unsympathetic scrutiny. It had shrunk until it was just a poor wrinkled little sausage, curled limply into its nest of damp hair.

Peter looked down at it, obviously embarrassed. She was sorry for him. He'd been so proud of his penis and now it had shrivelled away to a pathetic little nothing. She had been alarmed at the size of his erection – how could something of this size possibly squeeze inside the narrow, tight opening between her legs? It would cause the most awful pain. She tried to picture the thing drilling its way inside her, but here her imagination failed her.

Why didn't he keep kissing her? Why wasn't he stroking her until her flesh melted? Why did they have to focus on his silly penis?

They sat on a mat in a silence of mutual embarrassment until a surprising idea occurred to Theresa.

'You can't control it, can you?' she said.

'No,' he said. 'It has a mind of its own. I get erections
all the time and I think about it night and day.'

'It . . . you mean, sex?'

'Yeah. Sex. Doing it.'

'Have you ever done it before with a girl?'

'Yeah, I have a couple of times.'

Was he telling the truth or simply trying to impress
her?

'I jerk off every day.'

She was speechless for a minute, before squealing
in disbelief.

Every day? Wasn't he afraid of damaging himself?

He chortled at this. It dissolved their embarrassment.
He admitted to her that he often masturbated with two
of his friends.

'You do it in *front* of them?'

'Yeah. And sometimes we jerk each other off.'

She again felt disgusted and disapproving. But at
the same time – fascinated.

'Is it . . . is it exciting?'

He leaned back against an armchair and closed his
eyes.

'It's *incredible*,' he said. A huge smile broke out over
his face, making it seem beautiful and alive.

She wasn't afraid. Now her instincts told her that
whatever happened, Peter wouldn't hurt her.

How different boys were. She hadn't known if
she had sexual desires. How could you have desires
for something you had never experienced? She had
never thought about it, hadn't touched herself the way
Peter did with his friends. If she had fantasized about
a boy, the images had always revolved around talking,
cuddling, hugging. Holding hands. Kissing. Being seen
with him by her friends. She had felt very attracted to
Peter, to his looks, his cleverness, but was it love?

How did you know if you were in love? What did it feel like? Could she bring herself to have sex with a boy if she didn't love him? She wished they could have continued talking. She didn't feel ready to make a decision about whether or not to have sex.

She imagined him with his friends, the three of them pulling their penises out of their trousers and jerking at them in front of each other. And what did jerking mean? She saw their furtive gestures – a dark garage, the thrill of it, the camaraderie. The fear of being discovered. Her girl-friends didn't do that sort of thing. The very idea of displaying her private parts to a friend made her feel nauseous.

Peter opened his eyes. He pointed to his genitals.

'Why don't you play with my cock,' he suggested, 'and watch it grow.'

Theresa moved closer. She tentatively reached out and touched the strange little creature. It felt cold and slightly damp in her fingers. It wasn't nice to hold. She felt silly sitting alongside him, knowing he was studying her face while she touched him in this unbelievably intimate manner.

'Hold it like this,' he said.

Why am I doing this, Theresa asked herself. But she couldn't stop. There was a tingling sort of itch inside her, between her legs, that she had never experienced before. She kept stroking the funny veined thing until to her surprise it grew and hardened beneath her hands.

He moaned as she continued to stroke him. 'Keep doing it, *please* don't stop,' he begged her.

The thing was now rock-hard in her hands. If she let go of it for a second, it bounced back up again. He showed her how to move her hands up and down rhythmically. This steady movement seemed to excite him unbearably.

'Talk to me while you're doing it,' he pleaded.

'What about?' She was genuinely puzzled.

211

He was moaning and groaning now as if he were in pain, still begging her not to stop. The itch between Theresa's legs was stronger than before, but she didn't know what to do about it. Her knickers felt damp and slippery. She could smell her body scent, a peculiar new smell, and was anxious that Peter could smell it too. Why did her body always let her down? She felt like moaning too, but wasn't relaxed enough to imitate Peter's animal-like noises.

Suddenly his body arched and shuddered. And then he appeared to have a kind of fit – frowning, twitching, shuddering again, as if he were having a convulsion. She looked on concerned at first and then with enormous astonishment and interest as a jet of warm white liquid spurted out over his stomach and dribbled over her fingers. The liquid had a distinctive sour smell. She wrinkled her nose. Peter smirked with pride and then seeing her expression gave her a sheepish grin.

Close your mouth, Theresa, she told herself.

It had all happened very quickly. She scarcely had time to gather her thoughts and work out her responses when they heard the sound of a car in the driveway and scrambled to rearrange their clothing.

'Shit! They must have left earlier than they'd planned,' said Peter in a panic.

They were sitting reading companionably opposite each other on the two sofas listening to Pink Floyd when the van der Vossens entered carrying bags of fruit. They looked surprised to see her, although they had met her previously.

Mrs van der Vossen asked Theresa to help her make some coffee in the kitchen. She followed her, feeling apprehensive.

'Do your parents know you're here?' Peter's mother asked gently, when they were out of earshot.

'No.' Theresa felt bound to be truthful. Mrs van der Vossen gave her a shrewd look.

'I hope you know what you're doing,' she said bluntly. 'You mustn't let my son put any pressure on you. Do you understand what I mean?'

Theresa blushed. She couldn't look at Mrs van der Vossen. She was realizing to her surprise that it wasn't her son that Mrs van der Vossen was concerned about.

'I teach him to be responsible,' she said. 'I tell him to buy a condom if he has sex with a girl, but you know what boys are like. They never listen to their mothers.'

She pulled down a red biscuit tin from the top shelf. She lifted off the lid and gave Theresa some slim foil-covered objects.

'You be the sensible one,' she said. 'Have embarrassment now, and save having a pregnancy later.'

Theresa burst into tears and ran from the room. She grabbed her things from the lounge and scurried out of the house.

If this was her first brush with sex, it had failed miserably. Peter would never speak to her again, nor would his mother. She berated herself all the way home on her bicycle. She had behaved like an idiot, demonstrating with every word she uttered, every move she made, her ignorance and inexperience.

She remembered the extraordinary sensations she had experienced between her legs, the frantic, hectic feeling, the difficulty in breathing. She had been absorbed in the heat generated between her legs. And then the amazing sight of Peter's penis. She could scarcely believe now that she had actually done it to him. And the most surprising thing of all was that she wanted to do it again as soon as possible.

His hair was the colour of milk — like hers. It was the thing she liked best about him. But where hers was a tangle of wiry curls, his was like hanks of silk flopping down over one eye. His body was hard, lean and tanned. She knew because she had pressed herself against it and felt its foreign angles and hard muscle.

She was fascinated by him, but was it love? She had decided she definitely wouldn't have sex with a man unless she loved him. While she and her father were in the same town, she didn't see how she could have sex with anyone. Where did fathers get all their power from? Even the saints had trouble with fathers. St Barbara's chopped her head off. St Wilgefortis's father crucified her because she had grown a beard to repulse the suitor he had chosen for her. It was something to imagine, a bearded woman hanging from a cross. And all because she wanted to remain a virgin.

It wasn't difficult to arrange meetings with Peter. There were plenty of alibis. They fell into a pattern.

She refused to have him inside her. But she would watch, or she would masturbate him. He asked her to masturbate herself in front of him and she primly refused.

Their homework was laid out on the table in case they were ever interrupted.

The knowledge that they could be interrupted only enhanced the excitement. He told her the danger that accompanied every act further sweetened the climax for him.

Theresa bent studiously over her books, frowning and sucking at her pencil. Peter lay on the couch in front of her. He had a textbook in one hand and the other on his fly which he slowly unbuttoned. Without taking his eyes from his reading he lowered his trousers and underpants and pulled out his penis.

Theresa continued to flick pages. Every time he looked up her eyes were absorbed on a text. Every time he returned to his own book she stared at him, waiting for the tingling itchy sensation to crawl up her own legs and speed up her breathing.

He was aware of her watching him and his cock expanded with every hot glance he felt directed his way. Underneath the table she furtively touched herself through the fabric of her uniform. He said he found it exciting to know he was corrupting a convent girl.

'You're not corrupting me,' said Theresa. 'I'm choosing to further my education, that's all.'

He laughed. 'That's your story. I've seduced a convent girl,' he sang.

She wanted to box his ears. She wished she wasn't a convent girl. Her background was like a scar. A wound, a bruise. He wouldn't understand. Why hadn't her father told her that girls boiled with the same lust as boys?

She was scared of giving Peter any control over her body. He loved her superior manner. It amused him. 'You're a strange girl,' he observed. He had no idea how strange, thought Theresa.

Inside she felt wild. She longed to break out. She wanted to commit a reckless act, do something wicked.

'I'm not a notch in your belt of scalps. You haven't seduced me, it's the other way around. I've seduced *you*.'

How could she let him into the most private recesses of her body when she hadn't told him a single secret?

He liked to discuss Auden, Yeats, Greene, Steinbeck, Conrad and lately, Kerouac. He was only captivated by male writers. When she talked about Emily Dickinson or Margaret Drabble, he lost interest.

She put her pencil down. Peter heard the clatter as it struck the table. His fingers sped up.

The hand sliding up and down hypnotized her. She watched the head of his cock appear and disappear.

She yearned to run over to him and do something dramatic. As usual she restrained herself. Little beads of perspiration broke out over her forehead and she wiped them away. How hot the room was . . . And there was that hectic feeling again. She wished it could last and last. She also longed for it to intensify.

The pages turned more slowly. Peter's face was flushed.

She was almost in a swoon. Her hands fluttered over her pelvis and hips like wings before diving in to land. She was tantalized by her own fingers. She didn't care any longer if he saw. But he wasn't looking, so it didn't matter. The rule was, they focused on him. Did he know what it was doing to her?

'*My body is a temple.*' Of the Holy Spirit.

'What?'

She must have spoken aloud. She blushed.

'You don't believe all that crap, do you?'

'Course not.'

Maria Goretti had chosen to die at the hands of a knife-wielding rapist rather than submit to his beastly demands. Abuse the temple and you abused God, said her father.

She couldn't reconcile the two realities – Maria Goretti and holy temples and her present dilemma, a boy waving a fiery cock and her out of control. Being pure and saving yourself for your husband only concerned her because it had been rammed down her throat by her father. But what if she hadn't been taught it was wicked and a sin? Knowing it was wrong obviously wasn't something that came naturally. The *natural* thing to do would be to dive in and get involved. But if she threw away her religion, what remained? Mortal sin and hell for ever? Shit. What a choice. She was lost already. Why not admit it?

She continued to agonize.

She was still bemused by the idea that seeing his erection could fill her with such excitement. She liked knowing it was she who turned him on. Soon she learned to arouse herself by pressing her hand down firmly over her groin and rubbing it up and down. This produced some interesting sensations, causing her to feel almost sick with desire and frustration.

She knew she inhabited a castle far above Peter. It was a lonely position she had staked out for herself. She envied Peter his simple pleasure. Why couldn't she come down off her pedestal, from her high lonely place and join him?

She roused herself for the next part of the game. Teasing.

'I have a question about my work you could help me with,' she said, drumming a tattoo with the fingers of one hand on the table top.

'What . . . did you need . . . to know?' asked Peter faintly. He liked having what he referred to as 'intellectual sex'.

'Something to do with Conrad's actual *intentions* as opposed to—'

She heard a low moan. 'Pardon? What was that?' Peter moaned again. There was a crash as a book hit the floor.

He sank back, his eyes unfocused, staring at nothing, his body still trembling slightly.

She came and stood over him, dabbed a finger in the milky mucus. She licked it and pulled a face.

He pulled out a handkerchief already stiff from mopping up on previous occasions. Theresa watched, fascinated. It was a messy business. If he had come inside her, all that liquid would have been dripping down her vagina. At least she supposed it would. She was still not completely certain about what *actually* happened.

Her body gave an involuntary shudder. A million potential babies. The thought was indescribably revolting.

'And you do this every day?' she said, already sauntering back to the table. 'Extraordinary.'

'Yup. Sometimes twice a day,' he boasted. 'I just can't help myself. My cock leads and I follow. You've no idea how sexy it is having you watching me. I go into a frenzy. It's added a whole new dimension to sex for me.'

'Bully for you,' she replied. She looked across at his shrivelled penis and snapped her book shut.

Chapter Twenty

THE ALTERNATIVE

Catherine and Linda followed the track alongside the river until they had left the swimmers far behind. They heard shouts in the distance as the boys swung on ropes and dive-bombed into the water.

'Morons,' said Linda.

'Juvenile creeps.'

They changed into their bikinis. When Catherine glanced over at Linda's body she saw her friend staring at hers. That surprised her. She blushed and turned away.

Linda placed her towel alongside Catherine's, close enough so that it touched. Catherine didn't move away. She took a deep breath and waited.

Linda jammed a battered straw hat on her head and passed her coconut oil to Catherine.

'Would you do my back?'

Catherine loved the smell of coconut oil. It was the scent she associated with summer.

'Now you can do me,' she said when she had finished.

'OK.'

Instead of leaning over Catherine, Linda stood above her and gently lowered herself so that she was straddling her. She applied the oil in long sweeping strokes, being very particular about not leaving any exposed areas.

'You're really attractive, you know,' commented Linda, massaging Catherine's shoulders for the second time.

'No I'm not,' said Catherine.

'Can't you accept a compliment?'

Catherine thought about it. No, and neither could her mother.

'Can I touch your hair? I've always wanted to.'

Linda lay back down on her towel and removed her hat. They stared at each other for a long time and then Linda wriggled closer.

Catherine slid over too until their faces were almost touching.

'What are you doing?'

'What are *you* doing?'

'Nothing.'

'It doesn't feel like nothing.'

'It can be whatever you want it to be.'

'What's that supposed to mean?'

Linda giggled.

Catherine began to giggle too. Once they had started they couldn't stop. Tears streamed down their faces. They chortled and squealed and shrieked.

'You're so funny.'

'Not as funny as you.'

Catherine's hand accidentally touched Linda's. Linda grasped it.

As if a switch had been turned off, the laughter abruptly stopped. They drew close again and stared at each other solemnly.

Linda ran her tongue lightly over Catherine's lips. It was the delicate touch of a bird.

Catherine found herself responding. She opened her mouth. Linda's tongue gently entered and circled it, probing for Catherine's tongue, Catherine's teeth. A flicker of excitement shot up Catherine's groin.

Linda kissed her lightly on the lips. Her lips were warm, sweet. Delicious. They moved closer so that their whole bodies were touching, and clasped hands.

Catherine could feel Linda's body tremble against hers. She was flooded by a feeling of enormous tenderness. Gaining confidence she brushed Linda's neck with her lips.

'Your breathing has sped up,' whispered Linda.

'So has yours. I feel hot, as if I'm burning.'

'Hot to trot,' squealed Linda. 'I *knew* it. I don't know how, but I did. Join the club, girl.'

'What club?'

'The Girls' Club. No boys allowed.'

They kissed again. And again.

'I could kiss for hours.'

'Me too. Can I touch these?'

Boys, in Catherine's limited experience, never asked.

'You don't have to if you don't want to,' said Linda quickly.

Did she want to?

'Yes, all right.'

Linda unclasped Catherine's bikini top. Catherine scarcely dared to breathe.

Linda cupped Catherine's breasts in her hands.

Catherine felt the blood drain from her body.

'It's so personal,' she said in a shaky voice.

'It's so *exciting*.' Linda bent down and gently licked her friend's nipples.

'Oh my *God*.'

'I'm swooning,' moaned Linda.

Catherine's body tensed. 'You seem very experienced,' she accused.

'Not really. I learnt a lot from Mum's books. I know what to do *theoretically*.'

Catherine relaxed again. Being close with Linda felt like the most natural thing in the world. Surprisingly, her body seemed to know what to do without her having to think about it. She gained courage and daring with each new exploratory touch. Her pale thin body no longer felt as if it belonged solely to her. It had become a weightless thing, a separate being she didn't recognize. Is this me? she asked herself in disbelief. Me, feeling these strong, wonderful emotions, tingling, trembling, experiencing a shivery butterfly sensation? And not feeling ashamed?

'How long have you known?' asked Catherine. 'When did you first suspect?' The questions were a delight in themselves. Each wanted to hear the confirmation several times before being satisfied that it was all indeed true.

'You gave yourself away constantly,' smiled Linda.

'How? I thought I was alone.'

'You're not alone. I could see you weren't in the least bit interested in boys,' replied Linda. 'You were obviously faking it.' She stroked her friend's fingers one by one until Catherine thought she might pass out. She couldn't wipe the smile off her face. One of her legs was casually draped over Linda's. The sensation of touching the skin of another person was still new enough for her to be acutely aware of every subtle variation in contact and movement. She wriggled her leg a bit to see if Linda felt the same way. Linda immediately jiggled hers in response.

'It's wrong,' said Catherine, sitting up suddenly. 'We're committing a sin. My parents would kill me if they knew.'

'Who cares?' murmured Linda drowsily. She was almost asleep.

Catherine knew already what her father's views would be. She saw long hairy fingers pointing at her, crushing her opinions, driving them underground, screaming words like: 'Filthy, bad, disgusting. Wrong. Sick.' She would never tell him. It would be her secret. Theresa was the only other person she could confide in.

She was lucky. It was easier for her than for Theresa. Since her sister had shown an interest in Peter van der Vossen she had been guarded like the family jewels.

'Your father is jealous,' said Linda. 'That's my theory. He can't bear anyone else to have what he can't have himself.'

Catherine stared at her wide-eyed. 'Fathers can't love their daughters like that.'

'Mum said they can,' said Linda, and her hair swung over Catherine. She didn't have a father. It didn't affect her.

Theresa examined the condoms Peter's mother had given her. How long had she had them in her biscuit tin? They were probably full of holes — tiny pinpricks which invisible sperm could sneak through and race to meet the waiting egg.

She wondered if it were possible to go mad from frustration. Why did she both crave and at the same time despise the idea of allowing Peter van der Vossen to penetrate her?

'I don't know if I can hold out much longer,' she told Catherine. How long before he tired of their game and wanted more? And if she didn't give in he was sure to drop her.

'I don't want to do anything stupid,' she said. 'Imagine if I got preggers the first time I did it.'

'If you really love someone,' said Catherine, 'you can't control yourself.'

'And you'd know of course.'

'As a matter of fact I do.'

Theresa leaned closer. Their heads touched, eyes gleamed.

'What do you know that I don't?'

'I know about finger fucking.'

Theresa blinked.

'Linda taught me,' said Catherine.

'How does she know?'

'She just does. Her mother has books. Sexy books. When you look at the pictures it makes you want to do it.'

'Do it?'

'Yes. It makes you want to keep doing it until you think you're going to burst.'

'But you wanted to become a nun, a saint.'

Catherine laughed, her new high-pitched laugh. It was a sound that set Theresa's teeth on edge.

'Are you crazy?' replied Catherine. 'I don't believe in any of that rubbish.'

Theresa was aware of a shift in their relationship. She didn't like Catherine knowing more than her.

Her own virginity was like a millstone around her neck. Playing voyeurs with Peter van der Vossen somehow didn't compare to Catherine's new wealth of experience.

'Tell me what you do,' she insisted.

She wanted to know, but at the same time she also could hardly bear to listen.

Fingers, said Catherine. Tongues. Holding. Stroking. Rubbing. Biting. Licking. Sucking. And no fear of pregnancy.

Theresa felt a sharp pang of envy. She imagined Catherine and Linda's tongues thrashing and darting about like eels forging their way through a dark river. She pictured their fingers twining and untwining. It made her feel ill.

Her sister had been claimed. Now she belonged to Linda. They shared secrets. She was slipping away. Soon she would be lost to sight.

'I can't keep my hands off her,' said Catherine.

'You're too young. You don't know what you're getting yourself into.' Theresa heard a voice sounding like her mother, and she didn't care. She knew she was being unfair and couldn't stop herself. She felt reckless, half crazed by all the talking and thinking about sex and love and doing it with tongues and fingers. She knew her words pierced Catherine, who had opened herself up expecting a willing and supportive listener. Sensing her sister's withdrawal, Theresa gathered herself to attack.

'It won't last,' she coolly predicted. She wanted to make Catherine suffer, knowing that the following day she would be full of remorse and would do everything to make up for it. Catherine always forgave her.

'It *will* last,' insisted Catherine. How could it not work out? True love didn't fail. 'It's such *fun!*'

'Fun?' Theresa frowned. How could sex possibly be fun? It was fraught with dangers and difficulties. Everybody knew that. Catherine was sick. Really sick.

'You're not normal,' she hissed. And burst into tears.

'Lose your virginity,' advised Catherine. 'Get it over with. There's something else,' she added. 'I guess I should tell you. I've got to tell someone.'

'What?'

'I had my first orgasm,' confessed Catherine shyly.

'What was it like?'

'It's like a wave,' said Catherine in a dreamy voice. 'A wave that ripples through your entire body.'

Theresa longed to shake her sister until her teeth rattled.

Chapter Twenty-One

THE ANGER OF THE LAMB

'WHAT KIND OF DAUGHTERS ARE YOU?' His voice rose.

'Your daughters,' they replied, trembling before him.

'Act like daughters then.'

How did a daughter behave?

'PURE IN THOUGHT, MIND AND BODY,' he roared. 'PURITY. MODESTY. DECENCY. DON'T THESE WORDS MEAN ANYTHING TO YOU? HAVE I BEEN TALKING TO MYSELF ALL THESE YEARS?'

He banged his head against the wall. 'HAS NONE OF IT SUNK INTO THOSE STUPID HEADS OF YOURS?'

He banged his head again. A cut formed above his eye. He ignored it.

They were shocked, but they knew better than to reply.

'"This is the way of an adultress: she eats, and wipes her mouth, and says, 'I have done no wrong.'" Proverbs,' said Mr Flynn, staring at Theresa. '"How shall I again look upon thy holy temple?"'

The younger children hovered in the background, wondering what terrible crime their sisters could have committed to have provoked such a temper.

Tim clenched and unclenched his fists. He was fifteen now, almost big enough to take his father on if it came to it.

Beside him Theresa hung her head. How had her father found out? She didn't expect anyone to protect her, not now that Francie had withdrawn into herself. A timid voice began to speak, quiet and low at first and then firm as it gained confidence.

'"Love takes no pleasure in other people's sins but delights in the truth, it is always ready to excuse, to trust,"' said Catherine steadily.

She was no match for her father.

'"If your hand or your foot should be your downfall, cut it *off*,"' he retaliated.

Catherine swallowed hard. She couldn't think of a reply to this. Did he truly believe their hands should be chopped off as a punishment for what they had done?

He was hollow-faced and red-eyed. He waved a small black notebook in front of them.

'My diary,' whispered Theresa. 'Where did you find it? Give it back to me. It's mine. It's private.'

'Not any more,' said her father. '*Not any more.* We now know what vile filth goes on inside that head of yours, madam. We tried so hard, your mother and I, and what good did it do? I'm ashamed of you.' He made a spitting sound of disgust.

'And as for you, my girl,' he said, swinging around to face a bewildered Catherine. 'Words fail me, hell's teeth. Sluts! Get out of my sight. I don't want to know you.' He shook his head and clicked his teeth against his tongue. 'I think you should go straightaway to the presbytery. The priests will soon sort you out, quick and lively. My word, they will.'

Theresa tried to remember what she might have written about Peter and Catherine and Linda. All her thoughts, feelings, fears, doubts. Every significant recent conversation was in there, followed by a detailed analysis.

'No,' she bleated. 'I won't go to a priest.'

'Pardon?' Mr Flynn couldn't believe his ears. 'Say that again. I'm warning you, girl. You're sailing close to the wind. I'm in no mood to be crossed.'

'No,' repeated Theresa in a firmer voice.

Her father lunged forward as if to cuff her over the ears.

Tim blocked his path. His lips were pursed tight, his hands shaking. Theresa reached out, clasped one and squeezed it. 'Don't,' she whispered. He dropped his hands and rolled his eyes at her.

Francie began to cry silently, tears rolling down her face. Catherine held her.

And where, they all wondered, was their mother? Moping in her bedroom? Crying at the clothes-line?

Their father picked up his Bible. He ordered them to sit around him in the lounge while he read from Revelations. They seethed but were too afraid of his mood to refuse.

'"*Hide us away from the One who sits on the throne and from the anger of the Lamb. For the Great Day of his anger has come, and who can survive it?*"'

The anger of the Lamb. Seven lamps burning – the seven Spirits of God. There were creatures with six wings who had eyes all the way round as well as inside, and day and night they never stopped singing: 'Holy, holy, holy'.

And an eagle cried in a loud voice as it flew, 'Woe, woe, woe'. As he read the verses the smaller children became even more afraid and anxious, crushed by the weight of words. Theresa and Catherine had been so wicked that their father couldn't use ordinary words to describe it.

Theresa and Catherine were confused, angry and ashamed. Their father was reading from the Bible so it must be true. Their confusion increased because they didn't *feel* wicked. They didn't believe they deserved to be punished by either God or their father. The two became fused in their minds into one person. God and their father constituted one point of view, but what if there were others equally valid?

'"You whom my soul loves,"' he murmured, gazing intently at Catherine. She flushed. She didn't feel loved. On the contrary, she felt reviled and rejected. Perhaps her father wasn't referring to her. He seemed to love God more than any of them. It must be God his soul craved.

Francie's tears dried. If she screwed up her eyes, her father became the size of a pinprick, a mere speck. As he read on, she realized she couldn't feel anything any more, neither pain nor sadness. Nothing.

'". . . and the beast will turn against the prostitute and strip off her clothes and leave her naked; then they will eat her flesh and burn her remains in the fire,"' finished their father. He slowly looked around at each of them in turn.

Theresa and Catherine fell into an abyss. They could not think how to find their way out.

'Who will save us?' whispered Catherine.

'No-one,' said Theresa. 'We have to save ourselves.'

'It's all right for you,' said Catherine. 'You're leaving soon, but what about me? I have to continue living here.'

'You could go to Wellington and live with Nana,' suggested Theresa. 'Finish off your last year at college there.'

'And leave Linda behind? She's the only friend I have once you've gone.'

'You might have to choose,' said Theresa.

'I can't.'

Mr Flynn barged into their room as they were packing.

'Don't think you're leaving this house,' he bellowed. 'You're to stay here in your room until I call for you.'

'And when might that be?' Theresa asked, arms folded to hide her shaking hands.

'When I say so.' He turned on his heel and left them pulling faces behind his back.

'Quickly,' said Theresa. 'Get everything together, Cath. We're getting out now. We'll go together.'

They packed up their school things and stuffed

them into a bulging satchel. 'Francie can smuggle the rest of it out in stages,' said Theresa. She crammed underwear, pantihose, socks, shirts, gym frock, cardigan and books into a duffle bag.

When they had finished they quietly opened their bedroom window. Catherine climbed out first and Theresa passed their things down to her.

Francie silently entered the room just as Theresa was lifting her leg over the window-sill.

'Come here, Francie,' said Theresa and she gave her a hug and a kiss. 'Go to the church tomorrow at lunchtime,' she said. 'It'll be empty and we'll meet you there. Bring some of our things.'

Francie nodded solemnly.

'I'll distract him,' she said. 'I'll do one of my faints.'

'Good girl.'

Theresa turned back for a last look. Francie's lower lip wobbled.

'I love you Francie.'

'I love you too.'

Their father stood at the gate. He raised his arm and pointed his finger at them. Their hearts fluttered wildly. Wherever they went, there he would be – in front of them, behind them, around them, inside their heads. He would be reading their thoughts and knowing more than they did – just like God.

'If you step foot outside this property,' he barked, 'you can stay out. Don't come crying back to me. Get out and stay out! GOOD RIDDANCE! You're a couple of tramps – the pair of you.'

'Oh Terrence,' cried their mother running out, alerted by Francie. She put a restraining hand on his shoulder. He flung it away. He didn't see it.

Her depression lifted instantly. Now she was fully awake. Now she knew what she must do.

The whole street could hear. He didn't care. Rage and disappointment churned inside his chest. He knew

230

he was being reckless, but he couldn't stop himself. He knew he was backing himself into a corner. He had to continue, firing words as wounding as arrows into the stunned faces of his daughters. Did he love them? He couldn't remember. He felt betrayed.

'You're destroying the family,' he shouted. 'Destroying it.'

'It's you who are destroying it,' snapped his wife. 'You'll regret this. It's not too late. Stop this insanity. Bring them back.' Her voice was bleak. He was incapable of stopping when his blood was up. Didn't he realize he was driving them away?

'Terrence,' she warned. He didn't acknowledge her. He was lost.

'YOU BASTARD!' yelled Tim. He punched his father in the arm. Terrence slowly swung around, disbelief in his eyes.

'You hit me?'

'I'll hit you again, too,' threatened Tim.

The girls were already halfway down the street, stumbling and weaving crazily from one side of the footpath to the other, bags slapping against their hips.

Moira hesitated briefly. All her instincts pulled at her to follow them, to take a stand against Terrence. 'No, Tim,' she said sadly. 'It's not the way.'

She came to an abrupt decision, ran back into the house and snatched up the car keys. Francie went to follow her.

'No,' said Moira. 'It would be better if you stayed here.'

'I'm coming.'

Her mother nodded. 'All right then, go and tell Tim he's in charge until I return.'

Francie called to Tim. She pulled him away from her father who was slumped over the fence. She and her mother ran to the car before Mr Flynn could stop them. They locked all the car doors and began to reverse down the driveway.

231

Mr Flynn staggered up and blocked their way. His face was tight and pale, but his eyes remained dry.

Moira jerked on the handbrake. 'Come on,' she said to Francie. 'Get out of the car quickly and follow me.'

'OK,' said Francie, breathing rapidly. At that moment she would have followed her mother to the ends of the earth. They rushed past Mr Flynn and began to run down the road.

'He'll follow us,' puffed Francie, jogging alongside. Her mother seemed to have developed superhuman strength and was pounding along the pavement like a professional runner. Her face was red and perspiration was dripping down her chin.

'I've got the keys,' panted Moira. 'He's stuck there.'

She asked Francie where her sisters were headed for.

Francie thought for a minute. 'Linda's.'

'Do you know how to get there?'

'I think so.'

They kept running.

'You're a fantastic mother,' said Francie.

'I'm not,' croaked Moira. 'It's only adrenalin. I'll collapse later when I've done what I have to do.'

They rounded the corner and saw the girls in the distance. Catherine turned and saw them. She nudged Theresa, who also turned. They stopped and waited for their mother and Francie to catch up.

They cried intermittently all the way to Linda's.

'Coffee?' asked Linda's mother of the four tearful bedraggled faces in front of her.

'Yes,' they blubbed.

She tactfully took their bags from them and ushered Moira into a chair. The youngest girl was like a sleep-walker. Tiny little thing – obviously in shock. She held her mother's hand and wouldn't let go of it. No-one was able to speak for a few minutes. Linda had also started to cry in sympathy.

Linda's mother took a reviving nip of brandy in the kitchen. She decided it might be a good idea if they all had one, even the small girl, who she had been startled to discover was actually thirteen. She looked about ten.

'Now,' she said. 'Which one of you wants to go first?'

'I will,' said Theresa, taking a deep breath. 'Dad found my diary, and went completely berserk, and now he's kicked both of us out.'

Linda's mother looked to Moira for confirmation.

She nodded. 'Terrence never changes his mind, never goes back on his word.'

'He sounds like a hard man,' said Linda's mother.

She handed around a box of tissues and they helped themselves, sniffing and blowing their noses.

'I'm sorry we've all landed on you like this,' apologized Moira.

'I'm happy to help,' said Linda's mother and she looked as if she meant it. 'Call me Janice,' she added.

'Could Catherine and Theresa stay here for a few days while we sort things out at home?' asked Moira.

'Of course.'

Theresa didn't stay long. Her mother worked on her husband to pave the way for their eldest daughter to come home. 'Please Terrence,' she begged. 'The girl leaves home in three months. If you don't make up with her now, you'll lose her. We mightn't see her again.'

'All right then,' he agreed grudgingly. 'On condition she doesn't see that van der Vossen boy again. And no socializing until after the exams.'

'OK, Dad.' Theresa was too exhausted to argue. She had to live somewhere. Besides, her bursary exams were only a month away.

Janice said Catherine could spend her last year at

school living with her and Linda. They had a tiny spare bedroom. Smoking Nana promised Linda's mother she would send money for her granddaughter's board whenever she could. Linda's mother had said it didn't matter, but Catherine felt happier knowing she wasn't totally dependent on Janice's generosity. One day she would repay her grandmother and Janice.

Recently her mother had surprised her by quietly supporting Catherine living at Linda's if it was what she really wanted.

'I think they should be encouraged to go on to university. They're bright enough. They'll both get bursaries,' said Moira.

'Why should I support those two trollops? No, I think the pair of them should be out looking for jobs now,' said Mr Flynn.

'Over my dead body. I want them to have the opportunities we didn't have.'

Catherine missed her family.

'You can always come back,' said her mother wistfully. 'There'll always be a bed for you. And you can visit whenever you want.'

Catherine knew it wouldn't be the same. She felt a huge anger towards her father. If it hadn't been for him, she wouldn't have left. Her mother's love still tugged at her.

She made sure she visited before her father arrived home from work. She went often, but she was always relieved to be able to return to Linda's.

'Don't worry about the dishes,' said Janice. 'When there are none left in the cupboards we'll have a big wash-up.'

They were casual about housework too. 'We've got better things to do,' said Linda.

'I don't care if I live in squalor,' said Janice.

'Neither do I then,' said Linda, hands on hips.

234

How slovenly, thought Catherine. She found herself doing more than her fair share of the washing-up simply because staring at a bench full of dishes bothered her more than it did the others. The green Formica around the edges of the bench top was cracked and peeling around the edges, but Janice rarely stirred herself to repair anything. She preferred to put her feet up and read. She read for several hours every night, working her way through a carton of books each week.

And when Janice wasn't reading or at the library she wrote. Catherine would find her staring into space, a cigarette in one hand and a coffee mug at her elbow, thinking out the next paragraph. What she wrote was generally illegible to anyone but herself until she began to type her final draft on an ancient typewriter. At this stage the girls would beg to be allowed to read it.

'No,' said Janice, waving them away with her cigarette. 'Wait till I've finished, then you can read and criticize.'

'Aren't you ever tempted to sneak a look when she's out?' whispered Catherine.

'Certainly not. It wouldn't be ethical.'

She and Janice used this word often.

Catherine thought how much more quickly their tasks might have been executed if only they hadn't spent so much time squabbling over who would do them and how they would go about it.

Catherine was exhausted by the sheer volume of words. The only time they closed their mouths was when they read. And even then they were constantly reading choice bits aloud to each other. They seemed to think nothing of talking with their mouths full.

'If the ideas are flowing why waste time by stopping to finish a mouthful?' said Janice.

Catherine was repelled by the bits of food she could see bobbing about inside their mouths as they talked.

They shared the cooking and cleaning with scrupulous fairness. 'You can pitch in too,' said Janice.

'*Justify it!*' Janice would crow gleefully, pouncing on either of the girls if they got their facts wrong, or dared to pass a glib remark on a subject where she felt they should have known better. Or worse if they were guilty of what she termed 'woolly thinking'.

Catherine exploded one night over dinner after listening to the pair debate for fifteen minutes whose turn it was to cook.

'For God's sake!' she yelled. '*Listen* to yourselves.'

They swung around to stare at her.

'Why do we have to go through this every night? It's simple. You're the mother,' she said, pointing to Janice. 'Why don't you just *tell* her? Why must you discuss everything? It's so exhausting. It always takes so long. You *waste* so much time.'

Janice laughed. 'That's democracy for you. What group consensus is all about. Linda is seventeen. I can't impose my will on her over every little thing.'

'You don't care what she does,' shouted Catherine. 'You let her get away with murder.'

Catherine went to her room and stewed. Why was she so angry? She now had the freedom she craved and yet she couldn't seem simply to accept it and be grateful. She was consumed with resentment and uncharitable thoughts.

She'd been on her best behaviour for the first few weeks, anxious not to be a burden on them. She rushed to help at every opportunity, eager to do more than her share so they didn't regret having her as a boarder. Unfortunately she hadn't been able to sustain her good intentions. The effort always to be nice had soon proved too difficult.

She was horrified at the person who emerged when

her guard was down, the unlovable creature who survived deep inside her.

Janice and Linda decided in the end to prepare the meal together.

Linda wished it was just her and her mother alone again. How much easier it would be if they didn't have someone else's moods to take into account.

'What's up with Catherine?' asked Linda, slicing a cucumber.

'She's homesick, only she doesn't realize it. She doesn't understand her emotions. I suspect she's never been allowed to experience them fully before. Here, there are no limits on her. No-one to tell her what to do and think, and she's not used to it. She's probably scared stiff right now that you and I won't accept the real Catherine and will throw her out any time she disagrees with us.'

'It isn't easy for me either, you know.'

'But what sort of friend would you be if you rejected someone who needs us so much and who is desperately trying to discover who she really is?'

Janice stopped washing lettuce leaves for a moment and placed one of her hands over Linda's.

'Linda. It's important for us to be gentle with her.'

'Yeah, I know. She's so brittle and fragile I feel she'll break if I'm not careful.'

'Exactly. She doesn't need any more harassment. If you dig deeply enough beneath that brittle exterior I'm sure you'll find a very angry young woman indeed. No wonder her feelings scare her.'

'I'm sorry,' said Catherine.

'Don't worry about it,' replied Janice. 'We can take it. You don't have to be nice all the time. Not even a saint could be.'

'I'm no saint,' said Catherine ruefully.

'Just as well. Saints would be awfully dull to live with twenty-four hours a day, don't you think?'

'I don't know. I haven't thought of that before. I've always tried to be a saint, only it didn't work out.'

'We live by different rules here.'

'It's confusing. I don't know what you want from me, how to please you.'

'No-one asked you to please me.'

'But if I don't, will you send me back home?'

'No. Not unless you want to go.'

Catherine frowned.

Janice cocked an eyebrow. 'Yes?'

'Why are you being nice to me even when I've been bad?'

'Because you can't live a life dedicated to the truth if you're not open to being challenged.'

'What is the truth?'

'That's what I want to discover. It's why Linda and I argue and discuss things all the time. You have to work it out for yourself. Everyone does.'

'Catholics know the truth already. They're the one true Church.'

Janice smiled. 'They, or we?' she asked shrewdly.

'I'm not sure. I don't know what I think any more. Dad said I would rot in hell because of what Linda and I did. Do you believe him?'

'Definitely not. I don't believe in hell and damnation.'

'You're not angry with me?'

'No. The relationship with Linda has been good for both of you.'

Catherine's relationship with Linda had altered since she had moved in. Now Linda seemed more like a sister than a lover. Catherine hadn't expected this. Why couldn't feelings stay the same? Why had her desire for Linda burst forth and then disappeared? She still loved her and wanted to be her friend, but that was all. All those delicious and unexpected responses in her body had vanished. Now when she committed the forbidden act and touched Jean she felt nothing, not even a flicker. It was becoming harder to remember those sensations. Perhaps she would never feel like that again.

Chapter Twenty-Two

FLESH AND BLOOD

Catherine thought she was coping well with the huge changes in her life, but as the weeks went by Janice and Linda became concerned for her.

'What is it?' Janice asked Catherine.

'I've been thinking about my father,' she replied.

'And does thinking about him make you sad?'

'My father is devout,' said Catherine. She chose her words with care. She wanted to get it straight in her head.

'Devout?' enquired Janice.

Catherine felt her throat constrict. How could she explain so that it made sense to a non-Catholic? She repeated the word over and over again in her head – *devout, devout, devout* – as if she could make it justify his actions, discover the driving force behind his behaviour.

But no matter how hard she tried she could not explain or rationalize her father's behaviour. He remained a mystery to her. There was no longer any choice but to create a life in defiance of him. A life of order and symmetry, one in which beauty and truth mattered. Her father believed he was a good person, a just man, but he behaved as if he were sole custodian of the truth. She knew there had to be other versions. There was Smoking Nana's version of the meaning of life. Janice and Linda had presented her with another. She had to find her own. If it took her whole life she would do it.

'He can stick his devotion to God up his jumper,' she told Janice.

Janice laughed.
'With bells on.'

Moira Flynn didn't offer to help Theresa pack. She sat on the bed and watched, peering at everything that went in. Soon she leaned over, unable to resist any longer. Theresa could smell her perspiration. She smelled something else too – pain and fear. Her poor mother.

An address book was tossed into the bag, followed by an old black beaded cardigan.

'You can't take that.'

'Why not?'

'It's mine,' said her mother and snatched it back from the bag. 'What else have you got in there? Go on, show me, I want to know.'

'It's mine, all mine,' shouted Theresa, flinging her body protectively over the bag. 'The cardigan's too small for you. What's the point of keeping it buried in a drawer where no-one ever gets to see it? You said it'd be mine one day.'

'Let me see.'

'It's none of your business.'

Without pausing to think, her mother tipped the bag upside down so that its contents spilled out over the bed.

Mrs Flynn grabbed a crimson purse and unzipped it with a flourish. The rubber diaphragm fell out of its plastic container and rolled down onto the carpet. She bent down and picked it up, flexing it between her thumb and forefinger.

'What's this?'

Theresa groaned. Her mother flopped back on the bed as if she had been struck. Theresa felt like a criminal.

'The family is breaking up,' cried her mother.

'*Mum,*' said Theresa. There was a little flip of panic as reality hit her. She began to cry too.

241

Gently she took the diaphragm off her mother. 'You'd rather I didn't get pregnant, wouldn't you?'

Mrs Flynn decided she would prefer not to know how Theresa came to be fitted with a diaphragm.

'I can't do anything right,' she cried. 'I've done everything wrong. I'm a failure as a mother.'

'Don't be silly, you know you're not.'

Mr Flynn always laughed dismissively when Theresa mentioned her plans for the future. 'Being a mother is a full-time career,' he said. 'There's nothing more important than bringing up the next generation of young Catholics. You won't have time to go out to work once you're a mother. My word, no. Not if you do the job properly.' He tweaked her on the cheek. Theresa pulled away scowling.

'In a year or two you'll find your cock-eyed notions have changed,' he predicted. 'You'll be happy to settle down with some nice young fellow and be a mother. I just hope you're as happy together as your mother and I are. Nature and biology have made a woman ideally suited to look after babies. A man's job in life is to be the provider and that's all there is to it. God made it that way for a reason.'

'I don't believe you,' shouted Theresa. She stormed out of the room, banging the door behind her.

Mr Flynn opened it again. 'Temper, temper,' he rebuked. 'I expect you to show a good example to your brothers and sisters, not behave like a spoiled brat just because life isn't set up expressly for your convenience.'

Tension grew between Theresa and her mother.

'I can't do anything right,' yelled Theresa.

'Stop questioning me,' retorted her mother. 'I don't have to justify everything.'

'Neither do I.' Her mother's thoughts were as clear as if they were her own. Why wasn't her eldest daughter beautiful, good and quiet instead of angry, clever and difficult?

Theresa's questions were inevitably returned either without an answer or with one she considered inadequate. Her mother, for her part, delivered volleys of frustrated complaints. The arguments usually ended with Theresa stalking off in frustration.

She decided one day to spell it out to her mother. 'I may as well be dead,' she said, 'if I don't find answers. Otherwise, there's no *point* to anything. Can't you *see*?'

Moira didn't see.

Theresa wished her mother knew more. Perhaps I'm not asking the right questions, she thought.

'Don't you want to be happy? Why do you always put yourself down and deny what you really think?'

'When you have eight children you don't have a choice.'

'That's not true, it's never too late to change and go after what you want.'

'Happiness and responsibilities – they don't go together. One day when you become a mother yourself you'll know what I mean. You'll understand what it's like to make sacrifices for your children.'

'I don't want to be a mother. Why do I have to make sacrifices? Does it make me a better person? I want to have choices, but you'd never understand that.'

Theresa made an effort to see things from her mother's point of view, but she failed constantly.

'Will you for once in your life tell me the truth!' she begged. 'Tell me what you actually *think* about your life. Is it so difficult to admit what you feel? SAY IT! For once, stop telling me lies and fairy-tales.'

Mrs Flynn took a deep breath. 'All right,' she said, 'I'll tell you. I love you all. But I *hate* being a mother. I have too many children. They always want something. And it'll be another twelve years at least before the last one of you has gone. Nothing ever gets finished.

I'm interrupted by someone every time I go to do anything. I spend every day doing tasks that I don't want to do, pretending to be happy. I'm not. The monotony is crippling. It often outweighs the pleasure of seeing you grow up. The anxiety sometimes leaves me utterly defeated. I'm constantly tired. After almost twenty years I still resent asking Terrence for every cent I spend. It's my money too, but he thinks of it as his. I spend nothing on myself. I make all my own clothes. I've only bought one new dress since I got married. *There.* Satisfied?'

Theresa hugged her. 'It's not what I want,' she said. 'Can't you accept it?'

Theresa pined for Catherine's company. She had suggested that Francie share a room with her, but her mother wanted to leave Catherine's bed undisturbed in case she should change her mind and come home.

'Unlikely,' said Theresa.

'You never know,' said her mother. She still yearned for her daughter's return, more than ever now that Theresa was almost gone.

'Why do you and Catherine both hate us so much?' her mother asked whenever Theresa rejoiced at leaving.

'I don't hate either of you,' she said and realized it was true. She didn't hate her father after all. Sometimes she loved him very much. And to her surprise, her father appeared sorry she was leaving.

'He loves you, don't you realize?' said her mother.

'I don't believe you. Why doesn't he show it?'

'He doesn't know how.'

What a tragedy for him, thought Theresa. He and his fearsome God would just have to get on without her.

Everybody cried at the station. Even her father wiped away a few tears. His mouth worked. He tried to speak and failed. He stood very close to her mother, his profile deliberately averted. She couldn't look.

244

'Write every week,' pleaded her mother.

'Of course.' Now she was crying too.

'You never know,' smiled her mother. 'Perhaps you might see all of us in Auckland one day.'

Theresa experienced a momentary flip of panic. How could she possibly escape her family if they followed her to the city?

'I'll believe it when I see it,' she replied.

The previous day, defying her father's edict that she not see Peter ever again, she had crept out to meet him at the river. They had greeted each other awkwardly. He seemed thinner than she remembered. She had heard from Mary Louise that he had replaced her with another girl-friend almost immediately. She was glad now that she was still a virgin. She couldn't believe that he had ever truly cared about her. It had been curiosity on both their parts. A childish relationship. Scarcely a relationship at all – an embarrassing encounter. Already she felt more mature than Peter, ready finally to shake him off and move on. Fortunately she wouldn't have to fear bumping into him in Auckland. He would be doing law down at Victoria.

Still, she didn't regret saying goodbye to him. It completed the circle somehow. Her father had done her a favour, after all.

She was impatient now to be away and free of her family. Love, compassion, grief, frustration – one emotion was swiftly followed by another. Her gut churned.

Catherine stared at her sister with an expression of such misery that Theresa was forced to turn away. Why didn't the train come?

'Don't forget your prayers,' urged her father. 'Remember the Good Lord, won't you. He never forgets you.'

Theresa quickly looked around to see if any of the other passengers had overheard. They were staring with indulgent smiles. She bit her lip.

Francie clung to her wrist. John, Andrew, Bub and Toots all sniffed miserably. They had made goodbye cards for her. She couldn't bear to look too closely at their gifts yet. Later. Tonight she would be sleeping in a strange bed, sharing a room with a complete stranger. She was overwhelmed.

Tim had a very stern look on his face in a pitiful attempt at self-control.

Oh God, thought Theresa, I hope he doesn't turn out like Dad. She ran over and gave him a hug. It was his dissolving face she carried with her as she turned to board the train.

Chapter Twenty-Three

NAKED NOVENAS

AUCKLAND 1973

Rose wore an ankle-length skirt made from an old floral curtain and a quilted satin bed jacket over a lace blouse. Both upper garments had been dyed a streaky black. The blouse appeared to be the top of a night-gown. Her lips and long nails were painted a violent purplish-red. She wore Chinese embroidered slippers.

She had high cheekbones framed by a tangled mop of orange hennaed hair. Theresa had been introduced to her new room mate by the hostel matron. Rose had already unpacked and settled in.

Theresa felt at a disadvantage. Rose seemed to have taken over most of the room already.

'A slattern of a woman,' commented Rose, as the matron departed in a miasma of cheap perfume. 'She has a tremendous drinking problem, as you'll discover.'

'Likewise, so do you,' Theresa was tempted to say, casting a critical eye at the bottles protruding from beneath Rose's bed.

'Care for a gin?' invited Rose, pulling out one of the larger bottles.

'Why not,' said Theresa. She had never drunk gin in her life.

She had already decided to throw away or alter most of the contents of her suitcase and start afresh. She would dye everything black.

'There are loads of fabulous junk shops near here,' enthused Rose. 'I'll show you where they are tomorrow if you like.' She described shops near the hostel, where there were many bargains in thirties and forties-style dresses, coats, hats and nighties to be found.

'Got anything to sell?' asked Rose shrewdly.

'A little.' Only her entire wardrobe.

Lou Reed was on the turntable turned up loud. They shouted to be heard above it. After Theresa had been with Rose for a week, she could see this was the norm.

'Loud music revs up the atmosphere. And Lou is *so* sexy. He has the most fuckable voice, don't you think?' said Rose.

'No,' replied Theresa. 'I think he's depressing. I prefer Joni Mitchell.'

Untidy piles of books and magazines were scattered about the floor. Among the debris Theresa spied a D. H. Lawrence and someone called Sartre.

Rose's bed was draped in black velvet and strewn with canary-yellow cushions. *The Glass Bead Game* was flattened out with a cracked spine on the pillow. Her wall was plastered with brown paper and decorated with travel posters. There was a new woven straw mat on the wooden floor. A Buddha sat enthroned on top of the dressing-table. In front of it Rose had arranged a shallow bowl of flowers.

Theresa was impressed. At home they hadn't been allowed to put pictures up on the walls. Pictures would leave pin marks. They would ruin the wallpaper.

'Are we allowed to put up whatever we want?' she asked.

Rose stared at her. 'Who's to stop us?' she asked. 'The bloody matron wouldn't care. As I told you, she's usually pissed. Do you like the décor?' She gestured towards the bed.

'It's not bad,' conceded Theresa.

'This space is my homage to Katherine Mansfield,' explained Rose. 'I've copied the details from her flat at Clovelly Mansions – you know, on the fringes of Bloomsbury. Of course it's not quite the same. I don't have a piano yet. There's not enough space. I want to forget that boring old New Zealand is outside the window. I imagine that I'm in London instead. Believe me, it does help.'

She yawned and lit up a Gauloise.

Theresa chose not to comment. Rose's remarks only added to her appeal.

She must write and tell Catherine. No, maybe she wouldn't. She would lead a secret thrilling life. Anything seemed possible now.

She noticed an old typewriter on the floor half buried under the piles of books. A little wicker basket overflowed with crumpled pieces of paper beside it.

'Are you going to be a writer?' asked Theresa.

Rose lowered her gaze modestly. 'I'm halfway through a novel.'

'What's it about?'

'A girl who gets fed up with New Zealand and goes off to London. She becomes a famous writer who has masses of lovers and ends up dying young in tragic circumstances.'

'It sounds fascinating,' said Theresa. 'You mean, sort of like Katherine Mansfield?'

'Not at all,' snapped Rose. 'It's completely different.'

'Have you ever been to London?' asked Theresa, sitting down on the bed.

'No.'

'Have you?'

'No.'

They both stared down at the pattern in the mat.

'How will you write the bits about London then?' asked Theresa.

Rose stood up abruptly.

'I can see you're a pragmatist,' she said in a chilly voice.

Rebuffed, Theresa quietly set about unpacking.

She hid her clothes at the back of the shared wardrobe. Rose's clothes took up so much room there wasn't a lot of space left for her things.

'Are you on the pill?' asked Rose.

'Not yet.'

'It's best to go on it straightaway. You never know, do you?'

Rose had probably had several lovers already.

'I've had a few,' admitted Rose. 'They weren't up to much. I'm still waiting for the grand passion. I've decided I can't be bothered with students. Now I'm looking for an older man. With a car, of course. Someone who can teach me things.'

Theresa bowed her head. She folded her sensible underwear in silence. What did she have to offer Rose in return?

Rose slipped into another stunning ensemble. Almost immediately she changed her mind. She stripped to her underwear again – a strapless bra, the merest wisp of black lace with an underwire. It was cunningly constructed to support her breasts and thrust them out into twin-peaked offerings. Her underpants were completely transparent.

Very sexy, thought Theresa. How did Rose afford it?

'It's a half-cup bra,' said Rose, acknowledging Theresa's admiring glance.

Theresa could hear her mother's voice in her ear. 'That girl has no shame.'

She added a half-cup bra to her mental list of things to acquire. She was to learn that Rose changed clothes several times every day.

Rose continued to preen. Theresa pretended not to look.

Rosary beads tumbled out of a pair of pale pink knickers and fell down onto the mat. Her mother must have optimistically stuffed them into the suitcase at the last minute.

Damn her mother. Face burning, Theresa snatched up the evidence. She wasn't quick enough. Rose's sharp eyes spotted the beads.

She looked up from where she was sitting on the black bed. She now wore a black silk kimono embroidered with gold and red dragons. She had removed the old polish and was painting her finger and toenails black.

She laughed. 'Well, excuse *me*, what have we here? The Chatterton madonna?'

Theresa shrank.

'A Mickey,' said Rose. 'I *should* have guessed. Are we going to have statues all over the place? Rosaries, penance and naked novenas? That would be a laugh.'

She came over and picked up the beads. 'Hey,' she said. 'These are cool. Can I borrow them?' Theresa nodded.

Rose added them to the strings of brightly coloured beads already slung around her neck and looked at herself admiringly in the mirror.

'Not bad,' she said. 'I might start a new trend.'

It was a lesson for Theresa. You could take things out of their usual context and appropriate them for a different use. It robbed them of their power and mystery. She studied Rose's Buddha with new eyes. It was someone else's god. What did Rose know about Buddhas? Probably as little as she did.

Several weeks later Theresa found herself alone on a Saturday night. Where were the exciting opportunities she had looked forward to, she grumbled to herself. Instead of getting on with her life she seemed to be paralysed. She couldn't understand it. Her studies were progressing well. She had even managed to gain a part-time job as a dish-washer at one of the big hotels for two nights a week. Along with her meagre bursary it was sufficient to seal her financial independence. She was beginning to make new friends. Male students looked at her, appraising her, although she felt uncomfortable under their gaze. She longed to return their looks, to be able to pick them up

251

and discard them with casual ease. The way Rose did.

She was far too serious, she told herself. Why did everything *matter* so much?

'Be yourself,' Smoking Nana had told her.

Which self? Bee-like creatures buzzed around inside her head – you can, you can't, you can. *Can–can't–can–can't.*

Twin ravens perched on each shoulder. Terrence and Moira. *Be careful, girl.*

She had never been alone before. She felt as if her insides had been sucked out and all that remained was hollow and fragile.

Rose was out with an older man with the requisite car. Her other friends were busy. It wasn't a waitressing night. A pending essay could wait. She wasn't in the mood for reading. She was broke.

She picked up Rose's Buddha and turned it over carefully in her hands. The statue felt cold and smooth. How had Rose come by such an object?

She studied one of Rose's travel posters. Egypt fascinated her. Perhaps she would get there one day with Rose, or perhaps not. She sensed already that Rose and her charm could not be relied upon. If a better offer came along Rose would be off without a backward glance.

Theresa returned to her side of the room. The monsignor's Bernini print dominated the wall above her bed. Her namesake had her head flung back, eyes closed, lips parted. The sculpted drapes were so lifelike they seemed almost to quiver. The completeness of the saint's surrender was nicely counterbalanced against the angel's readiness to plunge his arrow into her. The image expressed both longing and ecstasy. A private moment had been frozen for ever. Theresa wondered if she would ever lose control and abandon herself with a man to the same extent. Bernini's Teresa was the only image of sainthood she had ever been presented with that conveyed the possibility of sexual pleasure. Above the saint, with his arrow poised, the angel smiled with an expression of ineffable tenderness.

She remembered reading the nun's account of her meeting with the angel.

'In his hands I saw a long golden spear and at the end of the iron tip I seemed to see a point of fire. With this he seemed to pierce my heart several times so that it penetrated my entrails.'

St Teresa had been afire with her great love. The pain of the golden spear withdrawing was so sharp that she moaned. She wrote that the sweetness caused by the intense pain was so extreme that she hoped never to lose it.

Another masochist in a long line of masochists? Who needed them?

Theresa recalled another picture of St Teresa. It was a painting by Juan de la Miseria. It showed a middle-aged nun against a simple dark background. The expression in her brown full-lidded eyes was serious and watchful. She looked calm and intelligent. Her breeding was evident in the long aquiline nose. The eyebrows were dark, thick and curved, the lips full and the face plump. Her hands were clasped piously in prayer. A Latin scroll formed an aureole about her head and in the top corner of the painting flew a white dove.

When Theresa and Catherine were young they had spent hours attempting to decipher the expression on the saint's face. Was this how she looked while she was experiencing one of her mystical visions and dialogues with God? She had referred to her inner life as a 'kind of sleep'. She saw things and yet felt as if she were dreaming them. Her life had been a model for the nuns, an example held up to the children. A woman who changed life in Spanish convents, who dared to challenge the bishops. Yet despite her achievements, St Teresa had been only too human. She felt unworthy.

She anguished and doubted her visions, wondering if they were real or imaginary. At other times she was convinced, feeling herself guided, taken out of herself and propelled into extraordinary actions.

Theresa remembered something else about the saint, something that had certainly haunted Catherine. It was an image of their heroine entering a convent refectory on all fours, carrying a heavy burden on her back and led by another nunlike animal.

Was this her model? How often had she seen her own mother crouched cleaning, bending down to serve others, or on her knees to pray?

Theresa continued to pace the room. Thoughts flowed so quickly that most were lost before she could pursue them further. She wanted to make a new beginning, to throw out the old rules. She was tired of feeling lost.

The saint's imagery of the golden fiery spear was a cry of thwarted sexuality. It was clear now.

Rose referred to St Teresa as 'The Orgasm Lady'.

'It's what women look like when they're having a good fuck,' she said. 'As you'll find out.'

Rose said 'fuck' all the time. Just like Catherine's friend Linda. Theresa tried to imagine what would have happened in Rose's household if her parents had attempted to scrub her mouth with soap and water whenever she swore.

'How utterly *preposterous*,' declared Rose. 'I wouldn't have stood for it for a moment. The problem for you, Theresa, is you were totally repressed. It's why you have such difficulty now deciding what you believe in. You want someone to take care of you and tell you what to do.'

Theresa scowled. 'It's not true.'

Rose raised her eyebrows. 'Really?'

Waves of panic began to surge in her chest. She fought them, pacing more quickly. She tried to read, but the words swam together. She switched on Rose's stereo.

Soon the reassuring warmth of Carole King's voice filled the room.

Old and elusive childhood fears slipped in and out of her awareness. She had nowhere to go, no place to be in other than this room, and she didn't properly belong here yet. It would be the first of a series of transitory living places for the next several years, until . . . Until what?

She wasn't prepared for the avalanche of emotion which now overtook her, reducing her to hard racking sobs. It's all up to me, she thought, everything. Whether she smoked or drank. Gained weight or lost it. Completed her degree or dropped out. Fell pregnant or continued her studies. Continued to reach out and make friends or remained isolated.

She didn't want the burden of making all these choices and decisions on her own. She was too afraid of making a mistake on the way, of failing. Falling.

Do it anyway, said her inner voice.

'No! You don't know what's around the corner,' shrieked the ravens perched on her shoulders.

'Save me,' she cried to the walls crowded with images of faraway places, but silence, deafening silence, was her only response. Life went on whether she joined in or not. Her neighbour Harry was probably dropping acid, and too disorientated to talk. Rose would be fucking her older man somewhere. Her other friend Margaret was waitressing. Back home they would have finished reciting the Rosary long ago. Her parents would be asleep in front of the television. Catherine would be reading in bed in her room at Linda's, counting the months until she could come and join her.

Francie was in her old room now. Catherine's bed was still made up in readiness for her. Theresa's things were stored in a carton at the top of the wardrobe.

There was no going back, even if she wanted to. She was desperate for a morsel of comfort. She wanted someone to hold her and tell her everything was going to be all right.

She sniffed. There was no-one to do it for her. How did you go about reassuring yourself? How did you pretend you were big and strong so that eventually it became true and you didn't have to fake it any more?

'Breathe,' a little voice inside her instructed. 'Breathe.'

Can't. I've forgotten how to.

No, you haven't.

Can. Can't. Can. Can't.

Be careful, girl.

She had forgotten how to breathe.

She could die.

Ridiculous.

Breathe. Breathe.

She breathed. Everything passes, she told herself.

Everything.

Not long afterwards she began to notice references to the woman she thought of as the Virgin, her White Lady. Posters, articles, leaflets. From then on she began to collect information on Mary Blessed, zealously gluing cuttings into a black scrapbook. One clear fact soon emerged as she stacked the articles up alongside each other — not everybody agreed with Mary Blessed's opinions on women's position in the Church, the home, the workplace, or with her opinions about the Pope, abortion, or contraception. An organized and effective opposition group had been set up by a group of Christian conservatives who were bombarding her office with a campaign of hate mail and creating havoc at her public speeches and debates.

'How appalling,' said Theresa, reading excerpts aloud to Rose.

'How *very* New Zealand,' sniffed Rose. 'Full of rednecks and religious bigots. Theresa, we simply have to get out of here the minute we graduate or we will go barking *mad.*'

Theresa decided she simply had to see Mary Blessed, but she didn't confide her plan to Rose. She could just imagine the reaction: 'You think she's *who*?'

Maybe she was already barking mad, worried Theresa, but she found herself looking up Mary Blessed's address in the phone book anyway, studying a map and then selecting one of the several black dresses now hanging in her revitalized wardrobe, and slinging her shoulder bag on. A slash of carmine lipstick, and she was ready.

Chapter Twenty-Four

DEEPEST DESIRE

Theresa sat in a bus riding down Grafton Road with its dilapidated student flats, across the bridge, along the seedy length of the massage parlours and strip joints of Karangahape Road, and finally into Ponsonby Road. She climbed off the bus and walked to a back street where the headquarters of Mary Blessed were located. She saw several Polynesian women with toddlers carrying woven straw bags bulging with shopping, and passed row upon row of turn-of-the-century weatherboard villas with tall sash windows, jammed up alongside each other in the narrow streets. Verandahs were framed with wooden latticework – a contrast to her former home in Chatterton with its mean porch and small high windows.

The house was a newly-painted white villa with a blue wooden picket fence. For the first time it occurred to her that the journey might have been wasted. Arriving unannounced like this, she would probably be turned away. Mary Blessed mightn't even be at home.

The garden inside the fence was well tended. A large rhododendron carpeted the footpath with crimson. There was a row of lavender bushes and a native pittosporum with tiny cream flowers. A cluster of climbing pink roses spilled over the wooden verandah rails. She paused briefly to admire them before walking shyly up the steps to the cobalt-blue front door and with her heart beating a tattoo in her chest, knocked on it. Come quickly, answer, or I'll lose my nerve, she addressed the gold star painted on its centre panel.

A sharp-featured face stared into hers. 'Yes?'

Theresa gripped her shoulder bag to her chest like a shield. 'I'd like to see Mary Blessed, please.'

Inside, the villa was larger than she had expected. Most of the bedrooms seemed to have been converted into offices. Everything was painted white. The windows were draped in swathes of white muslin. There were tall vases of flowers — long-stemmed white daisies, blue irises. Theresa heard the cry of a violin and the murmur of women's voices. Occasionally one of the women would raise her voice and afterwards there would be the sound of laughter. Piles of books and magazines lay on every surface.

'Apparently Mary has been expecting you,' said the woman as she led the way to Mary Blessed's room.

'Me?'

Mary Blessed was seated on a blue chintz couch wearing faded flared jeans, boots, and a figure-hugging white cotton tee-shirt. Theresa gave her a tentative smile. Mary's hair had been tied back into a glossy plaited rope. Close up she looked very different from the woman who had left Chatterton so many years previously. For the first time Theresa began to doubt the identity of the woman in front of her. How could this powerful public speaker, this brave, visionary woman, be the same flawless, passive Virgin of her childhood?

Theresa gingerly lowered herself down on the opposite couch and placed her battered leather bag alongside her.

She tried not to stare at the huge nude reclining on the wall above Mary Blessed, but in spite of herself her gaze kept returning to the dark bush of pubic hair which had been painted in the shape of a heart. She was intrigued by the picture but it didn't match her image of Mary Blessed. The limbs were exaggerated and distorted. The woman was long-armed like

259

a gorilla. Her foreshortened thighs were fat stumps. Her breasts drooped. The mouth was a smear. The nude also didn't appear to have the correct number of fingers and toes. It was almost as if they had been painted as an afterthought.

She squinted to decipher the hand-daubed words scrawled at the bottom. *Women . . . are . . . mad.*

A woman in a long tent-like dress entered carrying a gold lacquered tea tray. She put it down and asked them if they would like their tea poured.

It was served in blue porcelain cups. Theresa sipped at the tea and selected a slab of carrot cake with lemon icing for herself after offering the plate to Mary Blessed, who declined. She hadn't touched her tea either. Theresa finished her tea and, at the urging of Mary Blessed, helped herself to more cake, realizing she was starving.

Now that she was actually in the presence of Mary Blessed, Theresa forgot why she had come. What were the questions to which it had seemed so imperative she find answers?

She could hear a phone ringing every few minutes in another room. She pictured the messages piling up.

'How can I help you? Why have you come to see me?' asked Mary Blessed.

Tears filled Theresa's eyes and slowly dripped down her face and onto her neck where they soaked the top of her black dress. What did it matter? She sensed Mary Blessed could see inside her to the person she really was. There was no sense in pretending.

'I've been waiting for you,' said Mary Blessed.

'How did you know I was coming?'

Mary Blessed didn't answer.

Theresa's fists clenched and unclenched by her sides. 'I'm sorry for being such a mess,' she said, weeping uncontrollably. She struggled to resist the urge to crawl over the space between them and rest her head in Mary Blessed's lap. She longed for the comfort of childhood.

How had it come to this? A quiet white room. A stranger with a dark rope of hair down to her waist leaning forward and encouraging her to speak when she was ready.

Theresa looked down and saw a dark abyss open up before her. She blew her nose loudly and finally began to talk. An avalanche of words, fire and brimstone, dreams and ambitions. She left nothing out. How confused she felt. How *angry*. Her feelings about her mother, her father, Catherine, Francie, Smoking Nana.

'Be yourself. Follow your passion, your heart's deepest desires.'

'And if I sin in the process?'

'I've never liked the concept of sin. It conjures up the notion of retribution and punishment. Rather mean-spirited, don't you think?'

Theresa blinked. 'But it's what we were taught. Everything was a sin. We sinned without thinking, despite our best intentions.'

'What purpose has it served? From what I can tell it's only made you anxious, afraid and guilty.'

'Are you saying I should forget all of it, throw it out the window?'

'I'm suggesting that you are now in a situation where you have the opportunity, if you so choose, to make a fresh beginning. To be reborn.'

'How do you choose what you will take with you and what you should leave behind?'

'Live in the present, take one day at a time.'

Theresa stared fixedly at the polished kauri floorboards. She twisted her damp handkerchief into a ball.

'There's so many things I'm not allowed to do. You're not allowed to live in sin, or have sex outside marriage. The Pope said so and he's supposed to be infallible.'

Mary Blessed raised her eyebrows. 'Really? I don't believe any man is infallible. Do you?'

Theresa hesitated. 'Well . . .'

'Do you?'

'No. I suppose not.'

'You have your answer.'

Just like that? Do what she wanted? Not worry about the consequences?

'I'll make mistakes.'

'It's only human. That's how you'll learn.'

'I don't want to repeat Mum's life,' said Theresa.

'Well, you don't have to marry the first man you go to bed with,' said Mary Blessed. 'And neither should you always have to live in fear of getting pregnant, no-one should.'

As the discussion had become more animated their voices had risen. Theresa was now striding about the room. She wanted to smash something.

'Of course they bloody shouldn't,' shouted Theresa. 'And another thing. I don't want to be a Catholic any more. I hate religion. I'm tired of the Bible and people always preaching at me. I don't want to hear another word about God *and* I'm fed up with always feeling guilty.'

She waited to be struck down for such heresy.

Mary Blessed clapped her hands. She laughed. 'Use your anger,' she said. 'Do your work. *Break* the mould. It's up to you from now on.'

'But how will I know what my work is? My task in life?'

'That's for you to discover.'

'How do I go about discovering it.'

'Let go of the guilt. You don't have to keep punishing yourself. What are you risking if you give the guilt away? By hanging on to it aren't you avoiding taking responsibility for your life? If you stop blaming your parents, God, whoever, and make your own decisions you're taking the first step in creating a new life for yourself.

'Don't misunderstand me, I don't have much sympathy for the institution of Catholicism either,' said

Mary Blessed. 'It is not kind to women. It does not treat them as equals. Men have all the power. Where are the women priests? Why not a woman pope? Why a pope at all?'

Theresa recalled the clippings about Mary Blessed in her scrapbooks. She was more curious about her than ever. If she wasn't the Virgin, then who was she? She had given no indication of recognizing Theresa and yet at the same time she seemed extremely familiar.

'The old doctrines and roles aren't always constructive. They no longer fit the way we need to be because they place too many unfair limits on women. We must all of us speak out more if there are to be profound changes in the way we run our lives.'

How did Mary Blessed live her own life? Did she have a husband or lover?

'Are you . . . do you have someone special whom you love?'

'Yes.'

'Who is this person?'

'I live with her here in this house.'

Mary Blessed stood up, indicating the audience was at an end. She hugged Theresa, enveloping her in the scent of roses.

Theresa wandered down the street in a confused state, narrowly avoiding being run over when she crossed a road. She felt overwhelmed.

In the weeks that followed Theresa often thought of Mary Blessed and the ideas they had discussed. One day she noted in the newspaper that Mary Blessed was billed as the leading speaker at a women's rally in Albert Park. Relieved to have a legitimate excuse for taking a break from swotting for her last exam, she persuaded Rose to accompany her there.

They both wore op-shop ankle-length nightgowns they had dyed black.

263

'Mum would have a fit if she could see me,' remarked Theresa, snatching one final glance in the mirror before they went out. She put on a black straw hat and pinned a red velvet rose onto its ribboned band. She then added black lace gloves and a long string of jet beads.

'There, that does it, I can go out in public now. We could pass for witches going to a funeral.'

'Rubbish, more like two Pre-Raphaelite princesses.'

Arm in arm the pair strolled up the hill to the park. The grounds were already packed with women. Buskers, clowns and food stalls were scattered about the grass in riotous profusion. Women who had arrived early to grab the best positions were sitting on rugs enjoying picnic lunches. Women smoked joints, fed babies, exchanged news, greeted old friends and acquaintances, drank wine, read books, or lay on their backs in the sun daydreaming. Idyllic except for the group of smiling women bearing placards and banners and singing hymns over in a far corner of the grounds. Everyone seemed to be making a determined effort to ignore them.

'They're the religious nutters,' said Rose, pointing. 'The ones who try to disrupt all of MB's meetings. Wonder what they'll do today, they're certainly outnumbered.'

Women continued to arrive in a steady stream. Soon there was standing room only and books and picnics had to be packed up to make way for newcomers.

A large woman with bleached blond hair and denim overalls was fiddling with the microphone on the small makeshift stage.

'Let's move closer,' urged Rose.

They squeezed through the crowd until they obtained a better view. The woman on stage was still struggling with the head of the microphone. It drooped every time she tried to prod and twist it into an upright position. She bent her head and spoke into it. 'Testing, testing, can you hear me out there?'

'Yes!' shouted the crowd.

The microphone drooped again.

The stage-manager pointed to it. 'This thing seems to be trying to tell me something, it won't perform.'

'Wring its neck,' suggested one woman.

The group of women nearest the stage roared with laughter.

Rose turned to make a comment to Theresa who was staring to her left with an expression of disbelief on her face.

'What is it?'

'It's *Mum*. And she's here with Carrie and Clara.'

She led Rose over to be introduced.

'What on earth are *you* doing here?'

'Same as you,' grinned her mother matily. 'We've come up for a few days. I meant to call you, but I wasn't sure until the last minute whether I would be able to get away. Isn't this fun?'

Moira Flynn looked happy and excited in her new green dress. It had probably been run up on the machine by Clara, who had no doubt donated the fabric as well.

Theresa gaped. Fun? Did that mean that her mother was in agreement with Mary Blessed's views? Theresa was temporarily lost for words. She was seeing a new aspect of Moira Flynn. Her mother actually possessed a sense of humour. Away from the inhibiting presence of Terrence Flynn she was witty, even to the extent of cracking jokes with her two friends, who were hanging onto each other apparently helpless with laughter.

Theresa didn't know what to make of it.

'I like your mother,' whispered Rose. 'She's quite a dag, isn't she? Nothing at all like you'd led me to believe.'

'She's a hard case, your mother,' gasped Carrie to Theresa.

A dag? Hard case? Theresa could only stare in bewilderment.

265

'What's the matter? Didn't think the old girl had it in her to kick her heels up, eh?' asked Moira Flynn, digging her daughter in the ribs.

Mary Blessed stepped up to the podium and the buzz of excited chatter was instantly stilled.

'It's wonderful to see so many of you here. Let's make today one of celebration.'

The women roared their approval.

There was an expectant hush when the last of the clapping and cheering had died down. And then, raising her head, Mary Blessed began to address the crowd.

'Do you deserve *rights*?'

'YES!'

'Do you *have* rights?'

'NO!'

'Do you have *status*?'

'NO!'

'Do you want to *change* things? Take *control* of your lives?'

'YES!'

Afterwards, Theresa could remember almost every word of Mary Blessed's speech. Sentences rolled off her tongue as smooth and rounded as river stones. Challenges were delivered in a voice sharp with anger. She played the crowd with the confidence of a musician at the peak of a career. She knew when to pause and when to shout. But she never berated them. Never complained that progress was so painfully slow, never suggested that some changes might never happen.

At least not in their lifetimes.

I want to be the best that I can be, thought Theresa. But how could she, one person, one woman, make a difference?

She squeezed nearer the stage.

Mary Blessed paused. Her eyes raked the crowd before coming to rest finally on Theresa's face. And in the fraction of a second before she leaned forward and drew the crowd into her orbit again, she signalled

Theresa with her eyes. The message in those eyes was so clear and so unexpected that later Theresa would wonder if she had imagined what she was being asked to do.

To continue Mary's work. To join her.

Placards and banners are waving like flags. There is heckling from a small group which has edged nearer to the stage. Some of them begin to clamber onto it and are pushed off by Mary Blessed's close associates. Women try to shout down the protesters. The atmosphere is chaotic.

Theresa is pushed up against one of the protesters. There is a blob of spittle on the woman's lower lip. Her eyes are lit up with the fervour of her cause. Theresa hears the word 'Satan', the phrase 'evil woman', and her heart starts suddenly to hammer in her chest. She finds herself pushing the woman away. The woman turns to look back.

'I'll pray for you,' she says.

Theresa pokes out her tongue.

Other women around Theresa are pushing and yelling at the protesters. Mary Blessed is shouting into the microphone, telling them that violence isn't the answer.

But neither is tolerance, thinks Theresa. Turning the other cheek is for fools.

The protesters have been forced to retreat. Undaunted they continue to sing. A hymn floats towards the stage.

After the speeches Theresa seeks out her mother's face in the crowd and, grabbing Rose, moves up to her. Their hands reach out and connect.

Hand in hand, Theresa and her mother stare towards the stage for one last glimpse of Mary Blessed. They present two almost identical profiles, one with red hair, the other with blond. Theresa's face, smooth and yet to be written on, her mother's already etched with half a lifetime's stories.

And then it is over. Mary is led away from the stage, surrounded, protected. Her face is partially obscured by her hair. What is she thinking? Where is she going next? Theresa longs to run after her, to pester her with urgent questions but already Mary has been swallowed up by the crowd.

Theresa, Rose, Moira, Carrie and Clara cling to each other – an island of sanity in the tangle of arms and legs. Strengthened by being linked, they are eventually able to push their way out of the crowd together. Around them they hear mothers calling for children. Friends seek lost companions.

'Come with me,' says Moira Flynn and she leads her emotional daughter in her long black gown to the shelter of ancient oaks and elms and there she embraces her.

Theresa pulls away. A frown crosses her mother's face.

'Couldn't you have worn something *nice*?' she says. 'Something that doesn't look as if it came out of the rag-bag?'

Theresa gasps as if winded.

'And your hair,' continues her mother. 'It looks like you've been pulled out backwards from a gorse bush.'

Have you looked at yourself in the mirror lately?

Theresa glares at her mother. Nothing has changed.

'Why can't you accept me the way I am?'

They take each other's measure.

Theresa shrugs. 'You know something. Your opinions regarding my appearance – I don't care any more. I like the way I am and that's what matters.'

And it's true. With every day that passes Theresa can feel the bonds loosening. She can walk away if she chooses. Simply realizing this is enough: it immediately robs her mother's words of any power to hurt her.

So why doesn't she walk away then?

It's the sight of her mother's face. The lines of suffering etched around the eyes and mouth. The poignancy of the new dress, her journey with Clara and Carrie. How can she walk away? She tucks her arm through her mother's.

'Mum, let's leave the others. They can join us later. Come and have a drink with me.'

Her mother hesitates for the fraction of a second. The ground rules have changed. Are there any guidelines?

She smiles, *yes*.

THE END

Sue Reidy was born in Invercargill, New Zealand, and attended a Catholic girls' school. She studied visual communications at Wellington Polytechnic School of Design, and has worked in the communications field full-time since graduating. In 1990 she formed her own design practice. She has gained recognition as a graphic designer, illustrator, writer and lecturer. In 1985 Sue Reidy won the BNZ Katherine Mansfield Short Story Award and in 1988 her short-story collection *Modettes* was published by Penguin Books. In 1989 she was elected to the National Council of PEN. In 1995 she was runner-up in the *Sunday Star Times* Short Story Award. Sue lives with her partner (a publisher) in Ponsonby, Auckland, surrounded by her paintings and artefacts, while a sub-tropical garden steadily encroaches on the house.